WHEN LOVE
GETS IN THE WAY

JANELLE MOWERY

D1113595

HARVEST HOUSE PUBLISHERS

EUGENE, OREGON

Cover design by Left Coast Design, Portland, Oregon

Cover photos © Alamy / iStockphoto / Shutterstock

Back cover author photo by Katrina Ashburn

The author is represented by MacGregor Literary Inc. of Hillsboro, Oregon.

WHEN LOVE GETS IN THE WAY
Copyright © 2011 by Janelle Mowery
Published by Harvest House Publishers
Eugene, Oregon 97402
www.harvesthousepublishers.com

Library of Congress Cataloging-in-Publication Data
    Mowery, Janelle.
    When love gets in the way / Janelle Mowery.
        p. cm.—(Colorado runaway series ; bk. 2)
    ISBN 978-0-7369-2808-3 (pbk.)
    ISBN 978-0-7369-4168-6 (eBook)
    1. Ranchers—Fiction. 2. Ranch life—Fiction. I. Title.
    PS3613.O92W48 2011
    813'.6—dc22

                                                    2010046513

Printed in the United States of America

    11 12 13 14 15 16 17 18 19 / LB-SK / 10 9 8 7 6 5 4 3 2 1

To my heavenly Father. Without Him, I am nothing.

To my sweet husband, who knows and puts up with my Grace-like quirks and loves me anyway.

ACKNOWLEDGMENTS

Thanks to all those whose touches made this book special: Marcia Gruver, Elizabeth Ludwig, Rod Morris, and Nancy Toback. A special thanks to Gary and Rachel Moon and MerriDee Shumski for their unending prayers and encouragement.

ONE

1873 Colorado Territory

Her mama once said that men thought with their hands long before the reaction reached their brain. Now, with this scowling fellow pointing a gun at her, Grace Bradley had to agree with the voice of wisdom.

He cocked his pistol. "Show yourself. And no sudden moves. I ain't afraid to shoot."

How on earth was she going to talk her way out of this one? Maybe hiding under the tarp tied over Cade Ramsey's wagon wasn't one of the brightest things she'd ever done, but desperation forced extreme measures.

Truth be told, it was his own fault she'd been discovered. He was the one who'd managed to hit every stinkin' hole in the road. Each bump jarred her bones into an unmerciful meeting with the lumber stacked in his wagon bed. The last jolt forced a loud gasp from her, and her final shred of hope for freedom had vanished with the click of the gun hammer.

"I said show yourself or I'll shoot."

"Hold your horses. I'm coming out." Hair draped her face, and she puffed it away from her mouth. "Put that gun away before you hurt someone."

Grace wormed her way to the back of the wagon, picking up slivers as she went, and with every inch of progress she schemed on how to get Cade to help her continue her flight. Then she'd disappear somewhere into the world and start a new life—free from Frank Easton, an overbearing brute of a man whose first wife, Maria, had disappeared without sign or word. How could Daddy even consider forcing her to marry Frank?

The tarp grew tighter as she neared the tail of the wagon. One attempt to stick her hand out to loosen the ropes earned her nothing more than chafed knuckles and a broken fingernail.

"Thanks for all your help," she huffed.

She lifted the tarp as far as it would go and heaved herself toward the sliver of daylight, hoping for enough strength to push through. The sudden release of the tarp sent her sprawling over the end.

She scrambled for something to catch onto, and her grasping fingers connected with cold, hard steel. An explosion blasted near her ear. She screamed as she hit the ground, ears ringing. A heavy weight landed on top of her, knocking the breath out of her.

Cade clamored to his feet to stand over her. Before she could get her bearings, he pulled her up by her arm. She stood blinking at the horses charging off in a cloud of dust, the careening wagon belching lumber and supplies in its wake.

Cade's jaw hung slack a moment before he clamped his mouth shut and holstered his gun. The expression on his face changed from annoyance to surprise. "Grace? What…?"

She looked from him to the retreating cloud of dust, then back at him. "Sorry?" she said with raised brows and the most convincing expression of innocence she could muster.

"What in tarnation are you doing?"

The look of little-girl helplessness on her face made most of Cade's irritation seep away. He glanced down the empty road, then back to Grace.

"Are you hurt?"

She shook her head and peered up at him, her brown eyes round in her pale face. She still wore the same dress from the funeral the day before, though now dusty and wrinkled.

Cade peeled off his hat and scratched his head. "What were you doing in the back of my wagon?"

She smoothed her skirt. "Hiding."

"What was that?"

Her chin lifted, and she stared him in the eye. "I said I was *hiding*."

"The question is why?"

She looked around. "Can I help you clean this up?"

Cade crossed his arms over his chest.

"Please? The quicker we gather this stuff, the sooner we can get moving again."

"What good will it do me without the wagon?"

She glanced down the road, then started walking. "All right, let's go get it."

He groaned and followed. All kinds of critters had crossed his path when he was young, needing some kind of aid. Why did it have to be a woman this time? One who left disaster in her wake, no less. He figured her assistance would be about as helpful as an avalanche in a snowstorm.

"Hold up." He moved in front to stop her. "You wait here, and I'll bring the horses back. It doesn't take two to catch them."

"You sure?"

"Yeah. Besides, they may have gotten pretty far, and those shoes don't look like they'd be much for a long hike."

She looked down, then nodded. "All right. I'll wait."

He took off at a brisk walk. In mere hours the sun would nestle into the Rockies, calling a halt to his day. He sure didn't need any more delays.

The horses had stopped not more than a mile away, though

they'd gone off the road to graze next to a swollen stream. Small chunks of ice floated in the rushing water, and a dirty snowdrift oozed moisture as the sun declared its victory over the long cold season. Cade could only hope the wagon wheels weren't bogged down in some mud hole.

He called to the team as he approached so they wouldn't bolt. They only glanced at him before continuing to nibble at the few blades of new spring grass. A quick inspection of the wheels revealed no damage. He climbed aboard and headed back, stopping to pick up anything that had fallen out during the horses' flight.

He returned to find Grace busy stacking the lumber and piling the supplies next to it. The gesture surprised him, though he was pleased at her achievement, right up until she dropped a board onto the stack. The *crack* sent the horses into another wild dance before he managed to calm them. He glared at her, only to receive another innocent look along with a shrug.

"Sorry."

He choked back a comment and set the brake on the wagon. Together, they loaded the lumber and supplies in no time…and without incident.

She darted another glance down the road behind them, then turned and looked him in the eye. "Can we go now?"

"Who's after you?"

"No one. I'm just ready to be on our way again."

"Why?"

"I'll explain later."

He lifted her onto the seat, then climbed up beside her and sat thinking for a moment.

"What are you waiting for?" she said.

"Sanity." He grabbed the reins and turned the wagon around.

"Wait. What are you doing?" She jerked on his arm. "You're going the wrong way."

He reined the horses to a stop. "At the funeral, you asked to go to Rockdale with me. I said no. Instead, you hid out in my wagon." He propped one hand on his knee and peered at her face. "You're not in trouble, are you?"

"No." She plucked at her bottom lip with her thumb and forefinger, brows puckered. "I'm not in trouble."

"You're not a very good liar, Grace. You might as well tell me the truth."

She craned her neck to peer down the road. "Why do you say that?"

"Well, for starters, the way you check the road every few seconds." Her gaze darted up at him again. "And because of the way you're almost pulling off your lip."

She dropped her hand to her lap and clasped it with her other hand. "I'm not pulling off my lip, and I'm not in trouble."

"So you're hiding out because…?"

She tapped one finger against her chin. Once more, her mouth opened and closed. She slumped. "I don't know how much I want to tell you."

"Well, right now, I'll take anything."

"Fine." She let out a gust. "I needed to leave town, and I didn't want anyone to stop me."

"And the reason you needed to leave town?"

"That's what I don't want to tell you."

Women! He slapped the reins against the horses' rumps.

Panicked, she jerked back on them. "You can't take me back there."

"At least tell me this. Did you know you were hiding in *my* wagon?"

"I felt pretty certain." She shrugged. "You rescued me once at the funeral. I thought maybe you'd help me again."

The vision of Grace being manhandled at her mother's funeral played through his mind. He still wondered what would have happened if he hadn't stepped in, despite Frank Easton's threats for interfering.

"So you want my help, but you won't tell me why."

She mashed her lips together tighter than a miser's fist.

"Tell me you at least left your father a note explaining your plans."

Grace looked away from him and fiddled with a button on her coat.

Cade threw the reins down. "You didn't leave a note? Your father knows nothing of your whereabouts?"

"He probably doesn't even know I'm gone yet."

He jerked the hat from his head, ran his fingers through his hair, then shoved his hat back in place. "So, more than likely, your father is worrying himself sick over you right now, isn't he? He just lost his wife, and now he may fear he's lost his daughter as well."

Tears appeared in Grace's eyes, and she gave him a stricken look.

They sat in silence while he sent up a plea for wisdom. "Neither of us is going anywhere until you tell me what this is about."

Her delicate hands clenched into fists. She huffed twice. "It's a matter of life and death."

"Whose?"

She peered up at him, desperation in her eyes. "Mine. So you'll take me with you, won't you?"

"Only as far as the next town. Then I'm going to buy you a ticket back to Pueblo and put you on the stagecoach myself."

"You're such a gentleman, Cade, and it's not the first time I've noticed." She straightened and smoothed her skirt. "I can't wait to meet your mother. She has to be a special woman for you to turn out so nice."

He gripped the reins until he thought they would cut into his palms. "I said you're not coming with me."

She frowned and propped her fists on her hips. "Well, I'm certainly not going back to Pueblo. Why do you think I left there in the first place?"

"I don't *know* why you left there in the first place. You won't tell me."

Grace's chin dropped to her chest, but the way her shoulders shook, she had to be laughing. He groaned and flicked the reins again. The sooner he got rid of this woman, the better.

He looked heavenward before fixing his gaze on the road. *This is my punishment, isn't it, Lord? I got angry with You over Kim, so now You've sent me this infernal woman as my discipline.*

Steel scraped against leather as he felt his pistol leave the holster. In the next instant, Grace turned, and an explosion deafened one of his ears.

❋ TWO ❋

W hat are you doing?"

Cade grabbed his gun from Grace's grasp just as the horses veered off the road. The pistol clattered to the floorboard. A shot from behind shattered the wood at his feet. He yanked on the reins to stop the horses, then flipped the straps around the brake. He shoved Grace from the seat to the ground as he landed beside her, keeping the wagon between them and the shooter.

A quick peek down the road revealed a horse and rider. Cade reached for his gun, then remembered he'd dropped it. He took a deep breath and lunged for the pistol. He grabbed it just as another shot whistled past his head.

"Who is that man?" he said as he crouched beside Grace.

"I don't know."

Cade peered at her through narrowed eyes. She stared at the ground.

"Then why did you shoot first?"

She shrugged, still not looking at him. "He scared me."

"Who scared you?"

This time she did look at him. "I said I don't know."

The shooter was too far away to hit with a pistol. The rifle lay under the seat. Cade cautiously stuck his arm over the side of the wagon and felt around, relieved when his fingers brushed the barrel. He wrapped his hand around it and yanked. Bits of wood showered his head when the next shot hit the seat.

He flopped to the ground, rifle dropping alongside. He scooted to his knees and readied his rifle before peeking at Grace from the corner of his eye.

"Just what kind of trouble are you in?"

She rose to her knees. "I told you I'm not in any trouble."

He grabbed her coat sleeve and jerked her back down. "You trying to get your fool head blown off? Stay down."

"Sorry." But with her lips in a tight, furious line, she looked anything but sorry.

"If you're not in trouble, then why is that man after you?"

"What if it's you he's after? You're the only one almost getting hit."

Cade ran his hand across his face and checked the man's location. He still sat on his horse in the middle of the road as if he had no fear of getting shot.

"We're not getting anywhere sitting here," he said. "You stay put. I'm going to make a run for those trees."

"But Cade, do you think—"

"Just don't move. I'll be back soon."

He scooted to the front of the horses. After one last check on the man, Cade dashed across the opening. Bullets sprayed the area. He begged his legs to move faster. Ten more steps. Five.

Cade plunged into the brush and sank behind a tree. A chunk of bark flew through the air from a shot above his head. He crawled deeper into the woods. Sure he'd reached safety, he stood and raced in the direction of the man. The crash of each step roared in his ears and likely announced his location.

When he figured he'd gone far enough, he veered toward the road and stopped behind a trunk along the edge of the tree line. Once he'd caught his breath, he looked for the shooter and found no one on the road.

The thunder of hoofbeats growing fainter made Cade's heart thump in dread. What if he'd blundered in leaving Grace by herself and the man now charged toward her? The thought made him rush out of the trees. He turned toward the wagon and saw no rider. A look the opposite direction revealed dust rising behind the horse running at full gallop.

Cade headed back to Grace and his wagon. Their escape from harm had been too easy, and that knowledge made him nervous.

Grace was no longer hiding but standing in the open. He didn't bother with a scolding but took her by the arm and led her back to the wagon. She didn't put up a fight when he lifted her onto the seat and climbed up next to her.

"We gotta go. I don't want to take the chance he'll be back with friends."

She spun to look back. "You think he might?"

He slapped the reins against the horses' rumps. "I hope not."

"Did you see who he was? Did you recognize him?"

"No. He was too far away and long gone by the time I came out of the woods."

She peeked behind them again. "So what do we do now?"

"Get to the nearest town and report it to the sheriff."

More fiddling with the button on her coat. "Do we have to?"

"We were almost shot. Of course we have to." He speared her with a look, suspicion on the rise once more. "Why wouldn't you want to?"

A shrug lifted her coat right before she ducked her chin into her collar. The tight line of her mouth let him know she'd give no explanation. Infuriating woman. Her silence might get them killed. His annoyance broke when she sighed, releasing a burst of vapor into the cold air, and rubbed her arms. He reached under his feet, pulled out a blanket, and handed it to her.

"Thank you." She wrapped it around her.

"Do you have any other clothes?"

"My travel bag is in back."

He shook his head. She must not have been in an all-fired hurry to leave if she managed to pack a bag.

"How much further to the next town?"

A twinge of guilt tightened his belly at the defeat in Grace's voice. He shoved the feeling away. He was right in this. She needed to go back and face her problems, and her father for that matter.

"We should be there within the next hour."

"Beulah?"

"No, Greenwood." He glanced at her. "Why?"

"I thought we'd be further along than that."

He smiled. "It must have felt like it, riding in the wagon bed and all."

She looked up at him, one eyebrow cocked higher than the other. "Did you manage to miss any of those bumps and holes, or were you looking to bust a wheel out here?"

He couldn't help but laugh. He looked back at the canvas-covered wagon bed. "How did you find room back there? I packed it pretty tight."

She made a face. "Don't I know it. I think every item in there weighs more than I do. I pushed and shoved until I made a hole I thought I could live with." She pulled the blanket tighter. "Sure am glad you found me when you did, though. I was starting to run out of air."

A cold wind blew across the plain and whipped through a patch of frost-browned grass. Cade clamped his hat down tighter and flipped up his collar, relieved the heavy snows were over. The Rockies up ahead still held their winter coat, but soon, even that would disappear.

In the silence, his thoughts clung to the woman sitting beside him. No doubt her troubles had something to do with Frank, though Frank didn't seem the sort to soil his hands. He'd likely hire someone to do his dirty work.

Cade used the guise of checking the road behind them to peek at Grace. Why wouldn't she talk to him? She said she'd explain. Maybe if he tried a different approach.

She leaned forward and looked into his face. "You never told me why you came to the funeral in place of your mother. Mama said they'd been close all those years ago. I figured your mother wouldn't miss the funeral." The blanket around her face muffled her voice.

"It was an accident."

"What was an accident? What happened?"

"My mom fell down some steps. Her hip is broken."

"I'm sorry."

"Yeah, me too." He didn't want to talk about it. "What about you? How're you taking your mother's death?"

"All right, I guess. She'd been sick for so long, I know she was ready to go. That made it easier." She sighed. "But I miss her."

They fell quiet again, and Cade pondered his own mother. He could have easily lost her in that fall down the stairs. He shuddered at the unbearable thought. She held the family together when he and his father would have gone their own way.

When they arrived at the outskirts of Greenwood, Grace reached to touch his arm. Bruises marred her slender wrist, a stark reminder of her heated words with Frank and the altercation that followed.

"Are you sure I can't get you to change your mind, Cade? I promise I won't be any trouble."

He took a deep breath. "I don't think it's a good idea, Grace, and I believe you should go back and talk to your father. I get the feeling there's something you two need to work out."

Her hand slid from his arm and dropped onto her lap. He admired her for not arguing with him. He'd expected a fight.

They rolled through town. He examined every storefront, the peeling paint making the buildings look as forlorn as the expression on Grace's face. The clanging of the blacksmith's hammer rang out above the rumble of the wagon. He was struck with a yearning to get back to work in his own livery.

The scent of roasting meat and baking bread drifted from the eatery they passed. His stomach voiced its appreciation followed by a similar noise from Grace. Speaking to the sheriff would have to wait. Besides, they should be safe in town. He stopped the horses in front of the establishment, set the brake, and tied off the reins.

"It'll be dark in a few hours, and I figure we could use a bite to eat." He jumped to the ground, turned, and reached for Grace, only to find her gone.

THREE

Grace shed the blanket and scooted to the ground. She'd be hanged before she let another man try to run her life. Men cared only about their own interests. Right now her interest was food. The name of the eatery beckoned to her from the window.

Faye's Foodstuffs
Fare and Fodder for Famished Folks

Simply reading the sign would work up an appetite. Maybe the owner needed a waitress. Grace shook her head at the thought. She couldn't say the words without tripping up, much less carry trays of fare and fodder.

Cade grasped her elbow. "I would have helped you down."

She pulled free. "I managed just fine, thank you."

She stepped onto the boardwalk and reached for the doorknob. Cade's hand beat her to it. The teasing aroma from outside became unbearable torture once she moved inside. She pressed her hands against her stomach, swallowed the sudden excess moisture flooding her mouth, and smiled at the attractive woman with blond hair standing by the door.

"I'll have whatever it is I'm smelling."

The woman laughed. "I'm Faye, and I guess we won't need these." She set the handwritten menus aside. "Follow me and we'll get that *smell* in front of you as soon as possible."

Her face heating, Grace followed Faye to a table and slipped off her coat. When she saw Cade headed toward her, she draped her coat over the back of her chair, flopped down, and scooted her chair toward the table. His eyebrows rose before he took his own seat.

"What can I get you to drink?" Faye asked.

"Coffee," Grace said.

Cade shrugged out of his coat. "Sounds good."

Faye left to get their coffee, but not before she tossed Cade a lingering smile.

Grace looked around. Sconces along the walls lit the room, and an individual candle burned at each table. A handful of patrons huddled at tables covered by red and white-checkered cloths. Her inspection ended when she noticed her companion sitting back in his chair, hands folded over his stomach, staring at her.

"What?" she finally asked when she could stand his gaze no longer.

"You're more upset than you let on."

"I'm fine." She snatched up the linen napkin, snapped it open, and draped it over her lap.

The door opened, and Grace's back stiffened. It was only an elderly couple who greeted Faye like old friends. When would she stop being skittish and get the shooting out of her mind?

Cade scrutinized her face, then leaned forward, resting his forearms on the table. "Tell me about Frank."

Her heart dropped. "What about him?"

"Who is he to you? A family friend, or maybe your fiancé?"

She choked on a cough. "Fiancé? Hardly."

"A family friend then? He and your father looked pretty close, the way they were talking together at the funeral."

"My *father's* friend."

Faye arrived with the coffee, and a waitress followed with plates of food. Their appearance gave Grace a needed reprieve.

Large portions of roast beef and mashed potatoes covered with rich brown gravy steamed from the dish. Green beans filled in the only available space left on the plate. Two thick slices of bread were propped on the side. She grabbed her fork and scooped up a mouthful of the potatoes.

"Great Father in heaven, Lord, we praise You and thank You for this meal we are about to partake of."

She stopped chewing, set her fork down, placed her hand over her mouth, and bowed her head.

"May it strengthen our bodies for Your service. I also pray, Lord, that You will allow us a pleasant time together before we must part ways."

Her head popped up, and she speared Cade with her gaze. Why did he have to keep reminding her?

"Grant us safety as we each return home. In Your Son's precious name I pray, Amen."

They looked at each other for several moments before she picked up her fork to finish what she'd started. The tender meat melted in her mouth, and she almost moaned with pleasure. A glance at Cade let her know he also found the food excellent. She told herself to slow down and savor each bite, but her stomach insisted on speed. In no time, their plates were empty.

Faye bustled across the noisy room and refilled their coffee cups, then scooped up the dirty dishes and balanced them on her forearm. "Could I interest you two in some fresh-baked apple pie?"

Cade grinned. "You've got my interest."

"I couldn't eat another bite," Grace said, "but what I've had was delicious. Don't get rid of the cook."

"I won't. That would put me out of business." Faye turned to Cade, and her interest and appreciation shone in her flirtatious gaze. "I'll be right back with your pie."

He sat back in his chair and patted his stomach. "Ah, I feel much better."

She nodded, picked up her coffee cup, and peered through the steam at her companion as she took a sip. He looked even better in his red flannel shirt and denims than he did in his good clothes at the funeral. A day's growth of whiskers gave him an appealing rugged appearance. His tousled hair, almost the color of her coffee, finished the virile image.

How could she get him to change his mind about her tagging along? She felt protected in his presence, although he could be an irritation at times. With very little money for a stage or train, Cade's wagon would have to do. She might need the meager amount in her handbag later.

His gaze dropped to her arm, and she was reminded of her still painful bruises inflicted by Frank's aggressive attempt to make her stay and talk to him. She moved her arm under the table and curled her fingers into the fabric of her skirt.

Faye brought the pie, and the scent of warm apples and cinnamon filled the air. Grace eyed the dessert, wishing she'd ordered one too. Cade slid the plate toward her. She waved it off.

"I'm too full, but it sure smells good."

He took a bite. "Mmm. This is great. Are you sure?" When she nodded her head, he motioned toward her with his fork. "You never finished telling me about Frank."

She set down her coffee with a thump. A tiny bit splashed over the side of the cup and dampened the tablecloth. "There's nothing to tell."

He continued to stare.

She sighed. Maybe if she confessed, he'd let her stay with him, though it was none of his business. "Frank would like to own me like he and his uncle own most of Pueblo." Worse yet, her father encouraged it, almost begging her to marry him. Grace clamped her teeth over her bottom lip. She didn't want to tell Cade about that yet. She wasn't sure what to make of it herself.

Cade scowled. "No man should treat a woman like I saw Frank treat you. Not for any reason."

She rested her arms on the table and clasped her hands around her cup. Might he change his mind after all? Cade scraped all traces of pie from the plate as she struggled for a different approach. Her thoughts settled on all the letters she'd read from his mother to hers.

"One of your mother's letters said you were getting married," Grace said. "Has that happened yet?"

He pushed his plate away. "We need to get going. It'll be dark in a couple hours, and I still need to talk to the sheriff before I buy you a ticket home." He stood and grabbed his coat.

She gazed up at him in surprise at the scowl on his face. Or was it pain? He moved to her side of the table and rushed her into her coat.

"Excellent food," Cade said to Faye as he paid the bill. He turned and held the door open for Grace. Not another word was said as they settled onto the wagon seat. He turned the horses and continued on his earlier path toward the sheriff's office.

Her anger rose. Of all the conceited, bossy…

"Will you at least tell me her name?"

"Whose name?"

"The girl you're going to marry."

A muscle twitched in his jaw. "I don't want to talk about it."

"I didn't want to talk about Frank either, but you kept pestering me."

He reined the horses to a stop in front of the sheriff's office and helped her to the ground. Cade jumped up on the boardwalk and entered the office. In seconds, he reappeared.

"Where's your bag?"

She motioned to the approximate location. He loosened the canvas and lifted her bag from the wagon, and then headed down the street to the depot. She raced to keep up. Cade approached the thin, balding man at the window.

"The sheriff isn't in his office. You know where I can find him?"

"You can't. He's out chasing outlaws."

Cade peered down the street as though he'd find answers to his problems there. Then he spun back around.

"I need a ticket to Pueblo for the lady here. When does the next stage leave?"

"It should be here in about half an hour, sir."

Grace poked Cade's side. "I told you I don't want to go back there. Why can't I go to Rockdale with you?"

He handed the man some money and took the ticket, then held it out to her. She refused to take it. He slipped it into her bag and pointed at a bench along the wall.

"You can wait for the stage right there." He set her bag next to the bench and turned back to the station master. "You'll look after her until she's on board?"

"Yessir. I'd be happy to."

Cade nodded and returned to her. "It was nice to meet you, Grace. I hope if we ever meet again, it will be under more pleasant circumstances." He tipped his hat. "I've got to be going."

She didn't say a word as he turned and climbed onto the wagon. Grace stared at his broad back as he headed down the street, then flopped down on the bench. *Now what am I going to do?*

Cade didn't get far before a man in a wagon parked in front of the mercantile flagged him down. He came to a stop and tipped his hat to the lady in the wagon, an infant nestled in her arms. "Need some help?"

The man jumped to the ground and extended his hand. "Name's Layton Woods." He motioned to his wagon. "This here's my wife, Katie, and the little one is Tommy."

Cade nodded to the woman again after shaking the man's hand. "Cade Ramsey. Pleased to meet you both."

Their faces were thin, and dark smudges shadowed their eyes. They looked too young for the weary lines that etched their features. If he had to guess, they'd been traveling for many a mile.

Layton shuffled his feet, not quite meeting Cade's gaze. He finally glanced up, then back behind them. "Begging your pardon for listening in on your conversation with the young lady back there, but I'm sure I heard her mention you're headed to Rockdale."

Cade fought the urge to turn around. "Yes, sir."

"That's west of here, right?"

He examined the man a little closer. He looked more nervous than dangerous. "It is."

"Well, sir"—Layton now met his gaze head on, his eyes pleading—"the wife and I are also moving west. I thought since we're both headed the same direction, maybe we could make the trip together. Between tales of attacks from Indians and bandits, my wife's a little shook up about heading into the mountains alone."

The idea of another wagon slowing him down didn't appeal much, but the mixed look of fear and beseeching on Mrs. Woods' face softened his heart.

"I think that's a fine idea, Mr. Woods. In fact, there's a tent town outside Rockdale full of folks planning to move out soon. If we hurry, you might get to head west with them."

A wide grin brightened his face. "Thank you, sir." He seized Cade's hand and pumped it as though trying to remove his arm. "And call me Layton."

"All right, Layton. Are you and your family ready? I'd like to get a couple more hours of traveling in before we stop for the night."

"Sure thing. And we just bought a few more supplies. We'll feed ya as thanks for your kindness." He scrambled up next to his wife. "We'll follow if that's all right."

"Perfect."

Cade couldn't resist one glance behind him. Regret slammed him as hard as the meeting of Grace's stare. He flicked the reins to get the horses moving.

Pleased to pass by the last house in town, he thought he'd be relieved to be rid of Grace, but guilt hung on him like the fog on the mountaintops. He tried to convince himself he'd done the right thing, that Grace needed to go home and talk to her father, but the bruises on her wrist and memories of being shot at haunted him.

"Frank would like to own me."

Cade shook his head and urged the horses on with another flick of the reins, more than ready to be home. Grace's father would protect her.

"Whoever sees his brother in need and closes his heart against him, how does the love of God abide in him?"

"But she's not in need, Lord, except she needs to go home."

"If someone asks for an egg, would you offer a scorpion?"

Frank's face loomed. Cade groaned and yanked on the left rein to turn back.

"I don't know Your plans, Lord, and I'm not sure I want to know them. But I feel it's Your will to bring Grace to Rockdale with me, so I'll obey. I may not like it, but I'll obey."

He stopped next to Layton's wagon. "I'm going back for the girl. I can't leave her sitting there. You can go on if you'd like. I'll catch up."

"No, sir. We'll wait."

He nodded. "I won't be long."

Grace still sat on the bench, looking as small and forlorn as ever. He pulled to a stop. They stared at each other until he held out his hand. She smiled, grabbed her bag, and scrambled up next to him.

"I hope you don't mind the cold," he said as he turned the horses around. "But I want to get home and that means sleeping under the stars tonight."

"I'll sleep on the back of a horse if that's your wish."

Her smile worked to soften his heart. "I think I can do a little better than that."

When they reached the Woods family again, Cade made the introductions, then they continued on their way. They rode in silence for the next hour. As the sun settled behind the mountains, shards of pink, purple, and orange glistened off the dew like myriads of colored diamonds. By morning those diamonds would be glittering frost. The twilight made it difficult to see, so he pulled off the road and stopped next to a stream. Layton stopped his wagon nearby, close enough for companionship but far enough for a little privacy.

Cade helped Grace from the seat. She motioned toward a stand of trees.

"Um, I need to...ah..."

"Go ahead. I'll get a fire started and set up your bed."

He and Layton unhitched and hobbled the horses before gathering wood. They soon had the fire going, and Katie went to work preparing their supper. Cade let her know he and Grace had just eaten and wouldn't need anything for the night.

He moved to the wagon and loosened the ties on the canvas, then propped two short pieces of lumber along the side and secured them. He lifted one side of the canvas and tied it to the tops of the poles, creating a temporary shelter.

He looked over his shoulder toward the trees. Grace had been gone a long time. He figured he'd give her a few more minutes, then check on her. After moving some of the lumber around to make room for her bedding, he grabbed his bedroll and crawled under the wagon.

A scream pierced the air.

He jumped, smacking his head on the underside of the wagon. He ignored the pain and lunged out from under the rig. Katie's hand stilled from stirring the pot while her other hand reached for the infant lying in a small wooden crate next to her. Layton pulled out a rifle. Cade motioned for him to stay with his family, then he raced toward the stand of trees where he'd last seen Grace.

❖ FOUR ❖

Cade stopped at the first large pine tree and listened. A light breeze rattled the dry needles overhead. Crickets chirped louder than usual. All the normal night choruses, but no sign of Grace.

At the memory of Frank clutching her wrist and also of the man shooting at them, he pulled out his sidearm and slipped further into the trees. He heard panting and a whimper, but no one materialized through the darkness. He advanced a few more steps. A snarl followed by another shriek propelled him through the underbrush.

Growls surrounded him, and he cocked the hammer on his pistol and fired one shot into the air.

He pushed through the brush. "Grace?" He heard her choke on a response. "Don't move, Grace. I'm almost there."

Twigs snapped, and the growling increased. The wolves were so close he could hear their teeth clacking. He took another step and bumped into something.

"Grace?"

She moaned. Her hands grasped at his arms, knocking his gun from his grip.

"Shoot them." Her voice held a tremor.

"I can't. You knocked the gun from my hand."

A wolf snarled, much too close, and Grace let out a strangled cry. He pushed her behind him and faced the beast.

"Grace, I've got to find my gun. I'm going to kneel down and feel around for it. I want you to stand still and don't make a sound." He waited for a response. "Grace?"

"You told me not to make a sound," she whispered.

His movements were slow so as not to alarm the wolves. He ran his hands along the grass.

"Cade? They're getting closer."

"I *know*."

"Do you have the gun?"

"Not yet."

"Well, hurry! I swear I can hear their drool dripping on the ground."

His search grew more desperate. He finally found the gun just as a wolf lunged. He pulled the trigger and heard a yelp and scream. The beast rammed into him as he fired a couple more shots into the pack. The rest of them scattered, yipping and howling.

He felt pain in his neck and shoved the foul-smelling animal away, but the pain continued. He reached up. Grace's nails were embedded in his skin. He placed his hand over hers and pried her fingers from his flesh. He stood, and she flung herself at him. Shivers wracked her.

He hesitated a moment, then wrapped her in his arms. "Shhh. They're gone now."

He holstered his gun and pulled her closer, holding her until the trembling ended and she stepped back. "Are you all right?"

She ran her sleeve over her mouth and eyes. The light of the moon made her face look pale, and her chin quivered with the sniffles.

"Yes. Thank you, Cade."

"You're welcome." He took her arm and led her toward the horses. "Let's get back to the fire before the wolves decide to return. Were you able to, uh…?"

"If I hadn't, I'd need to change clothes."

Layton raced toward them when they stepped from the woods. "Everything all right? You hurt, Miss Bradley?"

"She's fine." Cade answered when he felt a tremor shake her again. "A pack of wolves gave her a scare."

Once they reached the wagon, he grabbed the blanket and wrapped it around her. He held her at arm's length and tried to read her expression in the firelight. He took note of her disheveled hair and the dried leaves clinging to her coat.

"You sure you're all right?"

"No, but I will be. I just…" She gave a helpless shrug and looked past him. "Let me help Mrs. Woods. Maybe I can hold the baby or stir the pot."

He let her go, and Layton moved next to him.

"My missus planned to head out into the woods too. Now what do I do?"

"Take her. Don't go too far, though, and take your rifle. Just inside the tree line will be fine. I'll keep my back turned."

Doubt filled Layton's eyes.

Cade patted him on the shoulder. "She'll be fine. My gunshots ought to keep them away for the night. I killed one, and I'm sure I hit another."

"All right. But I'm not sure my wife will be as easy to sway."

He walked to Katie's side and crouched beside her, then the young couple headed into the dark, leaving Grace with the baby and the cooking. Cade moved to the other side of the fire and examined Grace's face. She stared into the fire, her lips a tight line, her eyes as wide as saucers. He felt certain if he gave a loud clap, she'd scream or crumble into a heap.

"Can I help?"

She didn't even look at him as she gave a slight shake of her head. "When they get back, I think I'll be ready for bed."

"Don't want anything to eat or drink?"

"Not really. I don't think my stomach would hold anything I managed to swallow."

Quite a confession for someone who tried to maintain a brave front. "I understand. If you'd like to go now, I'll watch things."

She didn't get a chance to answer before Layton and Katie returned. Grace made her apologies, said good night, and headed for the wagon. Cade followed, leading her to his makeshift shelter.

"I laid out some blankets in the bed of the wagon." He lifted her inside. "Is it all right?"

"It's fine, thank you."

He stepped back. "Call out if you need anything. Good night, Grace."

"Good night, Cade. And thank you again."

"You're welcome."

He moved to the fire and shoved several more pieces of wood into the flames after Katie removed their supper. Sparks crackled, shot into the air, and floated toward the stars.

Thank You, Lord, for Your protection tonight.

Nearby, an owl answered his silent prayer. Despite the dangers, he loved the feel of the ground underfoot and the night sky overhead. They made him feel alive.

"Sure you don't want to join us for some of Katie's fixings? She's a mighty good cook." Pride filled the young husband's voice.

"No, but thank you. Maybe I'll get to find out how good a cook she is in the morning."

He bid the couple goodnight, crawled under the wagon, and pulled his blanket over him. Grace tossed and turned above him.

He smiled. "Trouble sleeping?"

"Trouble getting comfortable."

"We could change places. You can sleep down here with the bugs, mice, and snakes."

Silence.

"Uh...no thanks. I'm fine right here."

"If you say so."

He rolled onto his side and fell asleep without hearing another sound from above.

FIVE

Grace gripped the seat and held on while the wagon bumped its way across a rough patch of ground. The ragged mountain skyline around them could have been the very path they traveled. The boards beneath them creaked and groaned in protest. They'd been on the road for two days, and her body felt every uneven mile. She imagined her muscles mimicking the noises of the wagon. Her bones ached for rest. She yearned to reach their destination, but what lay ahead?

She had never been away from home before, never out on her own. She had been a homebody out of necessity, taking care of her sick mother for the last ten years while her father worked in his gunsmith shop to provide for his family. Now her needs were her responsibility. The question she'd silently asked countless times over the years ran through her mind once again.

Oh, Mama. Why did you have to get sick?

The blast of anger that usually followed the question raced through her again, dancing between her mother and the God her mother worshipped. If God loved Mama as much as she claimed, why would He allow such a horrid illness to slowly drain her of life? And why didn't Mama fight it, or fight God for that matter?

Instead, she had slipped passively into the clutches of whatever

ailment affected her mind. The doctor's medicines did little to alle-
viate the headaches that sent her to bed for days. Later, odd speech
and behavior were a usual occurrence to the point they no longer
took her out in public. Then she became bedridden, soon followed
by a comatose state until she was nothing more than a small frame
sheathed in a thin layer of pallid skin.

Grace sat up straighter, turned her face away from Cade, and
scanned the mountains through a blur of tears. She had no mother
to teach her about life or how to be a woman. Now that she was on
her own, would she be able to take care of herself, especially with her
limited social skills? How many times would she make a fool of herself before she managed to learn what she didn't yet know?

The day before, Cade told her he knew of a couple, some rancher
friends of his, who needed a housekeeper and cook. Though she
appreciated his help finding work, she hoped she could stay and
help Cade's mother. Nursing the infirm held familiarity, and that
was what she wanted and needed right now. At least Mrs. Ramsey
wouldn't fade away from her injuries. And her mother's friend
would teach her what she didn't know without a hint of disdain
or humiliating laughter. Maybe she could get Cade to understand.

Grace blinked hard, then chanced a glance at Cade. They had
talked very little along the way, mainly conversing with Layton and
Katie when they stopped for breaks or to eat. She didn't push conversation, fearful he'd tire of her and leave her at the next town. He'd
taken the wolf incident well, even teased her, claiming he'd saved the
critters the trouble since she was but a mouthful apiece for the pack.

She liked Cade's humor…when he decided to show it. He kept
her at arm's length most of the time—except when his rock-hard
chest had pressed against her cheek while he held her, his gentle
arms calming her. It felt good to rest in such strength and security.

Her face burned at the memory, and she looked away to keep
Cade from noticing her discomfort. His feelings didn't match hers.
She was his burden, an obligation he couldn't wait to unload like the

rest of the items in his wagon. But the mountains now surrounded them, telling her they were getting near his home of Rockdale, and she needed more information, anything that would help settle her nerves. She drew a deep breath.

"How much further?"

Cade glanced at her like he'd forgotten she was there. "A few more miles."

"I guess you're pretty anxious to get home."

"More than you know." He gave her a strange look and cleared his throat before pulling his hat lower. He turned back toward the road. "It's home," he said in a low voice.

Grace smiled at his embarrassment. His slip allowed her to get a glimpse of his love of Rockdale. She'd lived in Pueblo as long as she could remember, and she didn't feel that way. But then Pueblo didn't look like this. Very little new vegetation dared poke its head out yet, but even so, this area of the Colorado Territory held a charm she'd never seen before.

The valley, at times dotted with a few buffalo, eventually gave way to small mountains leading into those that towered above them. The temperature dropped as they rose to higher elevations. Throughout the mountains, thousands of pines stood like sentries against the brown undergrowth. It held a quiet and majestic beauty.

"Yes, I can see why you love this area."

"What about you, Grace? Do you hunger to be back home?"

"No, I don't miss it. I've been thinking about my father, but I don't miss Pueblo."

"Rockdale is pretty quiet in comparison. You may wish you were back with all the people and activity of a big town."

"I don't think so." She sighed. "I watched life happen from our windows. No one but Daddy will realize I'm gone. It's like falling out of a crowded wagon and nobody noticing." She felt foolish for voicing her thoughts, but it was the only way she could describe the feeling.

Cade reached for her hand and gave it a quick squeeze, then flicked the reins again.

"What about Frank?"

"What about him?"

"When I was at your mother's funeral, he seemed pretty intent on you. I'm guessing *he'll* realize you're gone. I think that's why you keep looking behind us. You think he'll come after you."

"How do you know I wasn't checking on Katie?" He tossed her a doubtful look, and she huffed. "Frank knows we don't get along. I can't imagine he'd take the time to hunt me down." So that was a half-lie since she had a feeling he wouldn't be far behind. "Why can't some men accept when a woman wants nothing to do with him? Is he dense or desperate?"

"Most men can. But you've basically admitted you think Frank will follow." Cade clenched the muscles in his jaw and sniffed. "You still won't tell me what happened to make you run off. I've hoped you'd open up to me. Don't know that I could help, but I can sure listen."

They thumped through yet another hole in the road. Her tailbone felt as if it'd been shoved up between her shoulder blades. Cade sat there as though they rode on air while she wondered if she'd ever get the kinks out of her body.

"All right, I'll make you a deal. You stop hitting those holes, and I'll tell you what made me leave home."

The corner of his mouth curved upward. "Sounds fair."

She stared at him a moment, saying nothing.

"Well? I don't hear you talking, and there's a pothole up ahead…"

Just blurt it out and get it over with. "Frank wants to marry me."

He did finally turn then. "Why didn't you just tell him no?"

"It's not that simple. He's being persistent, almost demanding, and Daddy is pushing me to take him up on his offer."

"Does your father know how Frank treats you? Surely he saw what happened at the funeral. I can't imagine he'd want you to marry someone who would hurt you."

"I don't know if he saw anything or not. I doubt he noticed much that day." Why had she agreed to talk about this? It wasn't as though Cade could help with this mess. Or help heal her broken heart.

"What about your mother?"

"What about her?"

"What did she think about Frank? Did she try to talk your father out of encouraging the marriage proposal?"

A chill sent a hard shudder through her. "I don't think Mama ever met Frank. He's been in Pueblo less than a year. If they did meet, Daddy introduced them when I wasn't around. But I doubt that. I don't think Mama was aware of much for the last year, and I was rarely away from her side."

Cade yanked sharply on the right rein, making the horses veer and throwing her against him. It took her a few moments to right herself, and she felt her face grow hot.

"What was that for?"

"Just trying to keep up my end of our deal." He pointed his thumb behind them. "Didn't want to hit that hole." A slight smile curved his lips. "You all right?"

She fought the desire to look back to see if a hole really existed. "Yes. Fine. So tell me about your friends, the ones you want me to work for."

"Jace and Bobbie Kincaid. They've only been married a few months." He motioned toward the wagon bed. "All the lumber back there is for the house they're building. They could use your help now, but once the house is finished, they'll really need you."

"You said Bobbie doesn't like housekeeping?"

"Bobbie and housekeeping get along about as well as you and…"

"Go ahead, say it. You were about to compare her and housekeeping to me and Frank."

Cade stared at her. "*Me.* I was going to say they get along about as well as you and me." One corner of his mouth turned up.

She caught his lighthearted sarcasm and couldn't stop her own smile. "In that case, I guess her need of me is reaching desperation."

He chuckled, and she joined him in laughter, enjoying the brief sense of camaraderie.

"Bobbie loves the outdoors. Her mother died when she was young. Her dad worked on a ranch, and she stayed by his side whenever possible. He taught her to shoot, and she's better than most men I know. She even wears men's clothes. That took some getting used to, but everyone grew accustomed to it and learned to love her as she is. Well, except for her cooking."

"That bad?"

"Worse. Her first roast was like chewing on my saddle."

Cade went on to tell her a few more of Bobbie's attempts to learn to cook until Grace's sides hurt from laughter.

"They couldn't cut the bread? Really?" she managed to ask.

"Nope. Jace said it made an excellent doorstop."

"Oh, the poor thing. Knowing you, you probably teased her to death."

He grinned and winked, causing her heart to flutter, which surprised her. She'd enjoy life before being tied to anyone, especially a man. Except she needed money.

"So, how well did Bobbie take your teasing?"

"She took it well, then made herself learn to do better. Bobbie's pretty good now, but she doesn't enjoy it. She'd rather be out breaking and training their horses."

"I can't even imagine."

Grace pictured Bobbie as a big, hulking woman with dirty teeth and layers of muscle. She shuddered. What was she getting herself into? Was she desperate enough to take on a job so intimidating? And how would she ever learn about feminine niceties if the only person she spent time with could pass as a man?

"What about your mother?" Grace said.

"What about her?"

"Wouldn't you like me to stay and help with her?"

He gave a quick shake of his head. "She has plenty of help from our neighbors."

His tone let her know the conversation would go no further, and she wondered why. He pulled the wagon to the side of the road and waved Layton up next to them.

"If you take that path about half a mile"—Cade motioned off to the right—"you'll come to the tent town I told you about. Just tell them you're a friend of mine. They'll help you get set up."

"Thank you for all your help, Cade," Layton said.

"I didn't do much."

"You did more than you'll ever know. Much appreciated."

"I enjoyed the company." Cade tipped his hat to Katie. "I'll be out to check on you both tomorrow."

The young couple disappeared down the path, enveloped by the thick stand of pines. Cade slapped the reins against the rumps of his team, jerking them back into motion. In minutes Rockdale appeared, and Cade sat up straighter on the seat next to her. Even the horses seemed to know they were home. Their ears perked up and so did their pace.

She examined the storefronts as they rolled through town. They matched the bright smile on Cade's face. While some people all but ignored him, others hollered his name, and he waved and called a greeting. Her face warmed under their curious scrutiny. She tried to ignore them and continued her inspection of her new home, a fraction of Pueblo's size.

"This may be a small town compared to Pueblo, but you seem to have everything you need," she said.

"Yep, there's our church and schoolhouse, and coming up, the barbershop, laundry, and hardware stores." He motioned to the left. "Over there's the feed and mercantile store. Just past that is what will interest you…the dress and cobbler shop."

She smiled at the pride in his voice as she took in the houses mingled with the businesses. And the number of trees surprised her.

Cade pointed up ahead. "There's the hotel and restaurant. I think you'll find the food in there as good as what we enjoyed in Greenwood. Just past that's the telegraph and post office, should you decide to contact your father."

She glanced at him but otherwise ignored the comment. Each building looked clean and well-kept, much different from Pueblo. Further down the street, she noticed a stage depot and a livery, which she knew belonged to Cade.

Cade reined the horses to a stop and jumped to the ground as an older man strode out the doors. The two men embraced, clapping each other on the back. Was this Cade's father? They didn't look a thing alike.

"Glad you're back, Cade. How was the trip?"

Cade looked up at her. "Adventurous." He reached up and helped her from the wagon. "Matt Cromwell, I'd like you to meet Miss Grace Bradley. Grace, meet my former partner. He's selling me his half of the business."

Mr. Cromwell clasped her hand in a gentle grip. "Grace Bradley." He smiled and glanced at Cade before meeting her gaze again. "I know a certain woman who'll be thrilled to see you. She's sure been praying for you and your father, worrying herself almost sick. I half expected her to crawl to Pueblo just to see to your welfare."

Cade grasped Matt's arm. "How is my mother?"

"She's fine, just fine. Doc's happy with her progress, though he'll be glad to see you're home." Matt settled his hand on Cade's shoulder and gave it a squeeze. "She's eager to get out of that bed. Doc thinks you may have to sit on her to keep her there. He wants her abed for at least another month."

"Wanting up and around already. That certainly sounds like she's feeling better." He looked over his shoulder. "How's business?" He walked through the livery doors. "Where's Joseph?"

"He had everything finished, so I sent him home a bit ago."

She watched as Cade wandered through the livery. He ran his hand over the stalls, horses, saddles, and finally ended up near the bellows. He lifted some of the tools and examined them, a smile creeping over his face before replacing each.

He turned back to Mr. Cromwell. "Any more trouble while I was away?"

"Not really. Just the usual grumblings."

"And no one gave you a bad time?"

"Nothing I couldn't handle." Matt clapped Cade on the shoulder. "Give it a little more time. Maybe once they get to know Joseph better, the fuss will die down."

"I hope so. Joseph's a good man." Cade returned to her side. "I'll start back to work tomorrow. I want to introduce Grace to Mother, then I'll get her settled out at the Double K. I think Bobbie will be the happiest to see Grace."

Matt and Cade shared a laugh, and Grace's dread over meeting Bobbie grew another notch. She envisioned a bachelor's cabin with clothes lying everywhere, a thick layer of dirt covering everything, and large, ugly bugs leaving trails in the dust. A shudder ran through her.

"I'm going to take Grace home in the buggy," Cade said. "Do you need a ride, Matt?"

"No thanks. I've got Dancer. In fact, it's about time to close up shop and head on home."

"All right. Thanks for helping out."

"You bet. You know I've got to get my hands a little dirty now and then."

"Stop by any time. I always need help mucking stalls."

Matt made a face and turned to her. "It was good to meet you, Grace. Guess I'll be seeing plenty of you if you're working for Bobbie."

Grace managed a smile and nodded. "Yes, nice meeting you."

In minutes, Matt had his horse saddled and disappeared out the door. Cade wasted no time pulling his wagon inside the building, unhitching and feeding the draft horses, and then harnessing a fresh horse to a buggy.

"You ready?"

More than ready. Grace smiled and nodded, and they were soon headed back down the street. Five minutes later, Cade pulled to a stop outside a two-story, whitewashed house with pale green shutters. Two large swings hung on a porch that ran along the entire front of the house. Leafless rose bushes stood sentinel on either side of the steps.

Grace climbed out of the buggy while Cade grabbed their bags from the back. She followed him up the walkway and into the house.

He motioned to the left. "The parlor." He pointed to the right. "The kitchen. Upstairs are the bedrooms. I'll show you the room you'll use tonight. You can freshen up before you meet Mother."

Cade's pace never slowed, and she had to rush up the stairs to catch him. He placed her bag inside the first room on the left.

"Take your time. I'll be back for you later." He tossed his own bag in the next room before tapping on a door across the hall.

"Cade? Is that you?" The feminine voice sounded sweet.

Grace watched Cade disappear into the room, and it brought home the fact that she'd never see her mother again—at least not here on earth, though maybe in heaven if her mother's beliefs were right. She stepped inside her room, shut the door, and leaned against the wall. Her eyes and throat burned against the tears that threatened. She'd lost her best friend, her confidante, the only person who came close to understanding her.

Oh, Mama. What's going to happen to me now?

A lantern sat on the table by the door. She lit it and moved to the water stand to wash her face, but found the pitcher empty. She grabbed it and the lantern and headed for the kitchen.

The first rays of moonlight streamed through two large windows, blending with the soft glow of the lantern's flame. A large table sat in the center of the room. She set the lantern down and ran her hand along the wood. The smooth surface felt worn from years of use. She moved to the window and fingered the simple curtains, then pushed them aside to see the view. An empty street stared back. She continued to explore, enjoying her private acquaintance with Mrs. Ramsey's personality.

Counters ran along two walls, lending plenty of work area. A washstand stood next to a door that she presumed led outside. She moved around the room, touching the modest but tasteful decorations adorning the walls. The room felt homey and cheerful. The urge to stay here to work in a spacious kitchen instead of going to the ranch hit her full force.

A bucket sat at the end of the counter. Grace checked and found it full. She poured water into her pitcher and headed back to her bedroom. She raced to wash and change, knowing Cade might come for her at any time.

When finished, she opened the door, then sat on the bed and surveyed the room. It was much larger than her own back home, decorated in a soft blend of green and yellow. Curtains that matched the bedcover hung over one lone window. They reminded her of those her mother made back before she fell ill, the last ones she'd ever sewn.

Grace stood to look out over the street. Quiet darkness greeted her. Where were the gunshots, loud curses, and the shrill laughter of loose women? A smile played around her lips as she wondered if she would be able to sleep with so much silence.

A light tap brought her attention back inside. Cade stood waiting for her at the door.

"I wondered if maybe you'd fallen asleep," he said with a grin.

"I was just admiring your quiet street."

"I explained everything to Mother. She's waiting for you."

Grace followed him down the hall but stopped in the doorway. She expected to see a frail, sickly woman who looked older than her years. Instead, pink touched the woman's cheeks, and her lips curved in a vibrant smile. The only similarity between her mother and this woman was the joy that shone from their eyes. Grace's eyes welled at the thought.

"Oh, Grace." Ella Ramsey held her arms out to her. "Come to me, dear."

She stumbled into the room, knelt beside the bed, and leaned into the loving embrace waiting for her.

SIX

C ade slipped out of his mother's room and closed the door, allowing the two women to grieve in private. After stabling the horse in the small shed behind the house, he heated a pot of water and trudged with weary steps up to his bedroom. He left his door open so he could hear when Grace left, wanting to check on his mother one more time before he fell asleep. He sat on the side of his bed and ran his hands over his face. Fatigue took hold and sapped him of energy. He flopped back, enjoying the softness that swallowed him.

Quiet murmurs drifted from the room across the hall. He thought it strange that Grace had shown little sign of mourning until she saw his mother. Maybe that sight alone brought back memories she'd tried to forget. He swung his right leg up onto the bed and pulled the pillow under his head. His eyelids slid closed as he thought the day would never come that he'd figure out the mind of a woman.

The sound of a horse and buggy rolling by the window jerked him to a sitting position. He blinked several times and scrubbed at his eyes. A pink glow shone through the window announcing the start of a new day. He jumped to his feet, and a blanket dropped to the floor. He scooped it up and stared at it. His reflection in a mirror caught his attention, and he noted he was still fully dressed in the clothes he'd been wearing the day before.

He threw the blanket on the bed, disgusted with himself for falling asleep. What if his mother had needed something? He stripped off his shirt and moved to the basin. A shiver raced through him as he leaned over and splashed the frigid water over his face and neck. It took his breath away. He reached for the towel and scrubbed, but the action did little to warm his skin.

After putting on a clean shirt and denims, he moved to his mother's door and gave a light tap before entering. She turned her head toward him, stretched, and sent him a warm smile. No sign of her late night showed in her eyes or on her face.

"Did you get some rest, son?" Ella laughed when his mouth twisted at the sarcasm in her voice. "Grace told me you'd fallen asleep."

"I'm sorry."

"Don't be. I'm only teasing. That trip can wear out even stalwart men like you."

He kissed his mother's forehead. "Let me get you a cup of coffee."

His mother gripped his arm. "Wait, Cade. Have a seat. I want to talk to you first."

He slid the chair next to her bed and waited to hear what had her looking serious all of a sudden.

"It's about Grace."

He leaned back in his chair and nodded. "I figured this would come up. Just not so early in the morning."

"You know what I'm going to say?"

"You want Grace to stay here instead of going out to help Bobbie."

His mother gave a satisfied nod and smiled. "Well then, I guess we don't have anything more to discuss. I'll take that cup of coffee now."

He leaned forward and rested his elbows on his knees. "Oh, no. It's not going to be that easy."

"Sure it is. All you do is boil some water—"

"Mother. You know what I mean."

She chuckled and patted his arm. "Of course, I know what you mean. But Grace and I had a talk last night, and we both agreed she should stay here for a time. She can help me while I'm laid up in bed, and it'll give us a chance to get to know each other."

He sat back and remained silent, crossing his arms while waiting for her to finish stating her case. She didn't say another word, and the expression on her face looked as though she thought the matter settled.

"Are you finished?"

She nodded.

"Good. Now let me give you my view of this situation. You know as well as I do that you have more than enough help around here. Rebecca Cromwell will be coming through the kitchen door in a few minutes with a plate of food for you, followed by a dinner and supper plate throughout the day. Mrs. Robbins will drop by at least twice and probably feel inclined to do some cleaning while she's here. Then we have Annie Wallace, who spends a good part of her day here, along with her children, to keep you company just to make sure you don't get bored."

He leaned forward again. "Do I dare mention all the other townsfolk who stop by every day for a visit?"

"All right, all right." His mother waved her hand to make him stop. "So I have plenty of help. I still want to get to know Grace better."

He took his mother's hand in his. "And what about Bobbie?" He gentled his voice. "She has no one. She works all day out on the ranch, then has to come home and cook and clean late into the night, only to get up and do it again the next day. I know you love her, Mother, so why would you deprive her of someone who could make her life easier?"

His mother jerked her hand from his and frowned. She fiddled with the top blanket while she sat in silence. He allowed her time to think.

After several minutes ticked by, she looked up at him. "You always could talk circles around me."

He tried not to smile. "Does that mean you agree with me?"

She hesitated. "Yes. I don't like it, but yes, I think you're right. Bobbie does need someone to help her with the housework."

He did smile then. "Don't look so down, Mother. You know full well that Grace will be in town at least twice a week to get supplies and go to church. I'm sure Bobbie will allow her plenty of time to stop by for a nice visit."

"Yes, well, she'd better let Grace visit, me being so generous and all."

He winked and stood. "I'll get your coffee." He leaned down and kissed her cheek. "I love you."

She sent him a playful scowl. "I love you too...most of the time."

He chuckled all the way down the stairs. Clattering met his ears as he pushed through the swinging door into the kitchen. He expected to find Mrs. Cromwell inside. With only stockings on his feet, he slid to a stop when Grace stood at the counter setting a pot of coffee on a tray next to two cups. When she turned and saw him, she reached for another cup.

"Did you get enough rest?"

He could hear the smile in her voice. "Yes, as a matter of fact, I did. And you?"

"Plenty. That bed was much more comfortable than the back of the wagon."

He slapped his hand across his chest in pretended pain. "And here I pictured you camping out on the floor because you missed my ingenious bed-making abilities."

"Well, the thought crossed my mind, but without the horses snorting in the background and bugs landing on my face, it just wouldn't have been the same."

He laughed as he entered the room and accepted the cup of coffee she held out to him. "I'll be sure to mention that to Bobbie today. I'm sure she won't mind tethering a horse outside your open window."

Grace's smile faded while she stared at him. "You haven't seen your mother yet this morning?"

"I just left her room." He took a sip from his cup. "Mmm. This is great. I should have let you make the coffee while we were out on the trail."

"Did she tell you what we talked about?"

"You mean about you staying here instead of helping Bobbie?"

"Yes."

"It came up." He took another sip. "I talked her out of it."

"Why?" She set down the tray she had picked up. "Don't you want someone tending your mother? I'd take great care of her."

"I don't doubt that, Grace, but she doesn't need your help. She has plenty already, unlike Bobbie."

She leaned back against the counter and crossed her arms over her stomach. "Why doesn't anyone ever bother asking me what *I* want? First Daddy, then Frank. Now you." She turned to pick up the tray. "Well, we'll just see what your mother has to say about this." She headed toward the stairs, giving the swinging door a push with her foot.

"Grace."

He started to follow her but stopped when the kitchen door leading outside opened. Mrs. Cromwell sent him a bright smile while she balanced a loaded platter against her hip. He glanced over his shoulder at Grace's disappearing figure as the door swung shut, and then rushed to take the tray from his neighbor's arms.

Who does he think he is? Grace fumed all the way up the stairs. *Why do people keep trying to run my life? Well, it's going to end right now, today.*

She stopped in front of Mrs. Ramsey's bedroom door, straightened her shoulders, and took two deep breaths. She forced a smile, tapped on the door, and turned the knob without waiting for an answer. Ella sat in bed, her hands folded on top of the Bible lying open on her lap.

Grace tried to back out of the room without disturbing Mrs. Ramsey's prayer.

"Come back in here, Grace."

"I'm so sorry, Mrs. Ramsey. How rude of me to burst in here without waiting for your invitation. I promise, my mother raised me to know better."

Ella waved her into the room and gestured toward the nearby chair. "Oh, hush now. I'm sure your mother raised you to live up to your name."

Grace set the tray on the table next to the bed and tried not to laugh. "Well, maybe she didn't do *that* great of a job."

Ella chuckled and accepted the cup of coffee she handed her. "I take it by the look on your face when you entered that you've already run into Cade."

"Was it that obvious?"

"Only because I felt the same way you looked when he managed to convince me you were needed on the Double K." Ella reached to touch her hand. "As much as I don't want to admit it, Grace, he's right. I would be selfish to keep you to myself."

She clutched at Mrs. Ramsey's fingers. "There's nothing I can do or say to convince you otherwise?" Tears formed in the older woman's eyes, and Grace hated that she had caused them. They also gave the answer she didn't want to hear. "It's all right."

"I'm sorry, Grace. But as Cade suggested, we'll have time during the week to visit when you come into town."

She stared into her cup and nodded. "Men. Why is it they always get what they want and we have to live with their decisions?" She looked up at Cade's mom in horror. "Oh no, Mrs. Ramsey. I didn't mean to say that."

Ella patted her hand again. "You've learned much about men at a young age."

"Not that I've had much experience, but the men I've known tend toward overbearing."

"It'll change. When you fall in love and know that your man loves you in return, you'll realize they're doing the best they can to take care of you."

She started to shake her head before Ella finished. "I'm never getting married. I've had about all I can take of men and what they think is best for me. Don't get me wrong. I love my father and all he's done, but I think I can manage just fine on my own."

Ella smiled at her. "Well, just know I'll be praying for you."

She closed her eyes against the wave of sorrow that slammed into her heart. That sounded like something her mother would have said years ago.

"Grace? Are you all right?"

She opened her eyes in time to see Ella wince when she tried to lean closer to her. She set her cup aside and took Ella's from her shaking hand. "Are you hurt? Do I need to get Cade?"

"No, dear. I just moved more than I should have. I'm fine." Ella looked up and must have figured that Grace was unconvinced. "Really, Grace. The pain recedes much faster than it used to. I fully expect to experience pain when I first start walking again."

She sat back down and fiddled with the hem of her sleeve. "You know, Mrs. Ramsey, we spent so much time last night talking about my mother and your friendship with her, I never was able to ask you something." She looked up and met Ella's gaze. "Do you mind if I ask how you were hurt?"

Ella looked away and smoothed the bed cover. "It was an accident, the result of an old woman acting foolish."

Grace sat silent, hoping she would continue.

Ella sighed. "I was pestering Cade, lost my footing, and fell down the stairs. My poor son feels guilty about it, but I want to make something clear right now, Grace." Ella turned to face her, and her eyes took on an intensity that Grace could feel. "That boy was in no way at fault. Don't let him or anyone else tell you otherwise."

There had to be more to the story. Just what was it that happened at the top of those stairs?

The bedroom door opened and jarred Grace from her thoughts. Cade's gaze connected with hers in a way that made her feel he was searching her very soul. She looked away, alarmed at how the idea disturbed her. A woman about the same age as Ella entered behind Cade, her face beaming. The creases around her eyes and mouth made it apparent smiling was something she did often. Ella held her hand out to her.

"Rebecca Cromwell, come in and meet Grace."

Grace stood, and Rebecca enveloped her in a warm hug. "Ella has told me so much about you and your mother, Grace, that I feel I already know you."

She stepped back and smiled. "It's nice to meet you too."

Cade moved to the side table, removed the coffee tray, and replaced it with his mother's breakfast tray. "If you're ready, Grace, I'd like to head out to the ranch. I want to get back and open the livery at a decent time this morning."

"Let me get my coat."

"Rebecca made breakfast for us. Go ahead and take a minute to enjoy it. Trust me, it's great."

Trust you? She shook her head. "No, but thank you. I don't have much of an appetite this morning." She leaned down and kissed Ella's cheek. "I'll see you later." She turned. "And nice meeting you, Rebecca."

She slipped out the door and into her room. She took a deep breath and fought the urge to run for her life—and her freedom. But where would she go, and how would she get there without money? Maybe once she had a little more cash, she would feel brave enough to venture further into the world.

She headed down the steps and heard noises coming from the kitchen. She peeked inside and saw Cade washing dishes. The sight surprised her.

"I'm ready," she said as she pushed through the swinging door.

Cade grabbed a towel and turned, wiping a plate dry. He glanced down at her hands. "Where's your bag?"

"My bag?"

"Your travel bag. You'll need some clothes to change into out at the ranch."

She propped her hands on her hips. "You mean I'm staying there?"

He stopped wiping the plate and set it aside. "Well, of course you're staying. What did you think would happen?"

"That I would go out to meet your friends and then decide if it would work out."

"What's not to work out? I know you'll all get along great. Now run up and get your bag so we can go. I have the buggy waiting outside."

"Do I get a say at all in what happens in my life? What if I don't want to go out there? What if I don't like it? What if I want to stay here?" She took a trembling breath. "I want to work for your mother, Cade."

He walked toward her. "We went through this, Grace. Mother doesn't need your help. Bobbie does." He cocked his head to one side. "What is it that bothers you so much about working at the ranch? I thought you needed a job."

"I do."

"Then what's the problem?"

"I guess there isn't one."

He stopped in front of her. "So you'll get your bag?"

Her hands curled into fists. She wanted to scream. "Yes. You win. I'll get my bag."

She spun on her heel and pushed through the swinging door, then shoved it closed. She heard a grunt. She turned in time to see Cade holding the side of his face before the swinging door wobbled to its closed position.

What have I done?

She pushed back through to find out if he was hurt, only to bang the door into him again. Cade groaned and took two steps backward.

She grasped his wrist and tried to pull his hand away from his face. "Oh, Cade. I'm so sorry." She pulled at his hand again. "Let me see." Her attempt to budge his arm was like trying to move a stout tree. "Let me see your face, Cade."

He moved his hand away, and Grace gasped. His eye was already beginning to swell, not to mention the red mark on his forehead where she hit him the second time. She reached up and placed her hands on each side of his face, her thumb gently caressing the swollen area.

"I'm so sorry, Cade." Her voice came in a whisper as she fought back tears. The desire to kiss his eye was strong, right up until he grasped her wrists and pushed her hands from his face.

Cade heard Grace gasp right before she pulled free of him, turned, and ran out the door. Out of instinct, he took another step back, not wanting to get hit again. But stronger still was the tingling sensation her touch left on his cheeks. *What just happened?* How could Grace affect him that way when he had just been in love with Kim? He heard Grace's footsteps coming back down the stairs and moved to grab his coat.

She entered the kitchen, but he couldn't look at her, afraid his eyes would give away his thoughts. He avoided meeting her gaze as he held the outside door for her, and then again when he helped her into the buggy. Her silence didn't escape his notice. He commented on the unseasonably warm weather and received a mere nod. Either she was still mad at him or he'd hurt her feelings when he pushed her away. Whatever the reason, he decided it best to leave things as they were.

Grace remained silent for the first mile. Then she heaved a big sigh and glanced around as if just awaking.

"How much further?"

"A little over a mile."

She nodded and peered again at the countryside. "It's pretty out here."

"Wait till you see the ranch. Jace told me his dad decided to ask for a job from the first owner just so he could have a great view while he worked."

"First owner? I thought Jace owned the ranch."

"He does. Mr. Kincaid bought the ranch. It became Jace's when his dad died."

She adjusted her bonnet after a small gust of wind moved it back on her head. "I didn't see your father anywhere. Is he away?"

"Yes."

"On business?"

"Yes."

"What business is he in?"

He'd never complain about her being silent again. "Surveying."

"Oh." She fiddled with her gloves. "I guess a job like that keeps him away quite often."

"It does."

More often than he liked to think about. Jace's dad had been more of a father than his own while he grew up. At least Mr. Kincaid was around most of the time. Cade and his father never developed a bond like he saw in Jace and his dad, which is why he found it surprising his father got so angry when he didn't want to follow in his footsteps. He'd given up trying to develop a relationship with him years ago.

The realization that Grace still stared at him jerked his thoughts back to the present. He steered his mare down the embankment that would lead across a bridge onto the Double K.

"We're here."

He tilted back his head and inhaled. It would be good to see Jace, who was like a brother to him. They had grown up sharing every-thing, from thoughts, feelings, and toys to Jace even sharing his dad with him. And now Jace had found a bride in Bobbie, who had become like a sister to Cade.

He pulled to a stop next to the barn and waved at those working the horses in the far corral. He turned, helped Grace from the buggy, and led her toward his friends. Bobbie scaled the fence and jumped onto her horse's back. She spun her mount around and raced toward them at full speed.

"Here comes Bobbie." Jace wasn't too far behind.

Grace stopped. "Oh, my."

"What?"

"I thought she would be..." Her hand went to her face. "She's pretty."

Bobbie reined in her horse right in front of them, its hooves skidding in the dirt, and dismounted. "You made it back. It's good to see you again."

Cade opened his arms, and Bobbie launched herself into them. He spun her around and gave her a kiss on the cheek before putting her back on her feet.

"It's good to be back. You know I break into a rash when I get more than ten miles from home."

Bobbie laughed. She peered closer at his face and then touched his swollen eye. "Did you win?"

He cast a quick glance at Grace, who eyed Bobbie's horse with a look of more than a little trepidation. "I'm not sure yet."

"Cade." Jace dismounted, grabbed Cade's outstretched hand, and pulled him in for a hug and a few claps on the shoulder. "Glad you're back, old friend. It's not the same around town without you."

"Thanks." He turned and touched Grace's elbow. "I'd like you both to meet Grace Bradley. It was her mother's funeral I attended in Pueblo."

He tugged Grace forward, making her walk between him and the horse she'd been trying to avoid. She stepped on the toe of his boot in her attempt to stay away from the beast.

"Grace, this is Bobbie." The two shook hands. "And this is my longtime friend, Jace Kincaid."

Grace moved to accept Jace's hand, but when Bobbie's horse followed her, she let out a tiny shriek and spun around behind Cade. The horse trailed her, its nose pointing toward the skirt of her dress. Grace continued using Cade as a shield, edging around him in an attempt to stay a step ahead. He tried to stop her but she slipped from his grasp.

"Hold up, Grace. Mack won't—ow!" Cade tugged at his foot, but the horse's hoof pinned it to the ground. He shoved at the horse, then tried to reach the reins. "Get off, Mack."

Grace darted behind Bobbie, grabbing her arms from behind like a shield. Bobbie held up her hand.

"Stop, Mack."

The horse obeyed, but he sniffed at Grace again. Bobbie freed her arm from Grace and grasped Mack's reins. Then she turned to face their guest. "Do you have some sugar in your pocket, Grace?"

"What?"

"Sugar. Mack loves anything sweet and can sniff it out anywhere."

Grace reached her shaking hand into her skirt pocket and pulled out a small cloth bag. Mack's ears perked up.

"It's candy," she said and opened the bag. A pretty pink color washed across her cheeks and a timid smile touched her lips. "I have a sweet tooth too."

Bobbie burst into laughter. "I wondered why he took an instant liking to you." She reached into her coat pocket, pulled out the ever-present sweet treat, and fed it to Mack.

Grace's jaw dropped open. "He likes me? I'd hate to see his reaction if he hated me."

Cade leaned on Jace with one hand and rubbed his sore toes with the other. What was it about Grace that got him into trouble? First spooking his horses, the wolves, then the door, and now his foot. The sooner he shook her loose, the sooner he'd be safe.

"Grace is looking for a job, Bobbie. I thought maybe you could use some help around here, housecleaning and cooking. You know, all the stuff you don't like."

Bobbie gave him a shove. "You're such a rat, Cade."

The push knocked him off balance, and he had to stand on his sore foot to keep from hitting the ground. "I thought you'd welcome some help."

"I would. And I appreciate you thinking of me." She turned to Grace. "How about it? Will you stay? I'm not at all demanding, much easier to look at than Cade, and I guarantee I'm much more pleasant to live with."

Grace laughed. It was the first laugh Cade had heard from her in a while, and he liked the sound.

"Well, you're definitely not the person I expected to meet."

Bobbie's eyebrows rose. "Is that good or bad?"

"Very good. Trust me."

Bobbie frowned at Cade, and he gave an innocent shrug. She turned back to Grace. "Does that mean you'll take the job?"

"Show me to my room."

Bobbie placed her arm around Grace's shoulders. "It'll be nice to have another female around here. You'll be more fun to talk to, and I know you'll smell better."

Jace crossed his arms. "Now hold on there."

Bobbie winked at them over her shoulder as they headed toward the house.

Jace clapped Cade on the back. "You coming in for a while?"

He shook his head and limped toward the buggy. "Not today. I need to get back to work." He grabbed Grace's bag, held it out to his friend, and nodded toward the house. "Tell her I'll be back again to check on her when I bring out your lumber." He patted Jace's shoulder. "I'll leave her in your capable hands. Just…be careful."

"About what?"

He rubbed at his swollen eye and held out his foot. "Strange things happen when she's around."

"*She* did that to your eye?"

Cade nodded. "And more. But I'll leave that for another day." He saw Grace turn back. He waved and climbed into the buggy, knowing he'd have at least a couple accident-free days.

SEVEN

G race rolled to her back and pulled the bedcovers from over her head. Roosters weren't supposed to crow until dawn. Wasn't that right? Jace and Bobbie's roosters must be blind.

She glanced out the window but only the light of the pale moon shone through. Why couldn't those infernal roosters see that? But no. Their crowing came almost nonstop, each feathered nuisance louder than the one before.

She shifted to her side, slid her head to the edge of the pillow, wrapped the other end over her ear, and draped her arm over the pillow. She groaned when she could still hear them. She flopped onto her back and peeked again at the window through half closed eyes.

This pillow could sure use more feathers. I wonder if Bobbie would like chicken for dinner.

The thought of Bobbie made her smile. She had prepared herself to meet someone as masculine as her name. What she found instead was a thoughtful, sensitive, and humorous young woman. What she lacked in femininity, she made up for in kindness and consideration.

When Cade left that first morning, she had wanted to chase him down, wrap her arms around his neck, and beg him to take her with him. Bobbie must have noticed her anxiety, for she led her into the house, and while showing her around, assured her that if at any time she wanted to leave, Bobbie would hitch up a wagon and take her back to town. Grace warmed to her new boss that instant. The two sat down, discussed her duties, and agreed on wages. Bobbie left her on her own then, something she appreciated. Better to settle in by herself than have someone looking over her shoulder.

That thought made her think of Cade. He popped into mind often, as if he hovered nearby, though he hadn't been back to the ranch since he dropped her off.

She got up and crossed the room to wash her face since getting more sleep seemed impossible, especially now that Cade entered her thoughts. Granted, she hadn't gone out of her way to be extra nice to him, almost fighting him at every turn. And they did get along about as well as a bear and a honeybee. But he could at least show up to check on her, maybe give her a chance to thank him for talking her into working for Bobbie.

The job was easy and similar to what she'd grown up doing. Except for the livestock. She'd never been near ranch animals before, and they unnerved her. She always kept an eye on them and gave them a wide berth. So far, they'd made no advances, but the way they looked at her, she felt sure they were only biding their time.

Grace groaned at the clatter of a pot on the stove. How could Bobbie function at such an early hour? Maybe she'd be ready to kill the roosters too. She made the bed before getting dressed. The scent of coffee drew her like a magnet to the kitchen. She'd need a whole pot after waking so early.

"Good morning." Bobbie's cheery greeting sounded as though she'd been awake for hours. "I'll slice some ham if you'll get the eggs going."

"Sure thing." Grace poured herself a cup of coffee and took a sip before fetching the egg basket.

Working together, they whipped up a quick and tasty breakfast, then hollered for Jace, who appeared from his office rubbing his stomach. As usual, Jace said the blessing before they started eating. Bobbie took her first bite, then pointed her fork at Grace.

"I forgot to talk to you about something last night."

Grace stopped chewing and held her breath.

"There's a tent town nearby with several families waiting to head west. I usually check on them once or twice a week, sometimes bringing them food and medical supplies. Most of them have only meager provisions left."

Grace quietly gave a sigh of relief and finished chewing her bite. "I know of the tent town. The couple Cade and I rode with stopped there."

"I heard some of them are sick. Would you be willing to fix up a couple pots of soup to take there, help them out a bit?"

"Sure. I'd be glad to."

"Great. I think chicken soup will sit best on their stomachs."

Bobbie dug into her breakfast with gusto, not noticing that Grace only picked at hers and ended up leaving half of it on her plate. Chicken soup meant she'd have to kill some chickens. Jace finished his breakfast quickly, kissed Bobbie on the cheek, and told her he'd see her at the corral.

After he was gone, Grace said, "Ah, how do I go about getting the chickens?"

"Oh, that's easy. Just leave them locked up until you catch a couple. Then you can let the rest out." Bobbie rose to put her plate and cup on the counter.

"Then what?"

Bobbie turned and studied her. "You've never killed a chicken?" At Grace's shake of the head, Bobbie smiled. "There's really nothing to it. Once you catch them, wring their neck, and then pluck them. After that, you just take out the insides and clean them up for cooking."

Grace raised her eyebrows at the idea of wringing a chicken's neck. "All right. I think I can do that."

"Great." Bobbie headed for the door. "If you need help, holler. But I think you'll do fine. We'll try to leave around eleven. Will that work?"

"I'll be ready."

"If there are any eggs you don't think we'll need today or for breakfast tomorrow, let's bring those too." With that, Bobbie disappeared outside.

Grace stood and started cleaning up the breakfast dishes, mentally preparing herself for the task ahead. The way Bobbie explained it, it didn't sound too difficult.

The rising sun cast a pink glow through the trees as she made her way to the coop. After only three days, she decided she loved living on the ranch. Surrounded by trees, creeks, and nature, the quiet security made her feel wrapped in a warm blanket. Her peaceful moment was shattered when one of the roosters crowed from the top of the coop. She jumped, glaring at the beast. What she wouldn't give to be able to wring *that* fowl's neck.

She opened the coop door just enough to squeeze inside. The horrible pneumonia smell of droppings, feathers, and dirty straw brought tears to her eyes and stung her nostrils. She'd have to clean out the coop soon so she'd be able to continue breathing. On such a cool morning, the heat inside surprised her and made the stench that much stronger.

She reached into the shadows where she knew the chickens perched. When her hand touched a leg, she grabbed hold and headed out the door with the bird squawking and flapping its wings. All the others joined in as if she'd caught them too. She slammed the door shut and grabbed the other leg before the thing shook loose.

Now to wring its neck. Surely it would be no more difficult than squeezing water out of a cloth. Grace knelt next to the coop and eyed the hen. It craned its head toward her and stared back, its beady eyes daring her to do more than let it go. She took a deep breath, released one leg, and reached for the neck.

Once she had the chicken by the neck, she let go of the other leg and grasped its scrawny throat with both hands. The chicken clawed at her coat and slapped her on both sides of her head with its wings while ear-piercing squawks poured from its beak. Her ears and cheeks stinging, Grace held it at arm's length and prepared to twist.

"What are you doing?"

The voice spooked her so bad, she screamed as she stood. The chicken flew from her grasp...right into Cade's grinning face, leaving a scratch before landing on the ground and tearing off, clucking frantically. Blood welled up in the cut on Cade's face.

"You scared me," Grace said, her already racing heart doing a double thump.

"*I* scared *you*?" He took a kerchief out of his pocket and swabbed at his cheek. "Why were you torturing that poor bird?"

She longed to exchange the chicken's neck for his. "I wasn't torturing it. I need to kill a couple chickens for some soup."

"By strangling them?"

Heat raced up her neck and filled her face. She pulled at the collar of her coat. "I've...um...never killed one before."

He stared at her for a moment, then roared with laughter. Too bad she didn't have another chicken to throw at him. He stepped around her, reached inside the coop, and pulled out a second chicken. He gestured to the one that got away.

"I doubt you'll ever be able to catch that one again." The grin on his face stretched wider than the Colorado Territory sky. "Let me show you how it's done."

With a couple flicks and a quick jerk, the headless body dropped to the ground and started flopping. Grace backed up against the wall of the coop, her hand over her mouth.

"I can't do that. That's awful!"

He stared at her for several moments, then headed toward the barn. "I'll be right back. Start plucking that one while I'm gone."

The chicken no longer moved...a definite plus. She nudged it with her foot. Nothing. She grabbed up the fowl and pulled on the feathers. They weren't any too ready to leave the body. Determination made her try harder. Soon, a cloud of plumes and down floated in the air, some landing on her coat and skirt, others scattering around her.

Cade returned and stopped several feet from her, a hatchet and block of wood in his hands. "You didn't use water?"

"For what?" She blew at a small feather threatening to land on her nose.

"If you dunk them in hot water a few times before plucking them, the feathers will come off easier."

"Oh." She motioned to his hands with her head. "What are those for?"

"These," he said, and dropped the chunk of wood on the ground and knelt over it, "will make your job a little easier."

He pulled a couple large nails from his pocket and pounded them into the wood about an inch apart, and then looked up and smiled.

"Ready?"

Distrust niggled at her. "For what?"

He disappeared into the coop and, after more scuffling and squawking, returned with another chicken and exchanged the live one for the half naked one in her hands.

"See those nails?"

She held the bird at arm's length and eyed him with more than a little trepidation. "Uh-huh."

"If you put the chicken's neck in between them and stretch it out a little, a quick chop with that hatchet will do the rest of the work for you."

Her mouth dropped open. "I can't do that."

"Sure you can. It beats strangling it to death." He nudged her toward the block. "Give it a try. I promise it's not as bad as you think."

She took the hatchet, holding it with thumb and index finger, her nose scrunched. The doomed chicken eyed her now just as the first one had.

He motioned to the wood. "It'll be quick and easy. And besides, the head has to come off anyway." When she didn't move, he shrugged. "Up to you, but you're going to have to get used to killing them sooner or later."

Dread filled her. After taking a deep breath and slowly exhaling, she moved to the block of wood. He squatted next to her and helped her place the chicken's neck between the nails. Then he took her hand holding the bird's legs and pulled, stretching out the neck.

"You're all set. Now, just give it a whack."

She took in another long, trembling breath, lifted the hatchet over her head, and...hesitated.

"It usually works better if your eyes are open."

Her breath went out in a whoosh as her eyes popped open. "Would you like to do this?"

He fought a smile and lost. He put his hands up defensively. "Just giving you some pointers. Wouldn't want you lopping off your hand by mistake."

If he didn't watch himself, she'd lop off something of his.

Smack. She flung the body from her as fast as she could and scooted away. Cade stood next to her, his arm going around her as she turned into his shoulder while the chicken finished flopping. When she heard no more noise, she peeked and found it motionless.

"You did great." The look on Cade's face was both serious and tender.

"Yeah?"

"Yeah." He waggled his fingers at her. "You left me intact."

She swung at him with her free hand but missed when he stepped away. She couldn't help but laugh. "Bobbie's right. You're a rat."

With a grin, he stooped to pick up the chicken. "Come on. I'll help you clean these up. Then I've got to get to work. I'm already running late."

Several hours later Grace still smiled about the incident as she sat on the wagon seat regaling Bobbie with the whole sordid story. She felt a teensy bit of pride that she actually went through with the task and felt certain she wouldn't have a problem doing it again.

Before she and Bobbie left, they'd separated the soup into three pots to lessen the chance of it sloshing over the sides on the bumpy road. Two large platters of biscuits were also in the back. Grace had no idea how many people lived in the tent town, but she hoped to make sure none of them went away hungry.

Shock rolled through her at her first glimpse of the small community. Sprawled in no apparent system were at least 30 covered wagons and tents, all surrounded by mud. The horses and other livestock milling around looked miserable and hungry. She wondered if they'd be strong enough to make it across the mountains.

Many families huddled around their campfires, soaking in the warmth. For the first time, Grace comprehended what little protection the canvas over their heads provided. A sick feeling washed over her for what they must have gone through. She hadn't given a thought to Layton and Katie Woods since they had parted ways. Instead, she'd been selfishly focused on her own petty problems.

Children ran toward them with smiles on their dirty faces as they hollered Bobbie's name. The moment the wheels stopped, Bobbie jumped to the ground and hugged every last one of them.

"Where are Betsy and Claire?" She looked around with a frown. "And Joey."

"They're sick."

Bobbie placed her hands on her hips. "Well, then, I guess I'll just have to go to them to get my hugs." She started walking away, then stopped and pointed to Grace. "Hey, kids. This is my new friend, Grace Bradley. She made some soup and biscuits for everyone. Go tell your parents we have some food for you."

The children squealed their delight and scurried off in different directions. Bobbie waved Grace down from where she remained on the seat.

"Come with me. You've got to meet these folks. They're a great bunch."

"What about the food?"

"They'll come and get what they need."

After her first few cautious steps, Grace gave up trying to save her shoes and hemline and trudged through the mud alongside Bobbie. She met several of the residents, knowing full well she'd never remember their names. Some of the children hung back, hiding behind their mother's skirts, while others followed them around chattering as if they'd known her for years. Bobbie came to a sudden stop, though, when a tall black man jumped from the back of his wagon.

"Joseph? What are you doing here? Is Belle all right?" Bobbie brushed past him to climb into the wagon.

"She took sick last night."

Grace listened to the faint mumblings coming from the wagon as she examined the broad shoulders of the tall man in front of her. Words failed her. The sheer size of him made her feel like the children who had followed them, and she understood the desire to hide behind someone's skirt.

Joseph grinned at her, his white teeth gleaming in the sunlight. "You must be the young lady Mr. Cade tol' me about." He held out his massive hand. "Pleased to meet you."

"I'm sorry. I—"

"Joseph Kline, ma'am. I works for Mr. Cade till we head west."

His gentle touch surprised her. "Oh. Yes, of course. Nice to meet you, Joseph."

Bobbie jumped from the wagon with a pot and handed it to Joseph. "Grace, would you mind watching over Belle for a bit? Joseph and I are going to get some of your soup and biscuits." She leaned closer to her ear. "Her skin looks pasty enough to have me worried."

Bobbie peeked back through the covering and pulled Grace

forward. "Belle, this is Grace, the friend I told you about. She's going to sit with you for a bit."

A weak and unintelligible response came back. Concern covered Joseph's face as he stepped to the wagon, but Bobbie stopped him from entering. "Grace has some nursing knowledge. Let her check on Belle while we get you two something to eat."

Without a word, Joseph helped Grace into their home before following Bobbie. The scent of sickness met her nose full force, and she hoped she could live up to Bobbie's confidence in her. She didn't have a lick of formal training.

She knelt next to the thin form lying on a thick pallet, covers heaped on top, and felt Belle's forehead. Steam should have been coming from her feverish skin. The quiet moan let her know her cool hand was welcome.

"Bless you, child."

The whisper rasped from fever-cracked lips, and Grace wondered how much water Joseph had gotten into her. She glanced around for a cloth to use as a compress. Unable to find any, she pulled off her apron, poured a glass of water onto it, and, after folding it many times, placed it on Belle's forehead. The poor woman gasped.

"Would you like me to take it off?" Grace said.

"No. Oh, no. It feels heavenly. Thank you."

"How about a sip of water?"

"It doesn't usually stay in my stomach long."

"Let's try just a small sip. If it sits well, we'll add a little more to it later."

She helped Belle sit up enough for a small drink, then laid her back down and replaced the compress. The woman's pulse throbbed in her neck, accentuating her frailty.

Grace was about to take the pot Belle had been sick in outside to dump it when gunshots rang out. They boomed from all around them. Grace threw herself on top of Belle and listened to her prayer for safety.

✳ EIGHT ✳

Grace lay in the wagon listening to the blasts. A shot ripped through the canvas. She wished she could somehow shrink herself. The horses' shrill screams made her flesh crawl. Or maybe the shrieks came from the women and children. The explosions were so loud, Grace wondered if the shooters were right next to the wagon. Belle's violent shaking made Grace's flesh tremble. Why in the world were they shooting…and at what, or who?

The shots ended as suddenly as they'd started. She expected silence. Instead, scared children cried and shouted for their mothers.

"All you men drop your guns, or we'll start shooting into the tents."

The quiet pause didn't last long. The cocking of a rifle crackled through the air.

"Do it now."

Muffled thuds let Grace know the men obeyed.

"You know what we want," a man's voice shouted. "Get it out here or your women and children start dying."

Part of her wanted to peek out the canvas and see what was happening. Most of her wanted to stay still and hope they didn't search the tents and wagons.

"I'll count to ten. Then people start getting hurt."

Whimpers and quiet sobbing drifted through the camp.

"One."

Almost all sounds stopped. Not even a bird sang from the trees.

"Two."

Belle's whispered prayer rasped through the wagon.

"Three."

Another gunshot went off, followed by a groan and a curse.

Terror made her want to run for the hills, but she knew her trembling legs wouldn't hold her up. Her stomach churned, and she almost heaved into the nearby bucket. *They didn't even wait till ten to shoot someone!*

"I suggest you move along. There's nothing here for you."

Was that Bobbie's voice?

"Get us the strongbox with all the money. Then we'll leave."

"There's no strongbox here."

That is Bobbie.

"That's not what we heard."

"You heard wrong. Now, no one needs to get hurt. Just take your men and leave."

In the silence that followed, Grace could almost picture the standoff between the gunmen and Bobbie. Were there any others helping her oppose them? She moved toward the opening in the canvas but stopped when Belle grabbed her arm and shook her head.

"Let me shoot her, Z. I can take her," a voice whispered.

"Shut up."

Another cocking of a rifle echoed through the camp. "Next time, I aim to kill." Bobbie's voice sounded strong and threatening. "I don't want to, but I will if you don't pull out."

"All right."

"But Z."

"Don't shoot. We'll leave."

Grace heard grumbling from one man and a groan from another. Hoofbeats thundered away from them. She waited until Belle released her arm before poking her head through the back of the wagon. Joseph raced toward them, plunged into the wagon, and pulled his wife into his arms.

Grace jumped to the ground. A few others emerged from their hiding places as well. Bobbie stood in the back of her wagon, the rifle still in her hands, peering in the direction the gunmen must have disappeared. Grace slopped through the mud to Bobbie's wagon.

"You all right?"

Bobbie looked down at her, then back to the hills. "Sure. What about Belle and the others? Anyone hurt?"

Grace glanced around the camp. "Belle's fine, and it looks like everyone else is too."

A man rode up to them, his horse dancing as though skittish from the gunplay. "I'm riding into town for the sheriff." He spurred his horse and tore down the path.

Fear that the men would shoot from a hiding place made Grace step closer to the wagon. She peered up at Bobbie's tense form.

"How many were there?"

"Three that I saw."

"Did you know any of them?"

Bobbie shook her head. "Their faces were covered."

"They didn't put up much of a fight, especially since you were outnumbered."

Bobbie relaxed enough to lean against the wagon seat. "I shot one man in the hand, the one doing the talking. Made him drop his gun. Would you mind getting it for me before the children find it?" She pointed to a spot at the edge of camp. "It should be right in that area."

The handle of the pistol stuck up in ready view, the barrel three inches deep in the mud. With thumb and forefinger, she lifted it and held it out in front of her while she headed back toward Bobbie. Even though her father was a gunsmith, the deadly weapons had always frightened her. The streets of Pueblo often echoed with gunfire, and then she would hear the awful tales of death at the hands of lawless men.

Several men clustered around the wagon, all trying to wipe their weapons clean. Layton Woods stood with them and nodded a greeting. Grace handed the pistol up to Bobbie. Joseph's pan still sat next to the pots of soup.

"Bobbie, I'm going to take Belle their soup and see if there are any others who didn't get some yet."

"Good idea. With all the men here keeping watch, I'll help you carry a pot around to each home."

They headed straight to Joseph and Belle's wagon. After filling the Klines' pan and wrapping several biscuits in a cloth, they climbed inside. Joseph slid over and let Bobbie take his place.

She laid a cloth over Belle's nightgown. "Let's see if we can get some of this chicken broth into you, Belle. If it sits all right, maybe Joseph can feed you more tonight."

While Bobbie held Belle's head, Grace managed to spoon a few sips into her mouth.

Belle shook her head. "That's enough for now. Thank you." Her tired voice rose just above a whisper. She reached for Bobbie. "Joseph said you shot a man."

"Only in the hand to make him drop his gun."

"You be careful, Bobbie. You hear me? Most men won't take kindly to a woman besting them."

"I'll be fine. I'm surrounded by men at home. And you know Jace watches over me worse than a new mama with her firstborn."

"I know. But I'll be praying."

Bobbie patted her arm. "Thank you, Belle. Now Grace and I are going to make sure everyone in camp gets some of her soup. We'll check back in on you in a couple days unless you need us sooner. Send Joseph if that's the case."

Belle looked at her husband, adoration shimmering from her eyes. "We'll be fine."

By the time they'd visited all the shelters and returned to Bobbie's wagon, the sheriff had arrived. Cade stood next to him, but rushed toward Grace and Bobbie once he saw them.

"You two all right?" His arm went around Bobbie's shoulders, but his gaze lingered on Grace as he waited for their answer.

"We're fine, Cade. No one got hurt."

"Yeah, that's what the men said."

The sheriff walked over to them. "The men told me what they know. Now how about you tell me your version, Bobbie. Did you know any of them?"

"I don't think so."

"Nothing about them was familiar? Their horses or clothing?"

"No, and I sure looked as close as I dared."

"Tell me what happened."

Bobbie set the pot of soup in the back of the wagon and sat next to it. "I was already up in the wagon bed when they rode in and fired the first shot. I lay down and crawled up to the front toward my rifle. First chance I got, I shot the pistol from the leader's hand." She grabbed it and passed it to the sheriff. "I don't think he had much fight left in him after that."

The sheriff tipped his hat back with a bump of his thumb. "Did he know it was you doing the shooting?"

Bobbie shrugged. "I guess if he's from around here he did."

After telling the men they should post a watchman every night, the sheriff mounted his horse, then turned to Bobbie. "I'll see if I can track them through this mud. Then I'll check with our gunsmith to see if he recognizes this pistol." He shook his finger at her. "You look after yourself, young lady."

Cade stepped between them. "I'll ride home with them."

"Good." With a touch to his hat toward the ladies, the sheriff rode out of the camp.

Bobbie stood up in the wagon and strode to the seat.

"Miss Bobbie?"

She swung around.

A man tugging a goat along next to him waved at her. To Grace, the goat looked none too happy and sounded even worse, what with all the racket it made with its bleating. It shook its head and tried to dig in its feet, but the man just kept jerking on the rope. The horns were easily eight inches long and looked much too pointed on the ends. Grace took several steps back.

"What can I do for you, Mr. Nickerson?" Bobbie said.

"I need a favor." He held up the rope. "Take this goat."

Bobbie pulled her hand back as if she'd been bit. "Now wait a minute."

"Ya gotta take it, Miss Bobbie. It's starving. I got nothing left to feed it, and there's no grass for grazing. I doubt it's strong enough to make it over the mountains."

Grace saw the hesitation in Bobbie's face and panicked. Surely she wouldn't take it home. The beast stood almost as tall as her. If she and the goat ever came face-to-face, there was no doubt who would win the battle. *Say no.*

"I don't know, Mr. Nickerson."

"Please, Miss Bobbie. The only other thing to do is to eat it, and you know how tough the meat would be."

Much to Grace's dismay, Bobbie took the rope.

"All right, but under one condition. I'll take it home and feed it, get it strong again for you. Before you head west, you have to take it back." The man remained silent, and Bobbie narrowed her eyes. "Is it a deal?"

"Sounds fair enough. I appreciate the help, Miss Bobbie. I couldn't stand by and watch old Jonah die."

Bobbie's eyebrows rose almost to her hat. "Jonah?"

"Wife gave it that name." He tipped his hat and all but ran from them.

Laughter made Grace swing around.

"You're too easy, Bobbie," Cade said. "I hope you know he has no plans on taking it back."

Bobbie scowled at him. "Oh, yes, he will. If I have to drag this animal on foot, he's coming back. Now help me truss him up so we can get home."

Cade's chuckles could still be heard between the goat's bleats as he helped Bobbie tie the goat's legs together and then heft it into the back of the wagon.

"Why don't you let it walk behind the wagon?" Grace said. If they did, maybe it would escape.

Bobbie wiped her hands on her pant legs. "I don't want it slowing us down. This way, I can go as fast as I please." She climbed onto the seat. "You ready?"

Cade helped Grace up next to Bobbie, then swung his leg over his saddle. "I'm ready when you are."

Bobbie leaned forward to see him. "Cade, you know you don't need to ride with us. You've got your own work to do."

"Yep, and the work will still be there when I get back. Another hour won't hurt a thing."

They rode the first little while without talking. The noise coming from the goat would have made conversation difficult, but the lack of chatter allowed Grace to think about the attempted theft, and her apprehension returned. She examined the landscape, looking for any sign of trouble. Her two companions did the same.

"So do you have any guesses as to who those men might have been?" Grace's hands clenched into fists. Now wasn't that just the dumbest thing to ask?

A look passed between Bobbie and Cade, and then Bobbie shrugged. "I thought I might know who it could be, but I didn't recognize a thing about any of them."

"You thought it might be someone from around here?"

There went that look between them again.

Cade moved his horse closer to the wagon. "There have been some people in town who've resented that I have Joseph working for me. I expected something to happen but hoped it wouldn't. Tension seems to grow daily."

"And you think someone from town could have gone out there to scare them off?" Grace said. "Wait. Is it possible someone realized Joseph stayed home today and that's why they chose this day to ride into camp?"

Bobbie flicked the reins, and the horses picked up their pace. "But you forget that I didn't recognize the men or their horses. Chances are they were just some outlaws who heard about the town. It's generally known that wagon trains headed west carry a lot of money to pay the wagon master as well as to start their new life."

"I heard you tell the gunman that there was no strongbox in the camp."

Bobbie smiled. "There isn't. Jace and I talked them into putting it in the bank for safekeeping until they were ready to move on. A couple of the men said today they expect the wagon master to show up soon."

"And you think the trouble will leave with the camp?"

"Maybe not." Cade's brows were drawn together. "I've thought about trying to talk Joseph into staying here, making Rockdale his and Belle's home. He's a great worker."

A lock of hair blew free from Grace's bonnet, tickling her cheek. Is that why Cade was staring at her? She tucked it back up inside. "You think he'll agree?"

"I'm not sure. Today might make him lean toward leaving. I'll talk to him when he comes back to work."

Bobbie flicked the reins. "In the meantime, we'll have to keep an eye out for strangers. No telling where those men will show up again."

They could be living among us. Grace shuddered at the thought. She pushed it aside and focused on their surroundings. In order to enter the ranch, one had to descend from one bank, cross a bridge over a small creek, and rise up to the other side. The process reminded her of the peaks and valleys of her life. She had a great childhood, a high point right up until her mother fell sick. The years watching her mother slowly fade away were the lowest times. Now that she made the move to take over her own life and ended up on the Double K, things were looking better again.

As they crested the other side of the bank, the feeling of arriving home overtook her. In the few days she'd worked on the ranch, an affinity for the place had grown deep in her heart, making her decide to find someplace just like this to settle into and make her own.

A murmur from Bobbie grabbed her attention. She followed her stare and saw Jace talking to someone she didn't recognize. Bobbie glanced at Cade.

"Speaking of watching for strangers." Bobbie slapped the reins against the horses' rumps, and they raced toward the newcomer.

NINE

C ade kept alongside the wagon, and his heart thumped in antic-
ipation of more gunplay. Bobbie jumped from the seat at almost the same time the team of horses stopped. Cade dismounted
and stood between the wagon and the stranger.

Jace pulled Bobbie to him, his arm around her shoulders. "I'd
like you to meet our new ranch hand, Tim Martell. Tim, this is my
new bride, Bobbie."

Tim smiled and gave a slight nod. "Pleased to meet you, Mrs.
Kincaid."

"Let me see your hands." Bobbie's fingers hovered near her pistol.

"Ma'am?"

"Your hands. Let me see them."

Jace stared dumbfounded at Bobbie but didn't say a word. Tim
slowly pulled his hands from his pockets, then held them up and
showed her both sides. Cade released the breath he'd been holding.

But Bobbie still gripped her pistol. "Where'd you come from?"

Tim glanced at Grace, then turned back to give her a longer look.
One corner of his mouth twitched before he tipped his hat and
jammed his fists back into his pockets. "I'm from Missouri."

"What brings you out here?"

Jace took a step away and crossed his arms, his brows drawn.

"Cattle, ma'am. I love working with them." He took another peek at Grace.

"So you have experience?"

"Some."

"What's that mean?"

Cade wanted to laugh. He'd never seen Bobbie quite like this. He gave Grace a quick look, and her large, frightened eyes drew his attention. He moved closer hoping it would make her feel safer.

Tim motioned to some nearby cattle. "I'd just started learning about wrangling when I got word my father died. With no one left to care for my mother, I went to work for her. My father left her a general store."

Tim turned back toward Grace, smiled, and opened his mouth as if to say something. But she was focused instead on the noisy goat in the wagon, her fingers pressed against her ears.

Bobbie leaned into Tim's view. "And your mother doesn't need you any longer?"

"No, ma'am. Least not the way I looked at it. She got remarried." He shuffled his feet and scratched the back of his neck. "I know it sounds strange, but I'd rather work on the south end of an ornery cow than stand behind a counter dealing with an angry customer."

Bobbie relaxed, even gave a faint smile. "Actually, that doesn't sound strange at all."

Jace rocked up on his toes, then settled back on his heels. "So does this mean you approve of Tim as a ranch hand?"

By the hard glint in her eyes, Cade knew Bobbie didn't trust Tim completely. But she nodded to Jace and held out her hand to Tim.

"Welcome to the Double K."

"Thank you, Mrs. Kincaid." He shook her hand. "I'm sure I'll enjoy it here." He tipped the rim of his hat toward Grace. "I already like the view."

Cade took a step forward, muscles tense.

"Cade, I need you to meet our newest ranch hand." Jace leaned close with his back to Tim. "I'll let him know the only thing he's to show an interest in is the cattle." He turned around. "Tim, this is Cade Ramsey. He owns the livery in town. He's a great blacksmith too. In fact," he faced Cade again, "I thought I'd given you enough work to keep you busy for a week. What brings you out this time of day?"

Cade glared at Tim a moment longer. "A problem at the tent town. I'll let Bobbie and Grace tell you about it, but I wanted to make sure they made it home all right."

Jace looked at Bobbie, who waved him off and mouthed, "Later."

"Did the problem have anything to do with the racket back here?" Jace peeked inside the wagon and then spun around and speared Bobbie with his eyes, his arms crossed once again. "You thought we needed a goat?"

"It's just temporary. A few days at most."

Cade clapped Jace on the shoulder. "I think this is my cue to leave." He stopped beside Grace. "Would you like me to help you down?"

She nodded and leaned into his arms. "I think you tied up the wrong end of that animal."

Cade chuckled. Once her feet touched ground, he leaned closer. "I meant to ask you this morning but forgot when I saw you strangling that chicken—"

"I wasn't strangling it."

"If you say so. But I wondered if you ever sent a letter off to your father about where you are. I'll post it for you if you haven't sent it already."

She rolled her lips between her teeth and looked away. He sighed and stepped in front of her.

"I'll wait if you'd like to write it now."

She shook her head. "I'll take care of it."

"All right. I'll check in another time, see how you're doing with Jonah."

"He won't be here that long."

"Right."

With a tip of his hat to Grace and a wave to Jace and Bobbie, Cade climbed in the saddle and rode away. Misgivings rode right alongside him at the idea of leaving that new cowhand on the same ranch with Grace. No one knew whether he was a decent man. He could have been lying about his past. And Lord knew even some decent men could weaken enough to overstep boundaries they never thought they'd go near. Especially where women were concerned.

Why do you care?

He urged his horse into a gallop and wondered at the question. He felt responsible for her. The day that devious little vixen burrowed into his wagon was the day she'd launched herself into his life, hitting the bull's-eye with the expertise of a marksman. If he didn't know better, he'd wager she'd planned every phase of her scheme, right down to using him along the way. Well, he'd just pry himself loose and see where she ended up. He wasn't about to get tied up with another female, no matter what the cause.

He veered his horse from the road onto the lane leading toward the tent town. At the edge of the camp, he slowed, unwilling to get shot by some nervous watchman. Several men were posted on wagons and near trees, most keeping an eye on the entrance and the hills. He nodded at them and stopped at Joseph's wagon.

"You in there, Joseph?"

The big man poked his head through the back opening, a grin splitting his face once he spied Cade. "I hoped you'd come back by here. You got the message about my Belle being sick?"

"Sure did." He peered around Joseph but couldn't see Belle. "She all right?"

"Comin' around. She kept down the broth Miss Bobbie and that little lady gave her." He jumped to the ground. "I thought all that shooting woulda tied her up in knots, but she just prayed her way through it. She's sleeping now."

"Glad to hear it." Cade dismounted and looped a rein around the rear wheel. "There was another thing I wanted to check on."

Joseph motioned for them to move away, probably to keep from disturbing his wife. "Oh? What that be?"

"I heard your wagon master finally made it over the mountains and will be arriving soon."

"Yep. That's the word going around. That's why I was glad you come back. So's I could tell ya."

Cade looked Joseph in the eyes. "I know you're planning on heading out with them, but I'm offering you a permanent job at my livery. If you're interested, that is."

Joseph stared, not saying a word.

"I know some folks in town haven't made life all that easy on you and Belle—"

"They ain't been all that nice to you either, which is why I can't figure on how you'd want to keep me around. With me gone, them people would start liking you again."

Cade leaned against a tree trunk and shoved his hands into his pockets. "Joseph, if I'm doing what I think is right, then the problem is no longer mine but belongs to the folks holding on to anger and hate." He reached out and patted Joseph's shoulder. "Besides, you're a great worker and good friend. I'll miss you and pray for you if you decide to move on, but I hope you'll consider staying."

Joseph's eyes welled, and his throat worked hard at swallowing. "Thank you, Mister Cade. Life ain't been easy, not even here. But your friendship sure makes it bearable." He glanced at his wagon. "Let me talk to the missus. If she be willing, I'll be taking you up on that offer."

Cade reached out, and they shook hands. "Let me know what you decide." He took a couple steps, then stopped. "And quit calling me mister. I've been telling you that since you started working for me."

One side of Joseph's mouth lifted. "Some habits don't break too easy."

"Don't I know it." A certain girl's face came to mind, his own bad habit he wanted to break.

After mounting his horse and giving a brief wave, Cade headed back to town. He'd have to work late to get caught up, but at least he'd have something to think about other than wondering who might want to steal the money from those living in the tent town. The rumors that had passed through Rockdale about a gang of robbers terrorizing the area became reality when someone broke into Bingham's Hardware and Exchange. Now an attempt had been made at the tent town. It seemed someone had taken a liking to their territory. He'd have to talk to the sheriff and mention Jace's new hired hand. Couldn't hurt to have him checked out.

As he passed the church, he wondered if Grace would be there Sunday. At the realization that she'd slipped into his thoughts once again, he groaned and ran his gloved hand over his face, wishing he could wipe her away as easily. What bothered him most, though, was how quickly and thoroughly she had managed to replace Kim in his mind, especially since they were supposed to have been married in a few weeks. Maybe it was best she ran off with that photographer.

Movement up ahead and to his right grabbed his attention. Reed Murphy sat in front of his parents' leather goods store, only the back two legs of his chair touching the ground as he leaned against the building and whittled a piece of wood.

Years back, he and the Murphy family had been friends. He and Reed practically grew up together. When the Murphys went through the pain and sorrow of losing their two oldest sons in the War Between the States, Cade and his mother spent many hours trying to help and comfort them. But bitterness rode on the family's shoulders. Though they remained amiable, the friendship ended the moment Cade hired Joseph. Worse, the town divided because of it, many siding with the Murphys while others praised Cade for helping Joseph. He hoped one day a healing would take place, but he couldn't see it happening any time soon, though he spent many hours praying for that very thing.

The front legs of Reed's chair thumped to the ground as he stood and moved to the edge of the boardwalk. He touched his whittling knife to the rim of his hat in a mock salute while a smirk curled one corner of his mouth.

"Afternoon, Cade."

"Reed." He rode past, shoulders hunched and head lowered.

Reed kept pace. "I noticed your livery is closed. Your help up and quit on ya?"

"Nope."

"What then? He just decides not to show up so you had to go check on him?"

Cade reined to a stop. "You were gone quite a while this last trip, Reed. Any luck on your latest hunt for gold?"

A grin spread over his face. "Nice way to change the subject." He spat into the street. "If you must know, it wasn't too bad. But like most wells, that spot ran dry."

"What spot?"

Reed snorted. "Like I'm going to tell you where to find my gold."

Cade shook his head and urged his horse on. "Not even remotely interested. Better luck next time, Reed."

"You know I don't believe in luck. I make my own."

Reed's voice faded. Shame pricked at Cade for feeling relief. He hadn't tried very hard to smooth things over. But this wasn't the first time he wondered at how Reed went about making his own luck. From the stories Cade had heard, many from his own father, finding gold was hard work and took a lot of time. Yet Reed managed to come home from each trip with enough color to make the time away worthwhile. Regardless of the amount of money he earned, hatred and anger had changed Reed into a man Cade preferred to avoid. Lord help him, but making amends would have to wait for another day.

TEN

Jonah swallowed a great fish.

Grace tucked her chin into the collar of her coat to hide from the chill of the morning air as she waited for Jace to arrive in the wagon. Sure, she knew the real version of the Bible story. Her mother read it to her on more than one occasion many years ago. But now, after the goat had gorged itself on Jace and Bobbie's hay since its arrival two days ago, the distended stomach made it appear the roles had reversed.

Tied to a post near the barn, the bearded animal walked toward her until it reached the full length of its rope. The goat jerked and pulled and danced in an effort to get free. Chest heaving from the exertion, it finally stopped the fight and eyed her as if she were to blame for its troubles. After glaring at her for several long moments, it lowered its head, showing off its long, ugly horns, and then shook them at her.

Jace pulled his wagon next to her, Bobbie beside him. "You two getting acquainted?"

"I don't know if that's what I'd call it."

He jumped down and helped her up, then climbed aboard again. "What would you call it?"

"His successful attempt at intimidation." She kept an eye on

Jonah until they'd passed. The goat never looked away, even followed alongside until the rope tugged it to a stop again. "I have a strong suspicion he's going to be trouble."

"Don't worry," Bobbie said. "I don't intend for him to be around long enough to become a problem. In fact, I think a trip to the tent town will be in order tomorrow, and old Jonah will come along for the ride. Only he'll walk this time."

Relief washed through Grace as the wagon started over the rocky road. Church. Apprehension trembled in her stomach, much like the flower-laden hat quivering on her head from a light gust of wind. She crammed it back tight on her head and shoved her hands into the pockets of her coat.

She hadn't been inside a house of God for years, and she didn't mind the absence. Resentment toward the God her mother loved— the same God that Grace had vowed to worship as a child—began shortly after her mother took sick. If the so-called God of love took such a pathetic interest in His people, then she wanted no part of Him. She only went along today because she couldn't think of a good excuse to back out of it as she had done the previous week. Besides, she wanted to keep her job and would do nothing to jeopardize her position.

As they passed the bunkhouse, Tim Martell stepped from the building. A smile spread over his face as he gave a quick wave.

"Morning, Jace, Bobbie." He peeled his hat from his head. "Have a good day, Miss Bradley."

Jace slowed the horses. "Would you like to join us, Tim?"

Grace looked down but watched him from the corners of her eyes. *No! Oh, please say no.*

Tim jammed his hands into his pockets. "Thank you, sir, but no. I'm kinda partial to my saddle. But I'll see you there."

Grace released the breath she held. That man made her skin all but turn inside out. She couldn't put a finger on exactly why. Could be the way he stared at her all the time. Anytime she was outdoors, she could almost be assured he'd be watching. He'd even find excuses to get closer. And his smile. It could just as well be a coiled snake for all the pleasure it gave her.

Bobbie tapped her arm. "That reminds me. We'll be leaving in about a week or so to drive some cattle to Pueblo. Would you like to come along? See your father?"

"No, but thank you for asking. Maybe you could stop in and give him a letter for me though."

"Sure. If that's what you prefer. We'll leave Tim and one other man behind to take care of the place while we're gone, so you'll be safe."

Safe? With that man around?

"That means you'll have to feed them since our cook will go on the drive with us. Oh, and that also means I won't be able to take Jonah back tomorrow." Bobbie looped her arm around Jace's elbow. "We planned to round up the cattle starting first thing in the morning, and we'll have a lot of branding to do. I'm sorry, Grace. But I'll sure try to haul Jonah back to his owner before we leave for Pueblo."

Grace hardly registered the information about the cattle and Jonah.

Except for the birds chirping from the trees and the hushed chatter of Jace and Bobbie, the rest of the ride to church was quiet. Grace didn't mind at all. It gave her time to mentally prepare for the sermon and a preacher who'd probably pound the pulpit to keep his parishioners awake. But the sight of Cade striding down the street made most thoughts vanish. He sure was a feast for starving eyes. That is, if a woman's eyes were starving, which hers were not. But she still didn't mind looking.

A grin spread across his face as he greeted them before helping her from the wagon. "Glad you could make it this week, Grace. I know my mother will be thrilled. She's been asking about you."

Horror struck at Grace's heart. She'd forgotten all about visiting Mrs. Ramsey, what with all the other commotion going on while learning how to deal with ranch life. "I—" She turned to Bobbie. "Will we have time to stop and see Mrs. Ramsey?"

"Sure." Bobbie looked at Jace, who nodded. "We'll make the time."

Cade touched her elbow and led her toward the church. "Or if not, I'll see Grace gets home."

"Thank you."

"Sure." He grinned again. "Nice hat."

She reached up and touched it, sure his voice held a trace of sarcasm. Before she could respond, a bird swooped from a tree. She felt it bump her hat before it returned to a limb.

"Of all the nerve." She ducked as it came at her again. "What's wrong with that bird? Why don't animals like me?"

"I'm sure it's not you, Grace," Cade said. "Maybe it's your hat."

"What's wrong with my hat?"

"Well, nothing really. It's just…"

"Just what?"

"Well…a bit flowery."

She planted her hands on her hips. "It's not my hat's fault. Even Jonah doesn't like me. He looks at me as though he'd love to use his horns to slam me into tomorrow."

"All goats look like that. Besides, it's nesting season. That bird probably thinks your hat would make a great home."

The bird trilled a few notes and then plunged toward her again, just missing her by inches. She glared at the creature for a moment, then turned the same look on Cade. Without hesitation, she grabbed her hat from her head and thrust it onto Cade's.

"Hey!" He leaned away and whipped it off. "What do you think you're doing?"

"It's an experiment. Put it back on."

"I don't think so."

Jace and Bobbie howled with laughter. Cade handed the hat back and motioned to the church with a tilt of his head.

"Come on. We're going to be late."

They hurried inside and found the pastor already behind the pulpit. Cade led them to an empty pew near the back, which was fine with Grace.

"Let's begin with a rousing rendition of 'Rescue the Perishing,'" the pastor said as he watched them take a seat. "And let's all stand."

Grace noticed he looked directly at her as he spoke. Did he think of her as perishing? A strong distaste for church arose, and she hadn't even been inside a full minute.

Cade bumped her with his elbow. "You're not singing."

"Trust me, you don't want me to sing."

"Why not? You probably sing like a bird."

"You're right. Whenever I try to sing, crows come flocking."

He reached for his Bible. In moments, he found what he sought and held the Scripture in front of her, his finger marking what he wanted her to see.

Make a joyful noise unto God.

Much as she wanted to scowl at Cade, she couldn't. She had to slap her hand over her mouth to silence the laughter bubbling up. Bobbie bumped her from the other side.

"Do I need to separate you two?"

Grace dropped her chin to her chest and shook her head, though the grin stayed in place. The scoundrel. But when she looked up to make a face at Cade, his eyes were fixed on something over her head. She turned to see what erased his smile. Tim Martell. She looked away as soon as their eyes met.

Did he believe as Jace, Bobbie, and Cade? The idea stunned her. She'd distrusted him from the moment they met. But now she wondered if maybe there wasn't more to this man than she first thought. Or was he playing a role to keep his job, just as she was? Only time would tell.

Shock rolled all the way to Cade's feet. The expression on Grace's face probably resembled his own. He faced forward, ashamed for casting judgment on a man who did nothing more than show interest in Grace.

Forgive me, Lord.

Everyone sat after the song ended, and the pastor gave the Scripture reference he'd be reading from. Cade leaned forward, curious to see if Tim would struggle to find the passage in his Bible, if he owned one. Relief wrestled with disappointment when Tim took only moments to find it. Maybe he should give the man a chance.

Cade forced himself to focus on the pastor's message. No easy task with the way Grace wriggled in the seat, not to mention how she appeared to be counting something on her fingers. A quick glance at her face told him she'd heard no more of the sermon than he had. He squared his shoulders, took a deep breath, and started reading the verses cited earlier.

Gunshots from outside ended all attempts at concentration and brought everyone to their feet.

ELEVEN

G race, you stay here with Bobbie," Cade said before hurrying after Jace, who was already out the door.

Anxious to see the cause of the shooting, Cade forced himself to pause when he noticed Tim Martell still sitting in the pew with his head down. All the other men were either gone or clamoring to get outside. Cade wanted to grab the man by the collar.

"You coming, Martell, or are you staying with the women?"

Tim's head came up, and he jumped from the pew. "Sure. I was just...praying."

Cade weaved his way through wagons and buggies toward the town's main street. Tim matched his stride. They stopped and peered around the edge of the furrier building. Other men were doing the same all along the boardwalk.

"I don't have a gun," Tim said.

"Most of us don't bring a gun to church."

When it appeared there was no immediate danger, Cade strode toward Reed Murphy, the only man standing in the street holding a pistol.

Tim followed alongside. "Well, don't you have a sheriff for this kind of stuff? It's probably just a couple cowboys letting off some steam."

Cade took in the drag marks along the center of the street. "That doesn't happen around here much."

"Oh. Dead town?"

"Not dead. Safe." *Most of the time, anyway.*

They reached Reed about the same time as the other men. Blood ran down his left arm. He raised his gun arm and pointed the barrel down the street.

"I think I got one," he said, the scent of sour whiskey on his breath. *Probably shot himself,* Cade thought.

Reed shook his gun again. "They went that way. Let's get 'em."

Cade grabbed the gun from Reed, which earned him a glower. "You're hurt, Reed. Let's find the doc and get you fixed up."

Reed studied his arm, surprise on his face. "Well, whadaya know." He gaped at Cade. "I've never been shot before."

The sheriff rode up and jumped from the saddle. "I was at the tent town and heard shots. What happened?"

Reed swaggered up to him. "I seen 'em, Morgan. There was four of 'em, all wearing something over their faces."

Morgan took a step back and waved his hand in front of his face. "Four of who?"

"Them men that shot up the land office. One was dragging something behind his horse. I bet they got that gold I brought in the other day."

Cade exchanged a look with Morgan before racing down the street.

"Yeah, you better run, Cade," Reed yelled after him. "I'll bet your daddy'll be none too happy to find out how good a job you been doing watching over his business."

Cade reached the front door and found it locked. He headed around the side. The back door stood open, and he stepped inside. Jace was right behind him. Dismay filled Cade at the sight of scattered papers and overturned furniture. He heard a moan and saw his father's partner writhing on the floor behind the counter.

"Mr. Owens? It's Cade, Mr. Owens. How bad are you hurt?"

The elderly man grabbed Cade's arm and pulled himself to a sitting position. Blood ran from his forehead. His thinning gray hair stood as though held at gunpoint. He grimaced and pulled his coat away to show blood on the side of his shirt.

"I been better."

Jace moved next to them. "Let's get him over to Doc's."

They helped Jeremiah Owens to his feet, but they didn't get out the door before Mrs. Owens charged inside.

"Jeremiah? Land sakes, what'd you do?"

"I'm all right, Harriet. Just a couple scratches is all."

She examined his forehead, then flipped his lapel back to peek at his side. "Looks like more than scratches to me."

"We're taking him to see the doctor, Mrs. Owens," Cade said. "Would you let us through?"

She fixed him with a squinty glare, then backed out of their way, mumbling something he couldn't understand. She followed close behind, even brushing Cade's heels every so often. Once outside, she moved up ahead of them.

"Didn't I tell you to come to church, Jeremiah?"

"Yes, ma'am."

"You wouldn't a gotten hurt if you'd a done what I said."

"Yes, ma'am."

"Victor said he wouldn't be back for weeks. Don't know why you were so determined to get them papers together for him today. They could a waited till morning."

"Yes, ma'am."

"My father's coming back?" Cade asked Mr. Owens.

"Course he's coming back," Mrs. Owens said. "Didn't you get a wire from Victor like we did?"

Cade's ears burned from the frown she sent his way. Being unaware of his father's comings and goings embarrassed him, but he also knew some of the agitation Mrs. Owens sent his way stemmed from her anger that he'd hired Joseph.

He cleared his throat. "I'm sure my mother has the wire." But he wasn't sure at all. More than once, his father contacted his partner without sending one word to his wife.

People now filled the street and boardwalk. Grace and Bobbie appeared out of the mob wearing worried frowns, and he motioned them closer.

"Bobbie, why don't you and Grace wait for us at Mom's? Just don't tell her about Mr. Owens. I'll do that when we're through here."

After a quick nod, they separated and disappeared. Cade opened the door to the doctor's office, and the smell of blood, sweat, and whiskey assaulted him. He saw Reed sitting on the table and pulling on his shirt. Sheriff Taylor stood nearby.

Jace stopped to keep the horde from following them inside, admitting only Mrs. Owens, who still lectured her husband on the woes of missing a Sunday sermon.

Doc Barnes all but shoved Reed from the table and onto a nearby chair before motioning Jeremiah Owens to take his place.

"Was he ever unconscious?" Doc asked.

Cade helped Mr. Owens lie down. "He's been awake since I found him."

"How about it, Jeremiah?"

The elderly man shrugged. "I reckon so. Everything happened so fast. One moment the men were there. The next, Cade was leaning over me."

"Tell me what happened, Mr. Owens," Cade said.

Mrs. Owens grabbed Cade's arm. "Why you bothering him? You leave him be."

He took a deep breath. "Mrs. Owens, your husband's been shot and his business robbed. Now's the best time to ask him questions while he still remembers everything."

She crossed her arms, her lips in a tight line. But at least she didn't continue to fight him.

The sheriff stepped in. "He's right, Mrs. Owens. Just let us ask a few questions, then we'll leave."

Cade turned back to continue his inquiry. "We won't keep you long, Mr. Owens. Just tell us all that took place."

Jeremiah Owens winced when the doctor removed his coat, then lay back, folded his hands, and cleared his throat.

"A message was delivered to the house last night from your daddy asking me to dig out some files for him. I decided to do it right away this morning so I wouldn't forget."

His wife moved forward and leaned over him. "I told him not to, but he wouldn't listen, as usual when it comes to his partner." She licked the corner of her handkerchief and wiped at the blood on his forehead.

"Now, Harriet, let me talk."

She huffed but stayed quiet, surprising Cade.

"When I got to the office, I noticed the side door open just a bit. I couldn't believe I'd do such a thing, but I am getting older, as I'm sure you already know. I've often wondered when your father will offer to buy me out of our partnership."

Cade patted his arm. "You're not that old, Mr. Owens. And my father trusts you completely."

Jeremiah waved a hand at him. "Well, anyway, without thinking, I barged on into the office and ended up staring down a big, black barrel."

"And that's when they hit your head, Jeremiah?"

"No, not yet. Now hush and let me tell it, Harriet."

"How many men were there?" Cade said.

"Four. All wearing white sacks over their heads."

He gasped when Doc started cleaning the wound on his side. "Careful, Doc. My skin's getting paper thin, and it feels like you're tearing it apart." He turned to Cade. "One of them grabbed me and threw me against the wall. Then he held his gun to my head and told me to open the safe."

"How much was in it?"

"More than I wanted them to have, so I told them they'd have to kill me first. Wrong thing to say, I know, but it was face either them for refusing or your daddy for obeying." He cast a quick glance at his wife and shook his head. "Won't ever do that again. Another man with the meanest eyes I ever saw shoved his face into mine and said that wouldn't be a problem. Then he smashed me on the head with the butt of his pistol."

He gingerly fingered the wound near his hairline. "I played like I was unconscious and lay as still as I could. That man told someone to get the horses while they pulled the safe outside. I peeked through one eye and saw three of them shoving with all they had to move it to the door. Then they tied a rope to it. At the last minute, that mean-eyed critter turned and fired a shot at me. Next thing I know, you're leaning over me. Guess the shock of being shot knocked me out cold."

"So they dragged the safe out of town?" Cade said.

"Near as I can tell, that's what they used the rope for."

Reed stood and leaned against the table, the smell of sweat and whiskey arriving with him. "So that's what they were dragging. I didn't pay much attention in all my trying to take steady aim." He puffed out his chest. "I figured if they were gonna shoot up our town, then I could shoot them up a bit."

The sheriff grabbed his good arm and pulled him away from Mr. Owens. "Did you recognize any of them, Reed?"

With a tug to free his arm, Reed slumped back down in his chair. "Like we told you, Sheriff, they were wearing hoods. But one was big. Had dark eyes." He gave Cade a smirk. "Made me think it was your colored friend. Bet Joseph was in on it."

Cade grabbed Reed by the shirtfront and pulled him off the chair. Reed all but drooled through his grin.

"Whatcha gonna do, Cade? Hit me? Truth always stings the most, don't it?"

The sheriff moved between them and pulled them apart. "Just calm down, Cade. I know Joseph wasn't involved."

"What?" Reed pushed back in front of the sheriff. "How you knowing that? You weren't here."

"No, I wasn't. I was at the tent town talking to Joseph, saying good-bye to him along with the rest."

"Good-bye?" Cade said.

The sheriff nodded. "They're moving out this morning. You didn't know?"

Cade shook his head. *So Joseph decided not to stay. He could have at least made one more trip to town to let me know.* He'd miss the help and friendship.

"Sheriff, I'm going to follow those drag marks I saw in the street," Cade said. "I'm sure all I'll find is an empty safe, but I've got to try."

"I'll get my horse and ride along. Maybe we can pick up a trail."

"Let's get going then."

If nothing else, Cade needed some fresh air. The proximity to Reed was more than he could handle.

TWELVE

D o you think Mrs. Ramsey heard the gunshots?"
Grace trailed Bobbie up the stairs toward Mrs. Ramsey's
bedroom. Bobbie slowed long enough to cast her a stricken look. "I
hope not." She stopped at the door, hand on the knob. "We're about
to find out."

They entered the room and ran into words. "Who did the shooting, and what was it about?"

Bobbie went to the bed and gave Mrs. Ramsey a hug. "Why,
Mrs. Ramsey, you look downright famished. I'll leave Grace here
with you while I go help Mrs. Cromwell finish getting your meal together. Besides, I know you've been waiting to visit with her again."
In seconds, she was out the door.

Grace stared after her. *Coward.* She turned and was speared by
Mrs. Ramsey's eyes. She headed for the chair next to the bed, mind
whirling for a change of topic.

"You truly are a woman of immense faith."

Mrs. Ramsey squinted at her. "What makes you say that?"

She sat and smoothed her skirt. "I figure it would have to take
a great deal of faith to allow Bobbie in the kitchen to finish working on your meal."

Slow in coming, a smile spread across the woman's face. "Now

Grace, you and I both know that was just an excuse to avoid my questions. But I must say, that was a wonderful attempt on your part at diversion." She leaned closer. "No more delays. Tell me what happened out there. Specifically, is Cade all right?"

"Oh, I'm sorry, Mrs. Ramsey." She reached for her hand. "It never occurred to me you'd think he was hurt. But he's fine."

"Thank you for that. Now tell me the rest. What was it all about?"

"I don't really know. Cade sent us here saying he'd check into things and then come and tell us what he found out." *And he better not leave me in the lurch like Bobbie.*

"Oh. All right." She leaned back against her pillows. "Now I can relax, and we can have a nice conversation. So tell me how you liked church this morning."

"Ah, it was…short."

"The service was short?"

"Yes, because of the sh—"

The look on her face must have conveyed her mistake. Mrs. Ramsey chuckled. "All right, let's try again. Tell me how you like living on the ranch."

"Well, I guess except for the animals, it's fine."

"What's wrong with the animals?"

Grace pulled some imaginary lint from her skirt. "I don't think they like me very much."

Mrs. Ramsey shifted in the bed. Grace felt certain it was to hide a grin, but she found genuine concern when she chanced a peek.

"Now what would make you say such a thing?"

She cleared her throat, the collar of her blouse suddenly much too tight. "I get the feeling when I walk across the yard that the chickens would like nothing more than to peck my eyes out. And barring that, they'd peel the skin from my ankles if they could get past all this material." She flipped her skirts for emphasis.

Mrs. Ramsey laughed outright. "Oh, Grace. I sure have missed visiting with you." She squeezed Grace's arm. "Cade told me a little about your first attempt at butchering a chicken. It didn't sound like you did too badly."

"I'm sure he was being kind and left out the worst of it. So when does the doctor think you'll be able to get out of bed?"

Mrs. Ramsey gave her hand another squeeze. "All right, my dear. I'll let you lead the subject to me since I get the feeling you don't want to talk about yourself. But be prepared. I have so many questions for you."

Where was Bobbie? How long did it take to put someone's tray together?

"About three weeks," Mrs. Ramsey said.

"Pardon?"

"The doctor said about three more weeks before he'll let me try out my hip. And even then it'll only be for short amounts of time at first. I can't wait. I'm getting very tired of these same four walls."

"I can imagine. My mother said the same thing many times."

"The poor dear. I wish I would have made more of an effort to visit her."

A knot formed in her throat. "She wouldn't have known you for the last year or so."

A clatter at the door came as a welcome interruption. She jumped from the chair and would have glared at Bobbie, but her boss refused to meet her eyes. Two other ladies followed behind her. One she recognized but couldn't recall her name.

"We're back."

Bobbie set the tray of food on the table beside the bed and helped Mrs. Ramsey sit in a more upright position, then placed the tray across her lap. She finally turned and faced Grace, her eyes begging for forgiveness, as she introduced her to Mrs. Cromwell and to Annie Wallace, Jace's sister.

"We brought enough food so we can all eat together," Mrs. Cromwell said. "A little female companionship is good for the heart. And I'm sure the men don't mind having the kitchen to themselves either."

Grace hurried to round up enough chairs, her nerves tingling. She just knew they would ask her a ton of personal questions. But as the meal progressed she found her assumption wrong. They ended up having a delightful time together. She noticed Mrs. Ramsey glancing at the door from time to time and saw relief wash across her face when Cade finally appeared.

"Hello, Mother. Did you get enough to eat?"

Mrs. Ramsey set her tray aside. "Now don't you try Grace's trick. I've been patient long enough. Tell me what happened."

"Grace's trick? What would that be?" He stooped and kissed his mother's cheek.

"Changing the subject. I allowed her to do it, but not you. What were the gunshots about?"

Cade smiled and winked at Grace, sending her heart on a bumpy ride.

Cade perched on the side of the bed and turned back to his mother. "Now, where were we?" The question earned him a swat on the arm. "Oh, right." He took his mother's hand in his. "The land office was robbed this morning."

Mrs. Ramsey gasped. "Was anyone hurt?"

With a nervous cough, Cade glanced at the ladies in the room. They stood and Grace followed their lead.

Annie patted him on the back. "We'll leave you two alone."

"No. Stay." He stood too. "You're going to hear talk around town. You may as well hear the truth from me." He motioned for them to take their seats, and then returned to the side of the bed. "Mother, Jeremiah Owens was shot during the robbery."

Mrs. Ramsey put her hand to her throat. "No!"

"But he's going to be all right. It was just a crease along his ribs. Well, that and they also hit him on the head with the handle of a pistol."

Tears filled her eyes. "The poor, dear man. We should do something for him."

"We're doing everything we can for him. The doctor said he needs to rest for a few days before he goes back to work." He clasped her hand and found it cold. "Trust me. He's going to be fine."

She nodded and dabbed at her eyes.

"They also took the safe. They dragged it behind a horse so it was easy to track. Morgan and I found it about a mile or so out of town." He took a deep breath. "They shot it until it opened."

"Did they take everything?"

"Just the gold, silver, and cash."

"Your father will be furious."

A rustle of skirts and then a soft click let him know the ladies had left. He appreciated their thoughtfulness.

His mom spoke his name, but Cade didn't look up until she touched his cheek. She was the only person who knew his muddle of emotions when it came to his father. Love and hate. Anger and compassion. Aching for acceptance and burning from rejection. As often as he wanted to hug his father, he wanted to punch him in the mouth.

"Don't let your father make you feel guilty for what happened." She smiled to soften the venom in her voice. "If he wants his business protected, he needs to stay home more. You've got your own business to tend to."

Dear Mother. She loved both her husband and son with the fierceness of a mother lion. She was also fair, and he loved her for it. But as with him, it was much easier standing up to Victor Ramsey when he was miles away.

"We always manage to work it out somehow," Cade said. "This time will be no different."

He knew she realized their way of working things out was to avoid each other. Tears rimmed her eyes again.

"Mr. Owens said Father was coming home soon."

Her head jerked up and she searched his eyes. "When?"

"Mrs. Owens made it sound like a few weeks. Maybe less."

Several emotions crossed her face before it softened with love. "It'll be good to see him again. It's been too long."

"Yeah." He slapped his hands against his knees and stood. "I hate to leave so soon, Mother, but I've got some things to take care of before dark."

"I know." She took his hand, pulled him down, and kissed his cheek. "You be careful."

"I will."

He bounded down the steps two at a time. Voices from the kitchen led him that direction, but he hesitated at the swinging door, knowing Grace was probably inside. He gave it a slight push first, then moved inside.

Joseph and Belle sat at the table.

THIRTEEN

Joseph! I thought you'd left."

The two shook hands as a smile spread across Joseph's face.

"We did." Joseph glanced at his wife. "But we turned back. It just didn't feel right to leave."

Belle stood and put her arm around Joseph's waist. "We both felt the same way, like God was holding us here, telling us not to go."

"That's wonderful," Cade said. "Thank You, Lord." He clapped Joseph on the back and put his arm around Belle's shoulder. "Are you hungry? Did you get something to eat?"

"Eating isn't our problem right now, Mr. Cade."

Cade motioned them to retake their seats and then sat at the table. "Tell me the problem. Maybe I can help."

Joseph took Belle's hand in his. "If we're staying, we needs a place to live. Our wagon'll do for a time, but we can't make it our home for good. I won't do that to my lady."

"I understand. I'll start looking for something first thing in the morning. I may know of a place, but it will take some work to get it ready. In the meantime—"

"In the meantime," Bobbie said, and stepped away from the counter, "you can stay at the ranch. Jace and I will be leaving soon on a cattle drive. I'd appreciate it if you'd keep Grace company while we're away so I won't have to worry about her being out there alone. You can use our room while we're gone. Until then, we'll come up with some way to keep you warm and dry."

Joseph stood. "Oh, no, ma'am. We cain't—"

"You can, and you will. I insist."

"I think that's a great idea," Cade said. "It'll give me a chance to get this other place checked out."

"Well…" Joseph scratched the back of his head. "If you say so."

"I do." Cade stood with Joseph and shook his hand. "Welcome back."

Jace and Bobbie had been gone only a day, and Grace thought the ranch was already falling apart without them. Well, maybe that was a slight exaggeration, but she'd never before run short of wood for the stove. She could ask Joseph to chop some wood, but the poor man came home so exhausted from working in the livery, he groaned just kicking off his boots. And she sure didn't want to ask Tim Martell. In no way did she want to be in debt to him.

Some of the logs lying near the barn didn't look too big. She'd seen the men chop them into manageable sizes many times, and it didn't appear all that difficult. A smaller piece lay at her feet. With very little effort, she placed it on the chopping block.

The men she watched usually spat on their hands and rubbed them together before grabbing the ax. She looked at hers but couldn't bring herself to do something so disgusting. She reached for the handle. It was bad enough just having to hold the instrument they'd touched.

The ax could have been a boulder, it weighed so much when she raised it over her head. She took a step back to catch her balance. With a deep breath, she planted her feet and swung.

The ax didn't budge, but the strength she put into the effort spun her around, almost pulling her shoulders out of socket. Cade Ramsey stood like a tree with one limb grasping the handle over her head. The look on his face told her to expect a scolding.

"What do you think you're doing?" she said.

"What am *I* doing? I'm trying to keep you from hurting yourself. I should ask you the same question."

She jerked the handle of the ax, but it didn't move. "I'm trying to get some work done. Now step back and let me get to it."

He yanked it from her hands. "I don't think so."

"Why not?" She reached to take the ax back only to have him hold it away.

"Grace, do you realize what this thing would have done to your leg had you missed?" He slammed the ax head into the chopping block. "If you need help, ask for it. Joseph or Tim could have done this for you."

She crossed her arms. "I didn't want to ask Joseph. He always looks so tired." She wasn't going to mention Tim. "Why are you here, anyway?"

He stared for a moment and then shook his head. "Jace asked me to keep any eye on things while he's away. And it's a good thing, too, by the look of it." He peered around. "Where's Belle? I doubt she'd let you do such a fool thing as this."

"She's cleaning the house. And it's not a fool thing."

"Right." With a tug, he pulled the ax loose again. "I'll chop the wood. You go work on something else."

Without another word, he shed his coat and hat and tossed them aside. Then he turned his back on her and started chopping. She watched for a few moments before heading toward the house. Where could she find a good swinging door when she needed one? One good push and she'd knock that arrogant tone right out of him.

Two baskets of wet laundry sat in the kitchen waiting to be hung on the line. She grabbed the load of bedsheets and headed back outdoors. In minutes she had the linens hanging in the warm sun and soft breeze.

She returned to the kitchen and cut up some leftover roast to make a hash for supper. Then she scooped up the remaining basket of laundry. After rounding the corner of the house, she screeched at the sight of a squirrel playing chase-your-shadow all over her newly cleaned sheets. The varmint not only had left its dirty paw prints everywhere but also had torn some holes.

She dropped the basket, her fingers curling into fists. *I'm gonna kill it.*

Cade blasted around the house and nearly ran into her as he strapped his sidearm and belt around his waist.

"What's wrong?"

Grace stared at him.

"I heard you scream. What happened?"

She turned away from Cade and watched the squirrel as it balanced its way across the top of the hanging sheets and leaped to the ground before racing up the nearby tree. Then it sat on a low branch looking back at her, its tail flicking as if in challenge.

She reached for Cade's pistol and almost had it free of the holster before he grabbed it from her.

"What're you doing?"

"I'm gonna kill it!"

A slow grin moved across Cade's mouth. It only fueled her fury.

"Give me the gun!"

"I don't think so."

"Why not?"

"Because I value my life."

She crossed her arms to keep from hitting him. "I don't plan on shooting you...yet."

"And I don't plan to put a dangerous weapon into the hands of a woman who leads accidents along by the earlobe."

Her mouth dropped open, and she clamped it shut as she propped her hands on her hips. "So how do you propose I get rid of that menace if you won't let me shoot it?"

He looked around the ground, stooped over, and picked up a rock. "Use this." He tossed it to her, winked, and turned to walk away.

She fumbled the rock several times before it landed in the pocket of her apron. She clasped it in her fingers, itching to test her aim on him.

He glanced back at her. "The squirrel is in the tree, not on my back. Try to stay out of trouble." Then he disappeared around the corner of the house.

She ran to the tree, but the wretched critter was gone. With a stomp of her foot, she pitched the rock at the tree trunk. That squirrel had to be male.

She took down the dirty sheets and pinned up the clothing in their place. She set the basket of sheets inside the house and headed back outside to the shed. Hoe in hand, she stood at the edge of the garden and groaned. Bobbie told her the ground hadn't been worked up in a while, and from what she could see, "for a while" actually meant "years." With no choice but to get after it, she attacked the dead grass and new weeds with a vengeance.

She didn't get far before movement to her right caught her attention. Jonah stood nearby munching on some tender spring grass while keeping an eye on her.

"Jonah, you dumb old goat. How'd you get loose?"

Grace inched her way toward the goat, only to stop when he lowered his head.

"Now Jonah." She shook her finger at the beast. "You have to go back to the barn. We can't have you running loose and causing trouble."

A few steps closer and she could see the rope hanging from his neck. The loose end looked ragged, as though he'd chewed himself free. She continued toward him, only to stop when he waggled his head at her again.

"All right, Jonah. Just be nice and we'll get along fine." If all went as planned, she'd grab the end of the rope and lead him back to the barn. Cade could take him from there. The thought had no sooner run through her mind when Jonah charged.

"Grace, look out!"

She glanced at Cade, and fear froze her feet in place. She had just enough time to turn before Jonah rammed into her thigh, throwing her to the ground.

She didn't dare move for fear the goat might hit her again. She peeked one eye open and found Jonah standing over her, his beard almost brushing her cheek. Everything in her wanted to grab that tuft of hair and yank out each strand.

"Grace!" Cade's panicked voice must have scared the goat. He trotted off, and Cade appeared at her feet looking down at her with alarm-filled eyes.

"Are you all right? Did he hurt you?"

She rubbed her thigh. "I think I'm still in one piece. That big dumb animal."

Cade offered his hand. "He's just doing what comes natural."

She scowled but reached to accept his help.

"Cade! Watch out!"

Jonah slammed into Cade's backside, pushing him over the top of her. He put his hands out to stop the fall and keep from crushing her. Then he rolled to the side of her and lay there, emitting a tiny groan.

"Are you all right?

Another groan. "I'm going to kill that animal."

"Now, Cade."

"You and I can have goat for supper."

She turned her head toward him, moving slow so as not to attract Jonah's attention again. "He's only doing what comes natural."

He looked at her, and she couldn't help the giggle that escaped.

"Very funny. Do these kinds of things always happen to you?"

"What kinds of things?"

He raised an eyebrow at her. "Never mind. Come on. You can help me catch that dumb beast."

"Are you sure it's safe to get up yet?"

He looked around. "I don't even see him."

She pushed to her knees.

"Well, well, well. If it isn't Grace Bradley rolling around in the dirt with a man."

She froze upon hearing the voice, one she'd hoped never to hear again.

"I wonder what your father would say."

FOURTEEN

There is no God. There couldn't be. Not if He allowed such awful things to happen to His creatures. Or if there were a God, He didn't care what happened to His people. This wasn't the first time Grace felt that way, and if today was any indication, it wouldn't be the last.

Frank Easton leaned against the side of the house with his arms crossed and a smirk on his face, but she could see anger burning in his eyes. She'd seen it before and, as usual, it made her queasy. Cade moved between them. She took a step closer to him.

"What do you want, Frank?" She knew, but she wanted to see if he'd be so bold as to mention it in front of someone else.

He pushed away from the house and headed toward her, his steps slow and precise. "Now, Grace. You really didn't think you could hide, did you?" He stopped several yards from them, pushed his hat back on his head, and propped his fists on his hips. "You know I always get what's mine."

"Yours?" Cade all but growled the word. "Grace isn't a possession, Easton. She's a person with choices, and she didn't choose you. So go back where you came from."

"Oh, I will. Just as soon as I convince Grace to come with me."

Tired of them talking about her like she wasn't there, Grace moved out from behind Cade. "I'm not going back with you, Frank. I've got a fresh start here, a new home."

"This isn't your home. You're just someone's hired help." He held a hand out to her. "I could give you so much more. You'd never have to work again."

Cade crossed his arms. "There's nothing wrong with good, honest work."

"I've found most men in a low position like yours usually feel that way, Mr. Ramsey. I guess you tell yourself that to feel better about yourself." He shrugged. "Can't say as I blame you."

Grace wanted to slap the haughty expression off Frank's face. He'd always been proud of his large house and the pristine suits he owned, like the one he wore now. She doubted he'd ever known a moment of hard work. He jingled coins in his pocket just to let everyone know he had money.

The springs on the back door squeaked, gaining everyone's attention. Belle eased out, her face revealing apprehension. "Is everything all right, Mr. Cade? Miss Grace?"

"Everything's fine," Frank answered with a wave of his hand. "Go on back inside."

Belle turned to do as told. Grace moved toward Belle.

"Stay here," Grace said. "You have every right to be here. It's him that needs to leave." She jutted her chin at Frank.

Cade took a step forward. "You heard her, Easton. Time for you to go."

"Is there something I can help you with, Cade?" Tim Martell had somehow managed to join them without being noticed. "This man bothering the ladies?" Tim's hand rested on his sidearm.

"I think I can handle this, Tim, but thanks for checking." Cade's eyes never left Frank for a second. "Oh, another thing. That goat is running around free. Why don't you see if there's a way to keep it from getting loose again."

"All right." Tim stood shuffling his feet.

Cade finally looked at him. "Is there something else?"

"Ah, yeah. Something happened in town I thought you'd want to know about."

"What?"

"The Murphy's business was robbed." Tim's eyes moved to Belle. "Reed is accusing Joseph."

Cade raced toward town as fast as he dared while trying to keep Frank Easton in his sight. He didn't want him doubling back. Thankfully, the man had offered to ride to Rockdale at the same time. Otherwise, Cade would have had to choose between staying to protect Grace or allowing Tim to. Neither option held much appeal, but Joseph needed him.

He recalled the way Grace's eyes begged him to stay while Belle's pleaded for him to help her man. Frank offering to leave alleviated the problem. Temporarily anyway. But the way he made sure everyone was aware of his generosity was tough to swallow.

One last glance back at Easton was all Cade needed. They were now close enough to town that he doubted Easton would turn back. Cade spurred his horse on. At first, the boardwalks and streets were almost empty, making his heart thunder along with his horse's hoofbeats. In no time, he found out why. Most everyone had gathered in front of his livery.

He reined his horse to a skidding stop, jumped from the saddle, and shouldered his way through the throng. Joseph stood near the doorway with Sheriff Morgan Thomas. Over the noise from the mob, Cade could hear them talking.

"Just let me lock up, Sheriff. Then I'll come with ya." A look of fear and humility hung on Joseph's face. His expression changed to relief when he spotted Cade, who finally managed to get to them.

"What's going on, Morgan? You aren't arresting Joseph, are you? You know as well as I do that he wouldn't rob any store."

The crowd pressed closer, led by Reed Murphy. "Of course he's arresting him. He has to. Just as he would any thief."

Cade turned on Reed. "Joseph is no thief."

"He is, and he better hang for it."

The mob cheered and echoed his words. Morgan stepped forward.

"Hold on, everyone. I'm not arresting Joseph. Not yet anyway."

"What!" Reed thumped Morgan on the chest. "Do your duty, Sheriff."

Cade moved next to Morgan. "What proof do you have, Reed? What makes you think Joseph did it?"

Reed's nostrils flared. "I wasn't talking to you, Ramsey."

"Maybe not. But Joseph is my employee and that gives me the right to ask questions." He leaned toward Reed. "What gives you the right to accuse him? Give me the proof against him."

Reed's jaw worked.

Cade looked at Joseph. "You know of any proof they might have against you?"

"No, sir. I was here all the while you was gone." Joseph nodded toward the crowd. "He can back me up. I was here when he come in a while ago."

Cade scanned the crowd. "Who?"

"That man right there."

Cade followed Joseph's finger and found Frank Easton staring back, a smirk on his face.

Morgan pushed past Reed. "Is that true, mister? Can you verify what he said?"

"Frank Easton, sir." The two shook hands. "Yes, sir. He was the man I talked to when I stopped by earlier."

Morgan nodded. "Thank you, Mr. Easton." He turned to Reed and crossed his arms. "All right, let's have your proof against Joseph. Otherwise I'm headed over to talk to your parents, get their side of it."

Silence.

Morgan shook his head. "Sorry about this, Joseph. I'll let you get on about your business. I'll be back if I have any questions."

"Wait a minute. That's it? You're letting him go?" Reed grabbed Morgan's arm and swung him back around. "I told you to arrest him."

Morgan shoved Reed's arm away. "Let me do my job, Reed. Get in my way and it'll be you I arrest."

Reed spat at Morgan's feet. "Never thought you'd turn on us for the likes of one of them, Sheriff."

"Let it go, Reed," Cade said.

Reed turned on him. "This is all your fault, Ramsey. You started it by hiring that colored boy. Get rid of him and I'll think about letting it go. Otherwise, you just opened a whole sack of trouble."

Cade almost smiled at the childish threat but thought better of it. "He stays."

"Then you have only yourself to blame for anything else that happens." Reed poked him in the chest with every other word.

Cade's hands curled into fists. *Help me, Lord. I want to flatten him in the worst way. I need Your help. Show me what to do.*

"Whadaya gonna do, Cade? Hit me?" Reed jutted his chin out. "Go ahead."

Peace descended over Cade like a soft rain after a long drought. His hands relaxed. "I don't want to fight you, Reed. I don't think you want to fight either."

"You're wrong there, friend."

Reed drew back and threw a punch. Cade caught his fist before it landed. Reed tried to pull it back, but Cade wouldn't let go.

"You're blaming the wrong person, Reed. You've been nursing a terrific hurt since your brothers died in the war. Joseph wasn't at fault for that. He was just as much a victim as your brothers. And now you're becoming a victim because you won't forgive and let God help you heal."

Reed jerked his hand free, but not before Cade saw the moisture in his eyes. "I don't need help. Not from you or your God. But you're gonna need plenty of it if you keep that black man around. You've been warned."

Reed spit once more and shoved through the crowd toward home. The throng broke up, some shaking hands with Cade and Joseph while others scowled at them and stomped away.

Frank Easton, his face without expression, returned Cade's stare for several long moments before patting his stallion's neck. "Got room for another boarder? I think I'll stay a while. This is quite an interesting little town. In more ways than one."

FIFTEEN

"M iss Grace?"

Grace cringed. Belle had called her that since she and Joseph moved in a week ago.

"Yes, Miss Belle."

Belle stopped beating her rug and stared, the dust hovering around her head in the still air. "You cain't be calling me that, Miss Grace."

With one final whack on her own rug, Grace wiped at the bead of sweat rolling down her temple on a day much too warm for this early in spring. "I'll quit if you quit."

Belle's stare continued, now with a frown. "I cain't drop the 'miss.' People won't like it."

Grace looked around and then shrugged. "I don't see any other people."

Belle opened her mouth. She closed it and thumped her rug again, then pointed the tool at her. "Now see here, M—. You ain't understanding. If anyone was to hear me call you just plain Grace, why, I don't want to be thinking on how they'd react."

"It shouldn't matter."

"Course it matters."

"Why?"

"Why?" Belle blew out a puff of air. "You know what folks is like.

They quick to keep us in our place. Just like that mean fella that come to see you today."

The reminder of Frank was about as welcome as a tub of water to a drowning man. By silent and mutual consent, she and Belle had started working together after his departure, but only after Belle dropped to her knees to pray for her husband. Grace hoped God loved Belle enough to hear and grant her wish. Lord knew He never heard a word of her own prayers on behalf of her mother. If she were to pray right now, it would be that Frank would just forget about her. But she'd given up on most prayers.

"Like I told you earlier, you have more rights here than he does. You're free now, Belle. You can do whatever you want."

Belle shook her head. "A signed piece of paper may say so, but they's a whole lotta folks who must not a seen or heard a that paper." She fingered the edge of her rug. "Besides, it's a show of respect to call you Miss Grace."

Belle wasn't going to get away with that little ploy. "Well in that case, I'll have to start calling you Miss Belle since I respect you too."

Belle inhaled so deeply, she about sucked in all the fresh air. "Why you sneaky thing." Then she smiled. "Guess I deserved that."

With a burst of laughter, Grace pulled Belle into a hug. "Yes, you did. And I can't force you to drop miss or mister with everyone else, but I insist you call me just Grace."

"All right, Just Grace. You win."

"You rascal." She thumped her new friend on the backside with the beater.

The two returned to their work of transferring the dust from the rugs to the air. Minutes later, Belle stopped and grabbed at the rug. She dropped her tool and used both hands to hold herself up.

"Belle? What's wrong? You sick again?" Grace put her arm around Belle's waist and led her to the porch steps.

"I be all right in a bit. It's happened before."

"What has?"

Belle mopped her face with her apron and then fanned herself with it. "It sho is hot today."

"Belle!"

"I be fine." A smile teased her lips. "In fact, I think I be better'n fine."

Grace peered into her eyes trying to read her mind. She gave up. "What do you mean?"

Belle leaned close. "I think they's a baby inside."

The words were spoken so softly, Grace had to play them through her mind again just to be sure of what she heard. She jumped up and squealed. "You're pregnant?"

"Shhh, child." Belle stood and spun her away from the direction of the barn. "Don't go screaming the news."

Laughter bubbled up. She clapped her hands and pulled Belle into her arms. "You're going to have a baby?"

"Yes'm, I do believe so. Leastways, that's near as I can figure what's causing all this ruckus inside me."

Grace held her at arm's length. "Does Joseph know? What did he say?"

A sheepish look washed over Belle's face. "He don't know yet."

"Belle!"

"I know, I know. I thought maybe I'd tell him today. That is, if he gets to come home."

"Oh, he'll come home. Cade will make sure of that."

Tim Martell barreled around the corner of the house and skidded to a stop, out of breath as he gaped from one to the other. "What's wrong?"

Grace and Belle looked at each other and shrugged.

"What're you talking about?" Grace didn't feel quite as irritated to see him as usual.

"I heard you scream."

"No. Oh, wait. That wasn't a scream. Not really."

"Not a scream, huh? Nothing's wrong?"

She shook her head.

He took his hat off, slapped it against his leg, and clamped it back on his head. "You ladies reckon you could save your playful shrieking for when Jace or Cade are here? I don't think my heart can take another scare like that."

Grace smiled. "I apologize, Tim. But thank you for coming to our rescue. Again."

He met her gaze full on. "Glad you're all right." He touched the brim of his hat. "Ladies."

After he left, the two exchanged a look and then burst into quiet laughter. Grace plopped down on the steps next to Belle, who leaned over and nudged her.

"I think he's sweet on you."

"Stop that."

"It's true. That Frank fella's gonna have plenty a competition."

"What do you mean, plenty?"

Belle pulled back and once again looked at her as if she'd lost her mind. "Most women would be plumb tickled to have three men scrambling for their interest."

"Three? That baby's messing with more than your stomach."

Belle put one finger in the air. "That mean Mr. Frank." She flipped up another finger. "Tim." She wiggled a third finger and smiled. "And that handsome Mr. Cade."

She choked on a laugh. "Cade? We need to get you out of the sun, Belle. I'm nothing more to Cade than a mosquito bite that won't heal, or worse. You should've seen his face when he first found me. You'd have thought he was staring at the backside of a scared skunk."

Belle's mouth dropped open. "I don't—" She jumped up. "Joseph!"

Thank goodness. Maybe God did answer prayers. Even unasked ones.

Joseph dismounted and scooped Belle into his arms. Grace looked away when the kissing began.

"Evenin', Miss Grace." Joseph still held Belle, but she pulled away upon hearing his greeting.

"Oh, Joseph. Don't go calling her that."

"Calling her what?"

"Miss. You keep using that an' she'll start calling you Mr. Joseph. I'll explain later."

He gave Grace a puzzled look, and then grabbed his horse's reins. "I gotta put the horse up for the night. I be right back."

"I'll come along." Belle winked at Grace and walked away with her husband, clinging to his arm.

Grace followed their progress until Joseph whooped, swung Belle around, and began raining kisses on her face. Then she stood and entered the house to start supper.

Belle would make a good mama. Motherhood was one role Grace couldn't picture for herself. Perhaps because she never planned to give it a try. That way she couldn't let her children down.

Cade rode onto the Double K still berating himself. Two days had passed since he'd last checked on the place. Too long. Especially now that Frank Easton knew that Grace and Tim were in charge of the ranch site. Granted, Tim showed up at a good time the other day, but as far as Cade was concerned, the man still had to prove himself. But everything looked well-kept. Maybe Tim really was a knowledgeable rancher.

Movement on the far side of the house caught his attention, and he headed that way. After dismounting, he tied his horse out of sight and moved silently toward the back, wanting to see if Grace was doing something she shouldn't. He found her chopping up the garden to ready it for planting. That seemed safe enough.

She had her back to him, and he decided to sneak up on her. Belle caught sight of him and lifted her hand to wave. He put his finger to his lips and shook his head before pointing at Grace. Belle smiled and nodded as she went about hanging out the clothes.

He took care not to step on anything that would give him away. He smiled when he heard her muttering about someone letting the garden be taken over by weeds.

He was only a few feet away from her, and he looked up just in time to get a face full of dirt and grass. He fought the desire to spit and sputter and did his best to wipe his soiled face. He glanced at Belle and found her doubled over with her hand over her mouth, eyes almost closed in silent laughter.

Grace, still grumbling about all the weeds, squatted and flung another clump over her shoulder before running her hand through the loosened dirt. He tried to dodge the projectile, but it caught him on the shoulder. A muted shriek gave him just enough warning to duck under the large worm that flew over his head.

"E-e-e-ew!"

Grace stood, turned, and flung something from her hand. A thick white grub hit him in the chest and tumbled back to earth. Before he could react, Grace, with a look of disgust on her face, wiped her hand on his shirt, glanced at her hand, and then wiped again.

"What was that?" She squinted up at him. Dirt smudges streaked her chin, cheeks, and forehead. She looked adorable. "Where'd you come from?"

Belle howled with laughter as she dropped onto the porch steps and wiped her tears with the corner of her apron.

Cade's jaw dropped open. He clamped it shut again for fear she'd fling something else at him. "If this is the way you greet your guests, I'll have to think twice about coming again."

She dropped the hoe, and her hands went to her hips, leaving dirty prints on her skirt and apron. "Well, it serves you right for trying to sneak up on me."

He grinned. "I can't argue with you when you're right."

Something dangling from the brim of his hat stopped him from saying more. The earthworm he thought he'd avoided inched along until it slipped off and dropped near the grub. Grace took a step back. He bent down, scooped them both up, and held them out to her.

"But did I deserve this?"

A shudder shook her from her head down. "I don't think anyone deserves that. Not even you."

He lunged and caught her hand in his. Then he turned her palm up and pretended to drop the worms onto it. She made a fist and struggled to get free, never taking her wide eyes from the worms.

"I think you ought to try to make it up to me in some way."

"Like what?"

He gazed up into the sky as if to think about it. "Cookies."

"What? Cookies?"

"Yep. Make me some cookies and I'll forgive you." He grinned in victory. "And I want to watch."

"Watch? Why?"

He dumped the worms onto the ground and brushed the dirt from his hands. "Has Bobbie ever told you about the time she made cookies using pickling salt instead of sugar by mistake?" By the look on her face, she had. "I'm not about to let you do that to me. Not even the dog would touch them. We ended up using them in a slingshot to scare away some annoying crows."

She dug her toe into the dirt. "All right. When?"

"That depends on your answer to a favor I need to ask."

A smirk pulled at her lips. "Another one?"

"Do you remember Rebecca Cromwell?"

"Yes. Nice lady."

"Yes, well, she's planning a day for several ladies to get together to work on some quilting, among other things."

Grace made a face. "I'm not very good at sewing."

"That's fine. What she really wanted from you was help with Annie's children. She wondered if you'd mind watching them while the ladies work."

A look of panic crossed her face. "I've never tended children before. How many?"

"Three. All of them Annie's." You'd have thought he'd just asked her to play with a skunk from the horror on her face. "I'm sure Belle would be willing to help."

Grace crossed her arms in front of her stomach. "Well, maybe. When would I need to be there?"

"Oh, you don't have to go to town. They thought it'd be better to bring them out here. Two weeks from Saturday. Will that work?"

Grace looked in Belle's direction, then turned back to him and nodded. "Sure."

"Good. I'll come early to pick them up. We'll make the cookies then."

"*We'll* make the cookies?"

He grinned. "Well, I can help keep the kids occupied while you get them made."

"What kind?"

"Molasses. And I like them chewy."

She curtsied. "Anything else, Your Highness?"

"Nope. That should do it."

"Am I invited to this little party?" Frank Easton stepped around the corner of the house, a broad grin on his face. "Every time I find you two together, you're playing in the dirt." Frank's eyes traveled the length of Grace, his disapproval evident. "I can give you so much more than this, my dear, if you'd let me."

By the expression on Grace's face, she wasn't any too thrilled to see him. "I'm happy here, thank you."

He looked down, rubbing the thin line of hair he called a mustache, before once again eyeing Grace. "For how long? If you're honest, you'll admit this is just temporary. I can make you happy for the rest of your life." He glanced at Cade and then moved closer. "Have dinner with me tonight so we can talk in private."

Her hesitation just about killed Cade. He turned toward her. *Say no.*

"I don't think so, Frank, but thank you for asking."

Frank nodded. "All right, maybe another time. What about the cookies? May I join you?"

"No!" Cade said.

Frank smiled but never took his eyes off Grace. "Grace?"

She glanced at Cade. "Not this time."

"Time for you to go, Easton," Cade said.

"Excuse me?"

"Jace asked me to keep an eye on his place. Since I doubt you're welcome here, I'm telling you to leave."

Frank's annoying little smirk returned. "I understand he'll be back soon, and I'm sure he's a much more personable young man. I'll come back when he returns."

"You do that." *But not until I talk to him first.*

Cade stood his ground until Easton disappeared. Then he looked at Grace. "So I can tell Rebecca you'll help?"

All the fun teasing from earlier was gone. When she nodded, he started toward his horse.

"Cade?"

He stopped.

"Thank you for being here...both times."

He turned slightly. "I'm glad I was." *More than you know.*

SIXTEEN

Grace couldn't stop her smile at the sight of Jace and Bobbie riding toward the house. Feeling secure again hung uppermost in her mind as she ran to greet them.

All pleasure plummeted the moment Bobbie pulled her into a hug and the scent of a cow's backside assaulted her nostrils. What exactly did they do on a cattle drive?

She took two steps away. "Glad to see you two back. I'll start warming water for baths."

Bobbie grinned. "Are you trying to tell me we stink?"

"Well." Grace drew a line in the dirt with the toe of her shoe. "You stay on that side and we'll get along just fine."

Bobbie took a step toward her, arms outstretched. "It's great to be back, Grace. I missed your humor."

She bit back a grin and forced a scowl. "I wasn't trying to be funny."

Jace moved next to her and put his arm around her shoulders. "It's good to see you again, Grace."

He smelled worse than Bobbie. She ducked under his arm and headed toward the house, stopping only when she was sure she'd reached fresh air.

"Thank you, Jace. I'll, ah, get the water going."

But the sight of Cade riding toward them kept her immobile. His smile stretched as wide as his face. He dismounted and grabbed Jace's outstretched hand and clapped him on the shoulder before pulling Bobbie into a hug. He never once acted as if they carried a stench.

"Glad you two are back. I don't remember you being gone this long before."

Jace tugged off his gloves and shoved them into his saddlebag. "Why? Did something happen?"

"Mostly the same."

"Reed?"

"Yeah. Someone robbed his folks' place, and he blamed Joseph."

"Another robbery?" Bobbie said. "Anyone hurt?"

"No."

"Morgan find any clues?"

"Nothing. It's got the town on edge more than usual."

Bobbie bumped Cade with her elbow. "So did you hear we were back and came to greet us, or did you come for another reason?" She cast a quick glance and a smile toward Grace, whose face flamed.

"Actually, I came to see if Belle wanted to ride out and see the house they're moving into. It's almost ready. But now that you're home"—he turned to Jace—"I need to talk to you about something."

"I'm listening."

"Remember me telling you about the reason Grace hid in my wagon?"

If she could have found a hole, Grace would have crawled in. Or another wagon would have done fine.

Jace glanced at her. "I remember."

"He showed up the other day. Frank Easton. Been out here twice that I know of."

"He try anything, Grace?" Bobbie said.

She shook her head.

"But if I read you right," Cade said, "you didn't want him here."

"That right, Grace?" Jace said.

"Yeah, pretty much. But I've got to admit, I've never seen this side of him before. He seems...nicer."

"Oh, please." Cade thumped his hat back with his fist. "You don't honestly believe that? How do you know it's not an act to get you to let down your guard? You forget those bruises on your wrist?"

"Frank just surprised me, that's all." She shrugged and pointed over her shoulder. "I'm going to go—"

She stared. Cade followed her gaze and then groaned.

"Tarnation." Cade slapped his gloves against his thigh. "I have a feeling that guy's been watching me and following me every time I head this way."

"Is that Frank?" Jace said.

"Yep."

Frank dismounted and held his hand out to Jace. "You must be Jace Kincaid."

"That's right." Jace turned and pulled Bobbie to his side. "My wife, Bobbie."

"Ma'am." Frank peeled off his hat, nodded, and replaced it. "Good to finally meet you both. Nice place you've got here."

"Yes, it is. What can we do for you?"

Frank rubbed his thumb and forefinger along his thin mustache. Grace recognized the move. He did it every time he was about to talk money.

"I don't know if Grace told you, but my uncle is a prominent banker in Pueblo. Maybe you used his place during your business there. Pueblo National? It's the biggest bank in town."

"We didn't," Jace said.

"Yes, well, I'm just here to introduce myself as his main assistant and offer our services should you need any."

Jace's eyes narrowed. "We won't."

Frank walked toward Grace and attempted to put his arm around her. She moved toward Bobbie and caught the slightest flare of anger in his eyes. He countered it with a smile before turning his attention back to Jace.

"Grace's father has even used our services. We've developed quite a relationship since then. You see, we don't look at our customers as just customers but also as friends." He paused, and Grace thought he should stop before he dug himself into a hole. "I heard you're going to have a house-raising soon. I can help with that. With money, of course. I've never wielded a hammer before, but I'll sure give it a try just for you."

"With all your snooping around, Easton, you should have asked a few more questions about the owner of the bank here," Cade said. "He happens to be Jace's brother-in-law. Like he said, he won't need your services."

Frank appeared taken aback. "Oh. Well…I guess I should have checked out the competition a little further."

"Competition?" Bobbie said.

"Yes. Like I told Cade the other day, Rockdale is an interesting little town. I've decided to stick around for a while. There's no telling what kind of opportunities might present themselves. Well, I guess I've done what I came for, so I'll take my leave."

When he reached his horse, he took one more look around. "This really is a nice place. What would you sell it for?"

"It's not for sale," Jace and Bobbie said in unison.

Frank grinned. "Everything has a price. You'll see."

He mounted up and rode off, leaving behind a cloud of dust, a bad taste in everyone's mouth, and a stench that far exceeded that of Bobbie and Jace.

Bobbie walked past Grace, grabbed the horse's reins, and headed toward the barn. "You were wise not to marry him. Stay here and we'll make sure he doesn't bother you."

An explosion and several echoes of the blast jerked Cade from sleep. He leaped from the bed and raced to the window. Darkness still held claim on the new day. He couldn't see a thing. He pulled on some clothes and headed for the door.

Many residents had already gathered at the bank by the time he arrived, some still in their nightclothes, all in a state of panic. Against the early morning sky, Cade could see a thin stream of smoke rising from the side of the building, the gray vivid against the pale pink.

The sheriff appeared through the smoldering hole followed closely by Pete Wallace. With his shirt buttoned up wrong, the tails still untucked, and suspenders hanging down his legs, the banker looked far different from his normal prim self. The smile on his face defied everything Cade expected to see. The crowd pushed so close, they bumped into him.

Sheriff Taylor raised his arms. "Quiet. Quiet down, now, so Pete can talk."

Pete jumped up on the boardwalk. "You'll all be happy to know the safe is still locked. No money is missing."

A cheer went up, almost drowning out Pete's last words. Questions were flung at him from every direction, all mingling into one loud roar.

Pete grinned and cupped his hands to his mouth. "There's nothing more to tell. Your money is safe. Go on home and get some breakfast."

No one moved to leave but stood around exchanging ideas on who blew up the bank and why they didn't take the money. When Joseph's name came up, Cade looked around for Reed Murphy. Unable to spot him, he moved to stand next to Pete.

"Where's Reed?"

"He came in yesterday to withdraw some cash. Said he wanted to go check on his claim, maybe do some prospecting while there."

Cade shook his head. "His parents were robbed last week and he takes off?"

The curtains in the window over the hotel sign wiggled. Frank Easton stared down at him. After what Easton had said about being a competitive banker, Cade's suspicions took wing. He looked for Silas Mahoney and spotted the hotel's owner chatting with Reed's father.

"Silas, can I talk to you a minute?" After Silas had joined them, Cade said, "Did you see Frank Easton, one of your customers, leave his room this morning?"

"No, and I'd know if he had. I was sitting at the front desk eating my breakfast when I heard the explosion. He never came by. Why?"

Cade glanced back up at the window feeling a good dose of disappointment. "Never mind." He spun back to Pete. "You're going to need some help fixing your wall. I'll dig up some lumber and get started."

"Thanks, Cade."

Morgan nodded. "And I'll get someone to guard the bank until the repair is finished. No need tempting the dishonest."

"Sheriff!" a voice called from down the street.

Morgan stepped onto the boardwalk next to Pete. "Yeah?"

The town's gunsmith, Jason Mawbry, stood in front of his shop. "There's a hole blown open in the back of my store. Most of the guns and ammo are gone!"

❋ SEVENTEEN ❋

It soon became clear that what Cade had thought was one explosion followed by its echoes was actually several individual blasts. The mercantile and saloon had also been hit. No longer did he think the thieves targeting the town would be only a short-lived squall. Now that the bandits had a whole store of weapons, it appeared Rockdale was in for a mighty storm with no end in sight.

Someone bumped him on their way past, waking him from the nightmare. He headed toward Sheriff Taylor to see if there was anything he could do to help.

"You didn't see anything?" The sheriff did a quick examination of Jason Mawbry's head as he asked the question.

"Nope. As soon as I came around the corner, I got walloped. Didn't have a chance to see a soul."

"You have a nasty bump back there. Better have Doc take a look."

"I'm all right. It's my store that needs mendin'." He rubbed the back of his head and winced. "When you gonna catch them men, Sheriff? Looks like they don't aim ta quit till there's nothing left. And I want my guns back."

Morgan started for the alley. "I'll get 'em. They're bound to make a mistake, leave something behind I can track. I'm gonna check your store before I head over to the mercantile. Maybe today's the day."

Cade followed him. "Four explosions. Same as the number of men who robbed my father's land office. I'm guessing it's the same four."

"I had the same thoughts. But why so many blasts?"

"I'm thinking diversion. Especially since they hit the bank. That's the first place everyone would go just to make sure their money's safe."

Morgan stopped at the end of the building and examined the area. "Makes sense. But they could have done the same thing with just two. I think they're starting to enjoy their mischief a bit too much, which is also why I think they're going to make a mistake."

"So you're as certain as I am that they'll be back."

"Much as I hate to say it, yes." Morgan peeked up at the rising sun. "Wish there was a little more light." He pointed at the ground. "How many sets of footprints do you see?"

Cade squatted next to him and peered around. "I see three. That must be where Jason fell." The dirt showed an imprint of a body with scuff marks all around. He glanced behind them. "Where's your deputy? Shouldn't he be here by now?"

Morgan rose and moved to where he could see the hole in the side of the building. Some of the boards still smoldered. "I'm sure he'll be here soon. I'll have him guard the bank until it's repaired." He inspected the ground around his feet. "No wagon marks. They must've loaded everything on their horses. Look." He knelt and traced one of the hoofprints. "See how deep the tracks are?" He stood and followed them. "I count five different sets."

"Five?" Cade moved to his side. "Any of them stand out? Special marks?" He scrutinized every one of them. "It's almost as though they've been filed down smooth so as not to leave marks." He rubbed the side of his face. "These guys know what they're doing. You've got your work cut out for you, Morgan."

Pete came around the building. "Any luck?"

"Not much." Morgan gestured to the tracks. "All we know so far is there's five of them."

"Great. Sure you don't want to hire more deputies? At least until this is over."

"I'd love to, but who?" Morgan shook his head. "Look, I've got a lot to do in a short amount of time. We'll talk about deputies later." He disappeared inside the shop.

Cade headed for the alley. "I still have to check the livery. Then I'll be over to lend a hand."

"Good. I sent word to Jace. We're going to need his lumber."

Cade stopped. "His house-raising is only a few weeks off."

"I know. I've already sent a wire to Pueblo to replace what we'll use. He'll just have to send someone to pick it up."

Joseph stood waiting for Cade in front of the livery. "I checked inside. Horses be a bit skittish, but all's good in there."

Cade patted Joseph on the back. "Would you mind tending the place today? I told Pete I'd help repair the bank."

"Don't mind at all, Mr. Cade. Prob'ly best, I 'spect."

Cade met his gaze and found sadness. He considered Joseph one of the most honest men he'd ever met. He squeezed Joseph's arm.

"You let me know if you run into any trouble. I'll be here in a heartbeat."

"I knows it. You's a good man."

"So are you, Joseph. Don't you let anyone make you believe any different."

He headed down the street, his mind racing. For the town to be hit so many times, each instance worse than the one before, it was as if someone held a grudge. If that were true, then it had to be someone local. But who? And why? With each step, he ticked off the names of the residents. None of them seemed like possibilities. But then he would have never thought they'd shun Joseph with such intensity. Time to become a little more aware of those around him.

Make some food and bring it to town? Grace stared at a horse as it stared back. What was Bobbie thinking? The food part was easy enough, but how in the world was she supposed to get it to town? She'd never hitched a horse to a buggy in her life. Never even watched it being done. Now, as the food sat at the back of the buggy getting colder by the minute, she looked from the horse to the harness to the buggy. Surely it couldn't be all that difficult. Right?

Bobbie had said the men would be repairing some buildings damaged early that morning, and they'd need something to eat to keep them going. Well, time was wasting, and the food wouldn't get there any quicker by her standing around wishing it so.

"Hey, boy."

Hands shaking, she reached out and touched the nose of the horse as she'd seen Bobbie and Jace do many times. The beast seemed to enjoy it, almost leaning into her caress. But most shocking was how soft it felt, almost silken. Maybe this wouldn't be so bad after all.

She unlatched the stall door, grabbed the halter, and led the horse in front of the buggy. It followed along as if it knew just what to do. Pride washed through her.

"Good boy." She patted its nose one more time. "Stay there."

She lifted the harness from the hook and headed for the horse.

"What do you think you're doing?"

She screeched and dropped the harness. The horse snorted, shook its head, and started for the door. Tim Martell stood in the way, a grin plastered across his face.

"Whoa, girl." He grasped the halter and led the horse back inside. "What are you doing, Grace?"

"I, uh…" It's a girl? She tipped her head for a quick peek underneath. Tim caught her, and her face flamed. "Bobbie wanted me to get this food into town for the men. I was trying to hitch up that horse."

Tim stroked the horse's neck. "Not this one."

"Why not? She hurt?"

He led the horse into the stall and closed the door. "She's a saddle horse. You hook her up to that thing and she'll give you the ride of your life." He moved further down the barn and opened another door. "Hello, Bunny." He rubbed both sides of the horse's head. "You ready for some exercise?"

Once he had the horse positioned in front of the buggy, he waved Grace over. "Let me show you how to do this. Not that you'll ever need to. There's plenty of men around here to take care of that for you."

She stared at him, unwilling to move closer. He fiddled with a leather strap and then heaved a sigh.

"I hope you'll believe me when I tell you I'll never hurt you, Grace. Never. I'll do everything in my power to keep you safe."

His eyes bored into hers. In that moment, whether from his tone or his eyes, something calmed her fears. She moved toward him, earning a smile.

"All right, would you grab that collar off the wall and slip it over the horse's head?"

She did as told. "Any certain way?"

"The side that was against the wall goes over the head first."

The two worked together, Tim giving quiet instructions while Grace followed each command with quiet efficiency. Satisfaction filled her as he praised each of her successes. He attached the last buckle, wrapped the reins around a pole on the buggy, and led the horse out of the barn, closing the doors behind them.

"You're all set." He held out a hand to help her onto the seat.

She raised her brows, eyes going from him to the carriage. "I... I've never driven one before."

"You'd never hitched one before either, and you handled that well."

She nipped at her lip and nodded. "I guess." Once in the buggy, she reached for the reins, her hands trembling. "If I don't make it back tonight, come looking for me. No telling where you might find me."

Tim burst into laughter. "You're quite a lady, Grace. Gutsy and poised at the same time. As far as I'm concerned, you're miles ahead of most women." He bumped his hat back. "I need to apologize."

"For what?"

"Bobbie gave me orders to make sure you got to town with the victuals. I meant to have the buggy hooked up before you got out here, but I was tied up with some chores. Imagine my surprise when I found you trying to do my job. But…please don't tell Jace or Bobbie. I really like working on this ranch."

"Keep my secret that I can't hitch a buggy and I won't say a word."

"Done."

After she slid over, he climbed in and took the reins, then handed them to her.

"But I…" She leaned away. "I thought you were driving."

"Aw, Grace. Where's that gutsy side I saw?"

She was unmoved.

"I'll be right here in case something goes wrong. I won't let anything happen."

She scowled, then grabbed the reins from him. *Men.* "Since this is probably the only way we're going to get there."

Everyone usually clicked their tongue when they flicked the reins. She gave it a try. The buggy lurched as the horse obeyed. She was surprised as well as pleased. She was doing it. Maybe ranch life wasn't so tough after all.

Tim leaned back and propped his boot up on the front rail. "You're doing great. Wake me if you need me."

"What?" She craned her neck and found him grinning. "Where's the whip."

"Bunny never needs a whip. She's a good horse."

"I didn't mean for the horse."

"I figured."

They rode in silence a ways, and the strain of driving had her breaking into a sweat. She'd planned to keep quiet on the trip to town, but now she had second thoughts. Besides, Tim turned out to be a much nicer and far less scary man than she first thought. Even slightly amusing.

"What do you know about the trouble in town?" she said.

"Not much. The messenger Jace and Bobbie sent said several buildings had a hole blown in them. No one was hurt. Other than that, nothing."

If the trouble hadn't started before Frank arrived, she would have wondered about him. She didn't trust him any more than she did that rotten goat, Jonah.

They passed the road that led to the abandoned tent town, and Tim gestured toward it. "I kinda thought the trouble would have left when the wagon train did. Guess they weren't involved after all."

"Why did you think they were?"

He shrugged. "Timing. One of the other ranch hands mentioned the problems started when they showed up." He shifted in the seat after she hit a bump. "Shame really. Rockdale's a pretty nice little town. But I'm sure the sheriff will get it figured out soon enough."

"Yeah. Hope so."

"Sure is pretty here, isn't it?" Tim made a show of looking around, spending an extra moment on the mountains off to their left. "Especially at the ranch. Don't think I've ever seen a nicer view than the one Jace has from his place. I doubt anyone could ever get so used to it they wouldn't notice."

She chanced a peek at the scenery before pinning her gaze back on the horse. Only tiny patches of snow remained on the highest points. A green haze of new growth almost gleamed in the sunshine, growing darker as it reached the lower elevations. She didn't think there could be a prettier part of the country than right here.

"I know what you mean. I've wanted to take a walk out and about, especially down by their lake, but I haven't had the time."

"You should. In another couple weeks, the berries will start to ripen. There's a big patch just before you get to the lake. I heard Beans talking about picking them." He held up his hand. "Wait.

Maybe you shouldn't go to the lake. If you beat him to the berries, we may not get the pies he promised."

She smiled and quirked an eyebrow. "A race, huh? I've never thought of myself as competitive but—"

"Don't you dare."

A laugh started, only to be swallowed when the horse whinnied and lunged to the side, taking them off the road.

EIGHTEEN

Grace jerked on the reins. Bunny reared up and shook her head. The reins were yanked from Grace's hands. Bunny sidestepped and then lurched ahead at a gallop. Grace caught a quick glimpse of a snake curled on the edge of the road as they whipped by. She grasped for the buggy rail with one hand and for Tim Martell's arm with the other.

"The reins!" Grace said.

He had them and gently sawed back on them. Bunny slowed and then came to a stop. Tim jumped out and hurried to the horse, talking the whole while in a soft voice. Bunny's head bobbed at first, but Tim was able to calm her. After a couple snorts, she returned to her placid self.

"Good girl." Tim patted her head and came back to the buggy.

"I saw a snake."

"Did you? That must have been what spooked her." He offered the reins to her.

She all but sat on her hands. "You do it."

"You were doing fine. It's rare to find a snake on the road. It was probably just out sunning itself on this nice day."

"That's all well and good, but I'm still not driving."

"All right."

Grace glanced back at the food to make sure it hadn't ended in a heap on the road. Though tossed a bit, it remained relatively intact. But her desire for conversation was destroyed. They said very little the rest of the ride.

What they found when they arrived in town left them speechless anyway. She could have been back in Pueblo, what with all the commotion. Every other time she'd come in, only a handful of people wandered about. Now she wondered how they'd get down the street without hitting someone.

"Grace! Tim!"

Bobbie waved to them from the boardwalk in front of the bank. Tim turned the horse in that direction and stopped as close as he could. Bobbie stepped down next to them.

"Let's get the food inside the hotel. Silas cleared an area and set up some tables. The men will be ready to eat soon."

Tim grabbed the pot of stew while Bobbie hefted the chicken and dumplings. Grace lifted the basket filled with biscuits and followed, keeping an eye out for Frank. She wasn't ready to confront him on her own just yet, though she knew that day would come. He would make sure of it. With all the furor going on, she doubted he would take that chance today, but one never knew with him.

Bobbie handed her a glass of water. "Would you take this to Cade? He asked if I'd get him one, but I'm going to help in here for a while."

"Sure. Where is he?"

"Working on the outer wall at the bank."

Getting across the street without spilling proved a challenge. Men on horseback as well as some driving wagons filled with lumber forced her to zigzag and even reverse her steps at one point.

Cade and Jace were the only two men working in the alley, but more were standing on the other side of the hole in the bank.

"Hi, Grace," Jace said.

Cade looked up from his sawing, sweat running down his face

and dripping from his chin. His shirt clung to his chest, forcing her to look away.

He smiled when he caught sight of the water. "That for me?"

"So I'm told."

She handed it to him, and he downed it in seconds.

"I could use a whole bucket of that."

"All right." She turned only to be stopped when he grabbed her arm.

"I didn't mean it. Just wishful thinking." He looked past her. "Hello, Tim. Need something?"

"Just checking in with Jace. Would you like me to stay here and help or head back to the ranch?"

"Why don't you go get a bite to eat first? I'll meet you there and probably have you work here a couple hours. Then you can head back to start the chores."

"Sounds good." He tipped his hat to Grace and sped across the street.

Jace pounded in a nail before turning to Cade. "Tim's turned out to be a great ranch hand. One of the best workers I've had. Hope he can stick around a while." He dropped his hammer on the stack of boards behind him. "My belly's telling me to feed it. Want to join me?"

"In a bit. I'd like to finish this section first."

"How about you, Grace?"

"I'll wait. But thanks."

Jace walked past them and called over his shoulder, "All right, but don't think I'm gonna save you any."

Cade slung a charred piece of wood at him, earning a laugh. Someone from inside the bank howled.

"There goes another thumb," Cade said.

Grace moved to get a better look at the hole. "What happened this morning?"

"We're still trying to figure that out. I woke up to four explosions, all pretty close together. I got down here to find a hole in the bank, the mercantile, the saloon, and one in the gun shop. Only place robbed is the gun shop. Didn't touch the money in the bank."

"Odd."

"Ain't it though? That's what we're still trying to figure out. The sheriff is off asking everyone who lives on this street if they saw anything." He lifted the board he'd cut and held it against the bare beams of the bank. "But it's more than a little scary to think men like that now have a whole arsenal to help them carry out their thievery."

The picture Cade drew caused a tremor of fear from her scalp to her toes.

"I'm sorry, Grace. I shouldn't have said anything, especially something that would scare you. I guess I'm just so worked up, I wasn't thinking"

"I'm all right." She forced a smile, then picked up the hammer Jace had discarded. She pounded the ball of it into her palm. "Want me to nail that board on?"

"No!" The board he held fell to the ground as he snatched the hammer from her. "Uh…I mean, you don't need to do that."

"I can hold the board for you then. Or would you rather I cut the next one?" She reached for the saw only to have him take that too.

"Grace, are you sure Bobbie doesn't need you? There are a lot of hungry mouths to feed over there. Besides, I'll be finished here soon."

"What? Look at the size of that hole. You won't be finished for hours."

This time, Cade grinned. "You're obviously not a carpenter. I can promise you it won't take hours to fix that hole."

"You're right. Especially if I help."

"Listen, Grace—"

"Just let me do something, Cade. Let me help rebuild my new hometown."

He stared at her for several moments, then smiled. "All right."

He bent down and picked up an end of the board he'd dropped. "Grab that side and hold it up against the wall."

The plank was much heavier than it looked, but determination won out. She shoved it next to the one Jace had been working on. "Like this?"

"Perfect. Hold it still."

Two nails disappeared into the wood in no time. Cade sure made it look easy. He slammed one more nail into place and moved next to her. After grabbing another nail from the pouch around his waist, he hesitated a moment before pounding it in place.

"You can let go now." He leaned down when she didn't budge. "That nail is holding it in place."

"Oh." She moved back a step.

He had only one more nail to drive home.

"Is pounding nails anything like whacking off a chicken's head?"

The usually well-aimed hammer missed its mark. Cade closed his eyes and let the hammer drop to the ground as he grasped his thumb. He bent over and pressed his hands against his legs.

Grace gasped. "Oh, Cade. That had to hurt." He never said a word or made a sound. "Let me see it."

He twisted just enough to turn away from her. She grabbed his elbow and pulled him back around. His face glowed red. Sweat beaded his upper lip.

"Take a breath, Cade, before you pass clean out." Something akin to a growl was all she heard. "What can I do to help you? Some water maybe? Should I get the doctor?"

Cade stood upright, took a deep breath, and let it out slowly. Then he placed his uninjured hand on her back and maneuvered her out of the alley. "Go see if Bobbie needs your assistance. If she doesn't, go ahead and get something to eat."

"But I—"

"Really, Grace, I insist. I'm almost certain Bobbie needs help."

She looked up at him to give him a good scolding for trying to get rid of her, but the stunned look on his face stopped her words. "What's wrong?" She followed his gaze and found a man standing in the street staring at them. "Who's that?"

Cade licked his lips and rubbed his palms on his pant legs.

"Cade?" She glanced between the two men again. "Who is that?"

"My father."

NINETEEN

C ade knew to expect his father. Just not so soon. So much for a couple more weeks to mentally prepare for him.

Though Cade stood nearly a head taller, his father was an imposing figure with a sturdy frame and intense eyes. Smiles were infrequent. Cade couldn't remember the last time he'd been on the receiving end of one. Or of a kind word for that matter. Criticism filled their conversations from the time he'd reached his teen years, right about the time he showed more interest in livery work than in following his father's footsteps. Because of the land office robbery, he felt certain more disapproval would be forthcoming. He'd soon find out if his prayers for the opposite would be answered.

A tug on his sleeve pulled him from his thoughts. Grace stared up at him, her expression a mixture of concern and curiosity.

"Aren't you going to go welcome him?"

"Uh, yeah. Of course. He just caught me off guard."

But before Cade could take a step, his father was surrounded by townspeople, all clapping him on the back or pumping his hand as they welcomed him home. With one quick glance back at Cade, his father allowed himself to be pulled into the hotel by those insisting he get a hot meal before he headed off to his wife.

"Well." Grace stood with hands on hips. "Maybe the folks didn't see you standing here. I'm sure they would have let your father come see you if they had."

He turned to go back to work.

Grace grabbed his arm. "Let's go over there. You two can sit together while you eat."

"That's all right. I'll just finish up the wall first."

"Cade? Is anything wrong?"

"No." Irritation rose, and he fought to keep it under control. Where to begin about what was wrong? But he didn't want to talk about it.

"Cade?"

"Oh, all right." He tossed the hammer onto the stack of lumber. "Let's go."

The tension in him rose and his feet grew heavier with each step toward the hotel. Inside, people milled from one end of the room to the other. Some men sat on the floor to eat while others stood balancing their plate. Yet his father somehow managed to find a seat. No doubt someone gave up their chair for him.

"Cade, get some food and come on over." Jace stood at the registration counter using it as a table. "We'll make room. You too, Grace."

He followed Grace to the long tables laden with all kinds of food and desserts and filled his plate. He turned to find Grace standing next to his father but looking at Cade, waiting to be introduced.

Since his father didn't attempt a handshake, he didn't either. "Father. Welcome home."

"Thank you. Who's the lovely young lady with you?" He stood and took Grace's plate from her, handed it to Cade, then clasped Grace's hand in both of his.

"This is Grace Bradley from Pueblo. She's working for Jace and Bobbie."

Victor Ramsey gave a slight bow. "A pleasure, Miss Bradley."

"Likewise."

"I hope we get a chance to visit one day soon."

"That would be nice. I've enjoyed getting to know your wife."

"Wonderful." He gave another bow. "I'll let you eat while your food is warm."

They headed toward Jace, but didn't get far before Grace reached for her plate. "I'm going to see if I can find Bobbie. They may need help cleaning up."

She spoke to him but her eyes were on the far end of the counter. Frank Easton.

"Want me to help you?" Cade said.

"No, but thanks. I'll try to find you later."

He kept an eye on her until she disappeared in the back of the hotel. Frank never made an effort to talk to her, though he watched her every move. Cade made his way toward Jace and settled next to him. He planned to make short work of the meal and take his leave. Only one bite managed to disappear before Frank's voice made him lose his appetite.

"You seem to be a well-respected man around here." Frank held his hand out to Cade's father, who took it. "Frank Easton's the name."

"Victor Ramsey. I own the land office here."

"Ah, the one that was robbed."

Victor turned and pinned Cade with his eyes. "So I've heard."

Cade forced himself to meet the gaze without flinching. Even his mother agreed he had his own business to run and didn't need to feel responsible for his father's. So why did a tremor just shake up his insides?

"I've noticed everyone is treating these mishaps as though they were the worst possible things that could happen around here." Frank strutted around the tables, gaining everyone's attention. "You should look at the bright side."

"What bright side is there to robbery and damaged buildings?" Mr. Murphy frowned and propped his fists on his hips.

Frank smiled, looking for all the world like a spider with a juicy moth caught in its web. "Why, it proves the town is growing. No smart crook would waste his time on a Podunk town when he can line his pockets by focusing on a larger target."

Silas Mahoney moved around to the front of his counter. "That's foolish talk. A man with evil intent doesn't care where he gets some money."

"That might be true of just any thief, but mind you, I said a smart crook attacks the bigger towns. Especially those that are growing." Frank stroked his thin mustache. "Think of it this way—if a town is growing, chances are there's plenty of money floating around. They're just itching to relieve you of some of it."

Cade didn't know why Frank didn't shave off that scrap of hair he called a mustache. It looked ridiculous. But then, as far as he was concerned, that word described Frank. Surely the men wouldn't believe the nonsense he spouted.

Frank propped one finger in the pocket of his vest and lifted the forefinger of his other hand into the air. "Now, this news may make some of you wish for a small town again. Let me assure you that you don't want that. Growth means wealth. It's good business. Show me a man who says he doesn't want to make money, and I'll show you a liar." He leaned on the table next to him. "What about you, Mr. Ramsey? Would you like to see the town continue to grow with money prevalent enough to run through your fingers like water?"

Victor leaned back in his chair, his lips tight. Cade couldn't tell if it was a smile or a grimace.

"Sure, but how do you propose to make that happen? We're not growing that fast, and we still have a small-town mentality."

"Ah, but that can change." Frank pushed upright again and shoved his hands into his pockets where he proceeded to jingle some coins. "What would you say to a new bank that would guarantee the lowest interest on loans? Or what about a new livery where competition would keep prices down and, in turn, allow you to keep more money in your pockets?"

Cade glanced around. Other than Pete and Jace, Frank seemed to have the avid interest of everyone in the room.

"Or even another hotel and restaurant for that matter." Frank started his pacing again, still playing with the change in his pockets. "I'm telling you good folks, there's nothing like a little friendly competition to keep a town growing. Why, I'd even like to help someone start up a sawmill in the area. Why keep running to Pueblo for your lumber? Progress, people. That's what growth is all about."

A cheer went up. A chair appeared for Frank to occupy…at Cade's father's table no less. The men crowded around, plying Frank with questions.

Cade pushed his plate away and headed for the door. Were these good folks about to line their own pockets by buying into Frank's spiel, or were they about to sign a deal with the devil? Time would tell, and Cade had every intention of keeping an eye on the clock.

Finally. After more than two hours of cleaning up the mess left by the men, Grace headed to Joseph and Belle's new home. She couldn't wait to get away from the hotel where Frank stayed. All his chatter about helping the town grow infuriated her. She could only imagine how Cade and Pete felt now that Frank threatened them with competition. And he had the audacity to make it look as though he only wanted to help the town. Anyone who knew Frank knew he didn't do anything to help anyone unless he could line his own pocket in the process.

Her heart battled over whether she should somehow warn the townsfolk or stay out of it and out of Frank's line of vision. He wouldn't appreciate her interference in the least. The possibility of his retribution terrified her right down to her toenails. If his wife could disappear without any explanation…well, she didn't want to finish the thought.

Grace had reached the edge of town and wondered if she misunderstood Bobbie's directions. The small house described to her was nowhere in sight. She wavered between turning back and going forward, then figured a few more steps wouldn't hurt. After passing a large clump of bushes to her left, the house came into view. She spotted Belle sitting in a chair near the front door. She looked asleep except for a dark object held to her chest. Only steps away, Grace heard quiet words pouring from Belle, her voice laden with emotion. Fear gripped Grace's heart. *Did she lose the baby?*

She took the last few steps and discovered that the dark object was a Bible. "Belle?" Grace touched her shoulder and made her gasp.

"Girl! You ought not be sneakin' up on folks like that." Belle clutched at her blouse. "Why, I think all my innards just turned wrong side out. I may even have to check my drawers."

"I wasn't sneaking." Grace fought the urge to laugh as she knelt next to Belle, the tears still shining on her cheeks. "Are you all right?"

"Oh, sure." Belle dabbed at her eyes with her apron. "Dealing with memories is tough sometimes."

"Memories?"

"Of my mama. She shoved this here Book into my hands as they hauled me away after selling me to a new plantation." She briefly pressed her lips against the leather. "That was the last time I ever saw Mama. We looked for her when we was freed, but they say she died." Fresh tears shone in her eyes.

"I'm sorry, Belle. I can't imagine how hard that must have been." Grace touched the binding. "I have my mother's Bible too. I'm sure I don't read it as much as you do yours."

Belle stared for a moment, then dropped her gaze and shook her head. "I canst read. Ain't been taught. So I just sit and hold this Book and try to remember all Mama tol' me. Most times it's comforting. Oh, my. Forgive my lack of hospitality. Let me get you a chair."

Grace stopped her when she moved to stand. "Stay there. I'll get it."

She entered through the open door into a small kitchen. The unmistakable smell of fresh paint reached her nose. The white walls

were almost bare of decorations, but she recognized the curtains
Bobbie gave them for the windows. The table and chairs looked new.
Pleased at least some of the residents loved and accepted Joseph and
Belle, she smiled as she caressed the smooth tabletop before grab-
bing a chair and heading back outside.

The sight of Belle's worn shoes sitting at the door made her stop.
One was in such bad shape, a stiff wind would either blow it away
or crumble it on the spot. She placed her foot next to them to get
an idea of their size, and then continued on her way out to chat until Bobbie came by to pick her up and take her home.

Belle looked up and smiled as Grace settled next to her. "So,
what'd ya think of the place?"

"I think it's wonderful. Small but nice. The real question is, what
do you think of it?"

Belle laid the Bible on her lap and rubbed her hands along the
cover. "Like you say, it's nice. Mr. Cade been wonderful to us."

Grace touched her arm. "I think I hear a 'but' in your voice."

She shrugged but wouldn't look up. "It's lonely. We had neighbors at the tent town. At the ranch I had you. I thinks most folks
here would rather we move on."

That was a polite way to say it. "Well, I don't feel that way. I'm
glad you stayed. I missed you only minutes after you left. It was
nice having someone around to talk to now and then. It's pretty
quiet until Jace and Bobbie get home." At least she knew how to
read to help fill her time. "Do you happen to have some paper and
a pencil?"

Belle sent her the strange look Cade often gave her. "Now, why'd
we be having that?"

Grace closed her eyes. "I'm sorry. I wasn't thinking." Then she
latched onto Belle's arm. "I want to teach you to read."

"But I—"

"I'll talk to the school teacher about borrowing a reader. They
shouldn't need it since school's almost out for the summer. Plus I

can get some paper and pencils. In the meantime, we can start right now by using a stick and the dirt."

"But—"

"Come on. Help me find a stick."

Belle stood and followed her toward the bushes. "I'm thinking you done lost a small piece of your mind."

With a laugh, Grace broke off a branch. "It wouldn't be the first time. Let's just hope I find it again. Otherwise there's no telling what might happen." She swung around and shook her finger. "And you don't need to comment on that."

"Well, shucks. You take out all the fun."

The two shared a laugh and a hug. Grace led Belle to the far side of the house where her scratchings would less likely be messed up. She wrote the entire alphabet in the dirt, both upper and lower case, explaining each as she scraped the letters. At the look of confusion on Belle's face, Grace smiled.

"I promise this will get easier and make sense as we go along. But first you need to learn these letters and the sounds they make."

"How'm I s'posed to remember all this stuff?"

"By saying it over and over."

Belle raised an eyebrow. "Uh-huh. And a hunnard dollars is gonna drop from the sky at my feet."

Grace propped her hands on her hips and stared at the sky. A good minute passed before Belle moved next to her and looked up.

"Whatcha doing?"

"Looking for that hundred dollars."

Belle bumped her with her elbow and burst into laughter. "You something else, girl. All right, show me more."

Belle's enthusiasm was short-lived as frustration rose with the difficulty of remembering the sound each letter made. An idea struck, and Grace squatted to draw pictures under each letter. She drew an apron and an apple, then moved to the next letter and drew a loaf of bread. Grace explained what she was doing, and Belle caught on immediately and began making all the correct sounds.

Grace sketched a terrible likeness of Jonah and had started on a hat when they heard Bobbie say behind them, "What are you doing?"

After they recovered from being startled, Belle looked at Grace, and she nodded that it would be all right to tell her.

"We was looking for Grace's mind."

Grace gasped and looked with astonishment at Belle. The little rascal.

"I'm almost afraid to ask if you found it," Bobbie said.

Grace was the first to get serious and explain her initial efforts to teach Belle to read.

Intrigued, Bobbie squatted and helped her finish the alphabet drawings. When done, she stood and glanced around. "Oh, my goodness. It's getting dark. We need to go. But that was fun. If you ever need help, Belle, you let me know."

Belle put her arm around Grace. "Thank you. But Grace is doing fine."

The two hugged. "I'll be back as soon as I can to check up on you. But next time I'll have paper so we won't have to play in the dirt."

Grace followed Bobbie to the buggy feeling needed again, of value to someone. It made her warm inside. And not only that, she'd made a friend, something she hadn't had since her mother fell ill, making her determined not to run again. She'd face Frank down and fight his advances with everything in her. He wouldn't be able to say or do anything to shake her resolve. Rockdale was now her home.

❋ TWENTY ❋

I f blood were purple, Grace might have been arrested on suspicion of murder given the look of her hands. Even her shoes were
stained with the berries she couldn't avoid stepping on, they grew
so thick. She wondered how long the color would take to wear off.
She'd never picked blackberries before, so the ache in her lower back
and the barbs tearing at her skin surprised her, but she had to admit she was having fun.

With her basket filled almost to overflowing, she was ready to
head home. But Belle said she wanted some berries too. Why she was
late, Grace didn't know, but worry began inching its way through
her, especially since her friend had been so excited about spending
the day on the ranch. She would give Belle a few more minutes to
show. In the meantime, she'd start filling her apron, but this time
she'd squat and give her poor back a rest.

A snort from behind made Grace stand with a smile as she prepared to scold Belle for making her do all the work. The bright sun
forced her to shade her eyes. The sight of Frank Easton sitting in his
buggy scraped her smile away. For the first time, no one was around
to help her.

Dressed all in black, he looked more evil than usual. The smirk
on his face didn't help the image. She bent to grab her basket with

her free hand while the other held up the end of her apron to keep from losing what she'd just picked. Without a word she stomped out of the bushes intent on getting at least a little closer to the house.

Before she took many steps, Frank turned the horse and cut off her escape. She veered the opposite direction, but Frank jumped from the buggy and grabbed her elbow, sending her basket tumbling to the ground.

She jerked her arm to free herself, but he held tight.

"What do you want, Frank?"

He reached into her apron, pulled out some berries, and shook them in his hand as though they were a pair of dice. "Now Grace, I've made no secret of what I want."

He tossed the berries into his mouth. The cocky slant of his hat added to his arrogant attitude.

"I'm not marrying you, Frank. I thought my leaving made that perfectly clear."

"Oh, my dear Grace." He ran his finger across her cheek. "I know you're nervous. Many young brides feel the same way."

She pulled away from him. "I'm not nervous. Because I'm not going to marry you."

"Ah, Grace. I'm a patient man, but you're certainly trying me."

"Then stop waiting and go on about your life. I want no part of it."

"But it's you I want, Grace. And you know I always get what I want."

His eyes held an intensity she'd never seen before, and he'd dropped his voice, making him more intimidating than ever. Had his first wife seen this side of him? No one knew. She'd disappeared mere months after they'd moved to Pueblo, and Frank refused to talk about her. Grace wondered if he'd wanted his wife as much as he seemed to want her.

"What happened to your first wife? Why isn't she still a part of your life?"

He looked down, his jaw clenching. "That's none of your business."

"On the contrary. I would think any future wife should be privy to that information."

"Did you just consent to be my wife?"

"No, not in the least. I'm just warning you for any future Mrs. Easton."

One corner of his mouth twitched. "Fight it all you wish, Grace, but you're the next woman to hold that title." He grasped her chin with his fingers and leaned toward her, his eyes intent on her mouth.

She wrenched away from him, dropping the berries from her apron. "Don't you dare."

He reached with both hands and seized each side of her face. "Oh, I dare. I have your father's permission."

He laid claim to her lips for only a second before something smacked him on the side of his head. Grace spun away while he ducked and dodged another strike. Belle stood with her large basket at the ready, her face filled with rage. A glance at Frank showed him in the same condition.

Frank stooped to grab his hat from the ground. "How dare you touch me!"

"I dint touch you. It was my basket. And if you lay another hand on Miss Grace, I be glad to whop you upside the head again."

Frank took a step toward her. "Look, girl, this is none of your affair. So why don't you just scurry your tail back to the hole you came from before you get hurt."

Belle tightened her grip on the basket handle. "I be staying right here."

Frank growled deep in his throat as he raised his hand. Belle swung the basket at him again. He snatched it from her, flung it aside, and shoved Belle to the ground. Grace dropped down between her and Frank, ready to take any hit he planned to deliver.

"Get out of the way, Grace. She's gonna get what's coming to her so she'll learn her place."

Frank reached for Grace, but she batted his hand away.

"Her place is right here. Yours isn't. Now go!"

"Not yet. We still haven't had our little talk."

"I'm through talking to you, Frank."

He grabbed her arm and yanked her to her feet. "You're through when I say you're through."

"Is there a problem here?"

Tim Martell sat atop his horse, his hand on his pistol, looking for all the world like the avenging angel Grace's mama mentioned from time to time. Grace thought if she peered hard enough, she just might find a halo hovering over his head. She jerked away from Frank's grip and returned to Belle's side.

"Tim, isn't it?" Frank said.

Tim nodded, his hand still on his gun.

"Well, Tim, you're not needed here, so be on your way. Grace and I have some business to discuss."

Tim leaned to look past him. "Grace?"

She shook her head, fear drying her mouth.

He sat a little straighter in his saddle. "I believe you're done here, sir."

Frank propped his fists on his hips, putting his hand dangerously close to his own pistol. "You're making a big mistake, son. I can make more trouble for you than you're ready to face, as I'm sure you already know."

Tim licked his lips and glanced at Grace. "Maybe so," he said, his voice betraying a slight tremble. "But if you continue on with this, the sheriff will have something to say about it." He motioned toward them with his head. "He already may if these ladies decide to talk to him."

The two men tried to stare each other down for several moments. Then Frank took a deep breath, dropped his hands to his sides, and turned to her, his eyes boring into hers.

"We really do need to talk, Grace."

His tone surprised her. Either Tim's presence or the mention of the sheriff had calmed him.

"About what?"

"Alone."

Did he think her dense? He'd already attacked her once. "No."

He took a step toward her. "Grace—"

She held up her hand. "Not now, Frank. I think you've said enough for one day."

The muscles in his jaw bulged. Then he nodded. "All right. But there's something you need to know, so don't let it wait too long."

"Goodbye, Frank."

He made a move toward the buggy, then stopped. "Would you like a ride?" He looked only at her.

Grace reached to take Belle's hand. "No, thank you. We'll walk."

His smile was tight. "Someday that stubbornness will get you into trouble, Grace." He climbed into the buggy and slapped the reins against the horse's rump, leaving behind a thick cloud of dust.

"You two all right?" Tim remained on his horse and urged his mount closer.

"I think so. Belle?"

"I's just fine now that wretched man done gone. You know he be back, don't ya, Grace? He all but say so."

"Thank you for your help, Tim," Grace said. "I'm not sure how that would've turned out had you not shown up."

"Glad I could help, though by the look on your friend's face, Frank would have been minus some hair and possibly some skin before it was all over." Tim smiled at Belle's chuckle. He looked toward the house and back. "Would you like me to get the wagon?"

"No, I think we'll be fine now, but thank you. In fact, the walk might do us some good."

He eyed them for a bit, then tipped his hat. "I'll be around if you need anything." He nudged his horse, leaving them on their own.

Belle stretched her back. "Don't know about you, but I ain't in no mood for berry picking now." She scooped up her basket. "Don't know that this would hold nothing nohow."

One corner of the basket hung open like a gaping wound. The handle didn't look all that sturdy either. Belle must have put everything she had into that hit. The whole idea of it made Grace smile.

"Are you sure you didn't get hurt, Belle?"

Belle waved her question away. "What say we salvage what we can of what you picked and head to the house?"

She didn't wait for an answer but knelt and started retrieving the spilled berries. Grace plopped next to her. She recalled Frank's kiss, and a shudder raced from her scalp to her ankles. She wiped her sleeve across her lips.

"I sure am glad you arrived when you did, but how did you get here?"

"Joseph brung me. Left me up at the house. When you didn't answer the door, I came here." She touched Grace's arm. "Sorry we was late. If we hadn't been, all this might not have happened."

Grace stood and helped Belle to her feet. "Knowing Frank, he'd have found a way whether you were here or not." They started home walking fast, both apparently ready to be where it was safer. "What time is Joseph coming for you?"

"Mr. Cade s'posed to take me home."

"Cade?"

"Mmm-hmm. When he heard we was gonna be baking all day, he offered to come for me. Says he was delivering things and would end up here." She elbowed Grace. "Said to give you a message."

"A message?"

"Yep. He tol' me to tell you he was ready for his cookies and today was as good as any to get them." Belle bumped her again. "I tol' you he was sweet on you."

Grace gave a mirthless laugh. "Trust me, Belle, he's sweet on sweets. Namely cookies."

She led Belle into the house, and they washed their hands, Grace scrubbing extra hard with little success against the berry stains.

"So do you like Mr. Cade? Even a little?" Belle said as she reached for the flour to start mixing bread dough.

Grace stared at Belle, who refused to meet her gaze. "I'm not getting married, Belle. Ever."

Belle looked up. "Why not?"

"I've waited a long time for my freedom. I'm sure not going to give it up now, especially not to some controlling man."

"Mr. Cade's not controlling."

"Not now, maybe." *And besides that, he's not a bit interested.*

"What you mean, you waited for your freedom? Ain't you always been free?"

Grace's heart jumped to her throat. How could she be so thoughtless? "Oh, Belle, I'm sorry. My lack of freedom was nothing like what you went through. I wasn't thinking when I said that."

Belle waved her floured-up hand through the air. "Oh, fiddle. I know you dint mean nothing by it. You's too nice to be cruel. I just wants to understand, that's all."

But did she really want to get into it? Talking about it with Belle would just dig everything up again.

"It was nothing, really."

"Now, don't be saying that. I can tell by the look on your face that something been eating on ya. And if'n it keeps you from getting hitched, then it must be something mighty powerful." Belle shook a flour-covered finger at her. "And that kind of power over you means you ain't free at all."

Grace dumped her dough onto the table and started kneading, feeling like the same thing was being done to her insides. "I just miss her, that's all."

"Miss who?"

She pushed a stray tress of hair out of her face with the back of her hand. "Mama."

"Oh. You tol' me she died not long ago. I'm sorry I made you think of her again." Belle thumped the dough with her fist. "But I guess I don't understand what that has to do with your freedom."

Grace added more flour to her hands and sprinkled some on her dough. "Mama used to be a lot of fun. We did everything together. Where she went, I went, even shopping and to church. She read to me a lot, especially from the Bible."

"So, she loved God."

"Oh, yes. She loved her Lord." The memory left a bittersweet taste in her mouth. She swallowed hard. "Then she started having headaches."

"Bad ones, I'd guess."

"Enough to put her in bed. At first just for several hours. Then it became several days at a time. Some were bad enough to make her sick to her stomach. And sometimes she complained of blurred vision. Daddy got worried enough to take her to some doctors in St. Louis."

Belle stopped kneading. "What'd they find out?"

When did it get so hot? A drop of sweat ran down her skin under her dress. She moved to the window and opened it wide, then did the same with the door. But she knew what ailed her wouldn't be helped by opening windows and doors. She returned to the table.

"Daddy said the doctors had seen this before, that Mama probably had something in her head that would eventually kill her."

"Oh, Grace. How awful."

"Yeah."

The two were quiet for a while, and Grace hoped the discussion was over.

"How old were you?"

She was wrong. "About eleven, I think."

"So it was a long illness."

"Yes." *Forever.*

Another silence. Maybe her short answers ended it.

"Talk about it, Grace. You needs to get it out. I sees it making you so tight, you might bust."

Grace stopped kneading long enough to look up. Belle's voice had been so soft, and her eyes were filled with care and compassion.

The sight almost brought tears to her own. She used her wrist to wipe at her cheek as she gave a long, heavy sigh.

"I don't know, Belle."

Belle reached over and squeezed her hand. "It be all right. You'll see. Just let it all out."

Where to start? "Well, things went on much the same for a while, except most of the fun had ended. Though she'd still read once in a while, Mama was afraid to leave the house not knowing when a headache would strike. She also started having seizures, and that embarrassed her. For a couple years, Daddy would do most of the shopping, but sometimes he'd give me money and a list."

If she didn't start kneading, she'd never get this bread rising.

"Sometime after that, Daddy asked me to quit school so I could take care of Mama. He said he needed to work more so he could afford to feed us. After I'd been at it a while, I came to understand he'd asked me to stay home full-time because he wanted to get away from it all. It could get overwhelming. You see, as time went on, Mama needed more and more help...with everything. The last few years, she was completely bedridden."

"You didn't have no help?"

"We did for a while. A couple ladies from the church would stop in once or twice a week. They even tried to help me with my school-work that my teacher brought by. When I turned sixteen, it all dwindled to a stop."

Belle cut her dough in half, shaped them, and placed each half into a bread pan. "And your daddy?"

"He stayed busy. He's a gunsmith. The larger Pueblo grew, the busier he got. Plus, he started looking into land ownership. Thought it would be a good and easy way to make money. He'd come home pretty tired. But he still took over Mama's care after he had something to eat. I could tell he loved her a lot and that her illness really ate on him. So much so that he started looking old."

Belle began mixing up pie crust. "I'm sure your mama didn't stay awake all day. What'd you do to fill the hours?"

What did she do? One corner of her mouth rose as she snorted. "Not much. I'd read for a while. And when I wasn't cooking or cleaning, I'd stare out the window and watch the people shop and visit." She couldn't count the times she had to wipe her nose prints off the window overlooking the street. Or the tears that ran from her cheeks onto the windowsill. The ache she'd felt in her chest all those years ago reappeared.

"I'd see my old school friends standing on the boardwalk visiting, and I knew I couldn't join them. I even doubted they remembered me. Then one of them looked up and pointed at me. I wanted someone to talk to, but Mama just lay there in her own world. Sometimes she'd say the meanest things. I'm certain she didn't realize it, but it could be awful at times."

Belle reached for Grace's dough. "Here. Gimme that 'fore you beat the rise clean out of it." She shoved the bowl of pie crust toward her. "You work on that. I'll finish this and then wash the berries."

Grace fought a losing battle with her tears. Belle came around the table and pulled her into a hug.

"I'm so sorry this happened to you."

"Thank you."

They went back to work without another word. The quiet started getting to her. Then Belle cleared her throat.

"You almost seem to resent your mama."

The comment all but slapped Grace across the face. "What? No, I loved Mama."

"Oh, I'm sure you did. But look how angry you got just talking about her. I could hear it in your voice. Or maybe it's God you mad at." Belle's tone held no condemnation, only concern. "Think on it some, Grace, and be honest with yourself."

She didn't want to deal with her emotions; she just wanted to get over them. Put it all in the past. What good would it do to bring it all up again? It hurt too much.

"All right, so maybe I was a little bitter about her illness. But it was just that, anger at her illness, not at her. It kept her from me. I needed her. And even though she was right at my fingertips, she just wasn't there." Her voice broke.

Belle put the last two loaves of bread in the pans and set them aside to rise. "Your poor mama. I bet she was mighty fearful."

"What do you mean?"

"Well, it be my guess your mama knew something was wrong with her. And knowing she had no control over it musta been scary. It would if it was me. Never knowing when something would happen. Feeling yourself getting worse." She dumped the berries into a bucket of water. "Yep. She musta been living in fear most of the time."

Heaviness settled in Grace's chest as she cut the pie crust in half and started rolling out one of the lumps. Mama always seemed at peace. But then, maybe she acted that way so as not to scare her. The heaviness turned to a throb. Grace had always been so wrapped up in her own misery, she never thought of what her mama was going through. Shame filled her.

"I knows it was tough on you, Grace. You done lost a big chunk of your childhood. That would make anyone mad. But you oughts to quit on it now. You been looking for freedom? You may be out on your own now, but you ain't free. You ain't never gonna be free till you forgive your mama and get straight with the Lord."

Her throat ached as she fought her tears. "Forgive mama? How can I do that when she's no longer alive?"

Belle moved to her side and placed her hand over Grace's heart. "Right here." Her voice was just above a whisper. "You forgive her right here." She turned Grace to face her. "I knows you loved her. But you gotta get rid of the mad you have at her. You do that, and you're well on your way to real freedom. Get right with God, and you'll be truly free even if you be locked up in a tiny room." Belle wiped her own tears away. "I knows this cuz I been right where you are. The law says I'm a free woman now. But God set me free long before that."

Belle returned to her berries. "All's I ask, Grace, is that you think on it. I'll help you all you want. All right?"

Grace smiled and nodded. Her heart already felt softer and lighter than it had in a long time. She put the pie crust into the plate, slid it toward Belle, then went to work on the second lump.

Belle dumped the berries into the crust. "How'd you meet that mean ol' Frank?"

Grace wiped away the moisture below her eyes. "Daddy brought him home one night about a year ago. Said they needed to talk about some business. Not long after that, Frank started coming around at least once a week showing interest in me. Nothing I said or did dissuaded him. When Daddy came to me trying to talk me into marrying Frank, I decided it was time to run."

Belle visibly shuddered. "I don't blame you."

The two laughed and went about their baking in a much brighter atmosphere. Once the pies were in the oven, they threw sandwiches together for dinner. While they ate, Grace laid out papers with some simple sentences she had prepared earlier and listened as Belle struggled through them, helping her sound out the words when necessary. A tiny thrill of pride rolled through her.

"You're doing great, Belle."

"Thank you."

They started to clean up, and Belle stuck out her foot. "You never said nothing about my new shoes."

Grace glanced at Belle's feet. "They look great. Where'd you get them?"

Belle leaned over and bumped her with her elbow. "Stop playing like you don't know nothing. I knows it was you." She hugged Grace. "And I thanks you."

Grace hugged her back. "You're very welcome."

A knock came at the door. The day had already been interesting, but she had a feeling it was only the beginning.

TWENTY-ONE

Grace answered the door and found Cade standing there looking very pleased with himself. And very handsome.

He grinned. "You going to let me in?"

"Oh." She stepped out of the way. "I just didn't expect you so soon." Not that she was complaining.

"Yeah, well, I wanted to make sure you didn't start on the cookies before I got here."

"I can't believe you don't trust me. What have I ever done to earn that?" By the look on his face, she didn't want to know. "Never mind."

"How'd the morning go?" He sniffed the air. "Get a lot of baking done?"

"Sure did." *And some healing too.*

She led the way into the kitchen. "Look who's here already, Belle. He's wanting his cookies."

"Then I guess we best get started."

Cade pulled out a chair and sat, showing he had every intention of watching just as he said he would. Grace went for a bowl and spoon.

Belle brought the flour and sugar back to the table. "You gonna tell Mr. Cade about Frank or you want me to?"

Grace almost dropped the bowl. Belle talked too much.

"What about Frank?" Cade said.

"Let's not get into it right now."

Cade narrowed his eyes. "Later then."

That sounded like a promise. She stirred the sugar and flour together, then added a bit of salt. "Grab a couple eggs, will you, Belle?" When Belle reached for the two eggs off by themselves, Grace said, "Not those two. When I cleaned the henhouse this morning, I found some eggs that might have been there a bit too long. Those two didn't feel right when I washed them this morning. I was going to toss them."

Cade stood. "I'll do it. That way I can say I helped."

"Don't hurt yourself doing too much," Grace said.

He waggled his eyebrows at her and strolled toward the door.

"Do you trust me enough to leave the room?" she said.

He turned with a grin. "Only for a moment."

He disappeared outside, then hollered something. Unable to hear him clearly, Grace headed his way. She saw him wind up to throw one of the eggs, but it made it only as far as his ear before it popped. A greenish-yellow goop oozed down the side of his face. He held his hand away and gave it a shake.

Grace tried not to laugh by biting her lip, but at the look of disgust on his face, she could contain herself no longer. A case of the giggles took hold as she went to the sink to wet a cloth for him. Cade followed her in. She caught the scent of the rotten egg and backed away as she tossed the rag to him.

He took a threatening step toward her. "If I didn't know better, I'd think you planned that."

She ran to the other side of the table next to Belle, who gave her a shove.

"Don't get me involved. I want nothing to do with that stink."

"Stink?"

"Yessir, Mr. Cade. You smell something awful."

"Well, thank you very much, Belle. I like you too." He wiped at his ear, then tossed the cloth into the sink. "So when do I get my cookies? I think I've really earned them this time, don't you?"

He sank into the seat he'd vacated earlier. Grace jumped from the chair she'd dropped onto and moved to the far side of the table before she finished stirring the mixture. Even after washing, Cade still carried an awful stench.

Grace dropped balls of dough onto a pan, and then removed the pies from the oven and placed them on the counter to cool, thankful that the sweet aroma had overtaken the smell of rotten eggs. Then she shoved the cookies inside.

Belle pulled out a chair, sat, and massaged her lower back. "How'd you two meet?"

"You wouldn't believe it, Belle," Cade said.

"Ohhhh, this sounds like a good story." She rubbed her hands together and leaned forward. "Tell me."

Cade started regaling her with the story of their trip, and his words flowed faster than a swollen river. Grace couldn't get in even one of her own.

"Then she terrorized my horses enough to make them run off, dumping everything out of the back of the wagon."

"Now wait a minute. It wasn't me that fired the gun."

Cade raised his hand to stop her. "I'm telling the story."

"Then you better tell it right."

"I was just trying to be a gentleman and keep you from sprawling all over the ground. That's what made the gun go off."

"And I sprawled all over the ground anyway."

He put his finger to his lips to shush her. Part of her wanted to hit him while most of her wanted to laugh. So she just clamped her mouth shut and continued working on the cookies.

The afternoon turned out to be one of the best Grace had ever experienced. Between baking bread, eating cookies, and drinking milk, she and Belle laughed so hard at Cade's stories, they were holding their stomachs.

Cade glanced at his pocket watch and jumped from the chair. "Oh, no. We've got to go. I told Joseph I'd be back by now."

"Already?" Grace said.

"It's almost five."

"Oh my. I hope Bobbie wants cookies for supper."

"You mean I don't get to take all of these?"

She couldn't help but smile. He sounded just like a little boy. "Yes, those are yours, but you're going to share with your parents, aren't you?"

"Maybe."

They hurried outside, and she held his bag of cookies while he helped Belle onto the wagon seat. "Oh, wait. We forgot Belle's pie and bread."

Cade followed her back inside. She picked up the pie to hand it to him but stopped when he touched her arm.

"Thank you for the nice afternoon. I really enjoyed it. Very relaxing."

Heat from his hand raced up her arm and into her face. "You're welcome."

Their heads were near each other, and Cade slowly leaned closer. He moved his hand from her arm up to her cheek. The thought that he might kiss her dried her mouth. She parted her lips, oh, so ready.

He cleared his throat and rubbed his thumb just below her eye before pulling away. "Ah…you had flour smeared on your face."

She ran her sleeve over the same spot. "Oh. Thank you." Her heart splattered on the floor.

He took the pie from her. "You didn't tell me what Frank was doing here."

"You already know. He wants to marry me."

"That's all?"

His eyes bored into hers, and she couldn't lie. "He…forced a kiss on me."

"What?" He stiffened as his eyes filled with rage.

"It didn't last but a second. Belle showed up and bashed him on the head with her basket."

The anger wavered as his lips twitched, then smiled. "Good. Just make sure it doesn't happen again."

He took the pie and loaf of bread, strode out to the wagon, and after tipping his hat, drove away. As he disappeared across the creek, she could only think that the one man she despised fought to kiss her, and the one she dreamed of kissing avoided it with everything in him. Why did men have to be so contrary?

I'm an idiot.

Cade had scolded himself so many times since leaving Grace, the phrase became as rhythmic as the steady clip-clop of the horse's pace. How could he have been so stupid? Kissing Grace would have set into motion a whole bucketful of trouble he didn't want, or need for that matter. Since Kim's rejection, he planned to give women a wide berth.

Yet he couldn't forget how the sight of Grace made his heart stumble. And her laugh sounded more beautiful than his mother's treasured bell made from fine china. But more than anything, the flour smeared on her cheek and chin made her almost irresistible. He could hardly keep his eyes from her lips.

Stop it, Cade! You're such an idiot.

"What's wrong with you, Mr. Cade?" Belle leaned forward to look into his face. "It's like I'm riding next to a shell that looks like you." She sniffed. "But smells worse."

He laughed. "Nothing's wrong with me. Just thinking about today."

"Mmm. It was fun, wasn't it?"

This afternoon would stand out in his memory for a very long time. Odd things always seemed to happen when he was around Grace, but today, he got to see a whole different side of her.

Stop thinking about her.

He flicked the reins, wishing he could as easily fling away thoughts of Grace. The town coming into view was a blessing. Then he could busy himself working with his hands and keep his mind away from where it didn't belong.

Joseph sat in front of the house waiting for them as they pulled up. "You late." He stood and moved to the wagon.

"I know," Cade said. "I'm sorry."

"Having so much fun you lost the time?"

"Something like that."

While Joseph helped Belle off the wagon, Cade jumped down and grabbed the pie and bread. He handed the pie to Joseph.

"Whew." Joseph waved his hand in front of his face. "You smell worse than that stray dog hanging around. You roll in something dead too?"

"Very funny."

Belle took the bread from Joseph's hand. "It's rotten eggs, honey. They popped on him."

"Oh." Joseph grinned and nudged him. "I guess it slipped my mind you were with Grace."

"Yeah, you'd think I'd learn, huh?" But no matter how much he warned himself, he couldn't seem to stay away from her.

Belle frowned. "What you two talking about?"

"Nothing," the two men said at the same time.

"I never passed Bobbie," Cade said. "She still in town?"

Joseph shrugged. "Don't know. I just locked up and came home."

"All right. I'll look for her as I head to the livery." Cade climbed back onto the seat. "Maybe I'll get lucky and see her."

"Is there a problem?"

"Nope. Just wanted to talk to her a minute." He shook the reins. "See ya tomorrow, Joseph."

Cade turned the horse toward the main street, ready to call it a day. He enjoyed seeing Joseph and Belle happy. He used to be excited at the thought of marriage. No more feeling lonely and dealing with wishful thinking. But all that died the day Kim walked away with another man. Now he planned on entertaining loneliness the rest of his days, though Grace gave him pause.

As he neared his livery, he jerked back on the reins at the sight of several stacks of lumber across the street. A man he'd never seen before stood next to them, counting and then writing something on a sheet of paper.

"Howdy, neighbor."

Cade turned and found Frank Easton striding down the boardwalk. *Neighbor?*

"Have you met Lenny?"

"Lenny?"

Frank's smile widened. "Yes. Leonard Gorman." He motioned to the man with the lumber. "My carpenter."

"Just what are you planning, Frank?" Cade said.

"Why, I thought I made that perfectly clear last week. I believe you were there and heard every word." He grinned and leaned on the lumber. "I'm going to build a livery."

"Here?"

"Sure. Why not?"

Cade gripped the reins until they cut into his palms. "Because it's right next to mine. That's why not."

"Which is the very reason I chose it. Perfectly logical choice, as far as I'm concerned. This way, the customers you turn away won't have far to go." He shrugged. "Besides, the space is available."

"So is all the area on the other side of town." Cade peered at all the wood, and suspicion rose. "How'd you get the lumber here so fast?"

"I wired Pueblo as soon as the meeting ended last week. Got Lenny scrounging up all the wood on hand and told him to beat it here as fast as he could."

And probably all but stole the orders out from all the other waiting customers, like Jace and Bobbie, by offering top dollar.

"You said you were going to build your own sawmill."

"In due time." Frank rubbed his finger along his mustache. "When I thought about it, I figured we'd first need enough livery room to house the livestock of all the incoming workers. Yep." He shoved his hands into his pockets and jingled the coins while rocking on his feet. "With all the plans I've made, we'll need lots of builders."

"What happened to helping others start up new businesses and lining the pockets of the residents with profits? Sounds to me like your plans are to line your own pockets."

Frank shook his head. "There's plenty of opportunities for others to earn their share. Take your father for instance."

"What about my father?"

Frank's brows rose. "Oh. He hasn't told you?"

A bitter taste filled Cade's mouth. "Told me what?"

There was that rotten smirk again.

"He's going to do the surveying for all the property I'm going to buy. I guess that makes me his boss."

Which also meant his father backed Frank's plans, including another livery. The news wasn't all that surprising, but the disappointment cut deep. He'd been waiting years to get that kind of support.

"But your father won't be the only one to benefit from this town's growth. If someone steps up wanting to build something, I'm more than willing to drop out. I'm sure they'd need a loan. I could help with that."

"So as long as you have your finger in the pot in some way, all is well."

"It's called business, Cade. You know that. Why bother with something if there's no profit in it?"

"Does Grace fit into that same scheme?"

"Ah, Grace. The real reason for all your questions and accusations."

"Does she?"

Frank leaned against a stack of lumber and rested one hand on his cheek. "She could certainly be deemed an asset to any man, don't you think?" He bumped his hat back on his head. "You know, there is one way you could be rid of me."

Besides shooting you? "How?"

Frank grinned. "Anxious, aren't you?" He crossed his arms. "Talk Grace into returning to Pueblo with me, and you won't hear from me again."

"Not a chance."

"No? Not even if it meant getting rid of your competition?"

"I wouldn't want my worst enemy to have to deal with the likes of you, let alone someone as sweet as Grace. Just leave her be, Frank. Forget about her."

"In your words, not a chance. I want her, and I intend to have her."

"Then we're at odds in more ways than one."

Cade slapped the reins against the horse's rump. He'd had enough of Frank. He'd never wanted to be rid of someone so bad in his life.

A twinge from the Spirit sent guilt racing through him. Hate would eat at his soul until it consumed him if he didn't do something about it.

Help me Lord. I don't think I've ever felt like this before.

Cade's fragile sense of peace shattered the moment he walked into the house and found his father standing in the hall, the usual look of disapproval on his face. He turned and shut the door, using the time to brace himself for what was sure to come.

"Playing during the day making you keep late hours?"

Why did his father suddenly care about the hours he kept? Cade bit back the sarcastic reply ready to jump from the tip of his tongue. "Something like that."

He tried to walk past, but his father grabbed his arm. Seconds later, nose wrinkled, his father released him.

"You start sleeping with your animals, son?" He pulled a kerchief from his pocket and wiped his hand.

"Right." He turned to leave.

"We're not finished yet."

"No?"

"No. You need to get home earlier."

"Why? Because if I hadn't been out late, I wouldn't have found out about the new livery going up that you're helping with?"

"I'm not helping with the livery."

"No, you're just helping the man who's causing trouble." And he'd never once offered to help his own son.

"I'm not doing much. And don't change the subject. Your late hours are keeping you from your mother."

Cade glanced up the stairs. "Was she looking for me?"

"No, but you have a responsibility to her."

Cade shoved his fist into his pocket. "And I did that while you were gone."

"So it ends the moment I get back?"

"Shouldn't it?"

Victor poked Cade in the chest. "You're the one who put her there."

Cade took a deep breath, forcing himself to remain calm. "It was an accident and you know it."

"And that makes it all right? You can just go about your life without giving it a second thought. What kind of man are you?"

"Stop it!"

His mother's voice spun Cade around. He found her standing at the top of the stairs.

"Mother, what are you doing out of bed?" He headed for her, his father right next to him.

"Stay there, both of you."

Her tone froze their steps.

"You two make me so mad sometimes." She wiped her hand across her cheek. "I know you two love each other, but I sure couldn't tell it by the way you act and talk toward each other."

Her voice quavered with emotion. "Victor, when are you going to stop being angry that Cade didn't want to follow in your footsteps? If you're honest with yourself, you'll admit that's why you act like you do. Cade didn't want to be a surveyor. So what? You once told me you didn't want to be one either, but you got into the business so as not to hurt your father's feelings. And you haven't been happy since."

Victor started to speak, but Ella held up her hand to silence him. Then she gripped the railing with both hands, so tight Cade could see her knuckles turning white from where he stood. Surprised by what he just learned, he turned to glance at his father, who jammed his hands into his pockets.

"Cade is his own man, Victor, and he loves what he does. You'd know that if you'd spend any time in the livery with him."

Cade swallowed, the lump in his throat making that nearly impossible.

"And Cade, you need to forgive." She pulled a handkerchief from her pocket and blew her nose. "Forgive yourself and your father. You and I both know that what happened at the top of these stairs was an accident. So stop beating yourself up about it. If I don't blame you, then you shouldn't either."

She wiped at her nose again. "And I know you've been hurt by the way your father's treated you, but it's time to be the godly man I know you to be and let it go, especially with what you've learned about him tonight. You both need to forget these last years and start fresh, right here, right now." She sniffled. "I love you both more than I could ever say, and seeing you two hurting each other breaks my heart."

Her last words were hardly understandable as she finally started to sob. Cade slid his sleeve across his eyes. A heart would have to be made of stone not to be moved. He turned to his father and found tears glistening in the corners of his eyes. He reached out and touched his father's shoulder. His father only nodded, his hands remaining in his pockets.

"You want to help Mother to bed or should I?" Cade said.

"I'll do it." The words came out in a whisper. His dad scaled the stairs two steps at a time, then he gently pulled his wife into his arms.

Cade watched them for a few minutes before he headed to the kitchen to give them some privacy. He dropped the bag of cookies on the table, sank onto a chair, and wondered if there was any possibility God could break down the wall between him and his father.

"Fire!"

The muffled shout came from outside the window.

"There's a fire in town!"

Cade sprang for the door praying no one was hurt.

TWENTY-TWO

C ade raced down the road, then cut through alleys to get to the main street, the glow of the fire beckoning from the far end of town. The same direction as his livery.

Lord, help the town get through this latest crisis.

The closer he came, he could tell his livery was safe. So what was burning?

A small crowd stood around the fire while several men scooped water from the trough in front of his livery. Cade pressed his way through. Flames still leapt from the stack of Frank's lumber, though the men had them dwindling. He reached for a bucket to help, but stopped when someone shoved a gun barrel in his face. He raised his hands.

"Come to see your handiwork?"

One corner of Frank's mouth was curled in a sneer. Two men stood behind him with their pistols aimed at Cade's chest.

"*My* handiwork?"

"You just couldn't handle the idea of a little competition, could you? Well, let me tell you, Ramsey"—Frank rammed him in the chest with his gun barrel—"this won't stop me. It only makes me want to work harder."

Cade pushed the gun away. The two men cocked their pistols.

He forced himself to ignore them and focus on Frank. "I didn't do this."

"Right." Frank looked around at the crowd. "Did you hear that? He claims he's innocent." He shook his head, then faced Cade again. "I don't believe you. You're the only one who has something to gain from this."

"It wasn't me."

"If it wasn't you, then it's someone you hired. Either way, you're guilty, and I'll see you pay." He turned to the crowd. "Folks, I know the Ramsey family has lived here a long time, but that doesn't mean someone can't go bad, even if something is done in a moment of anger or passion."

Cade shoved Frank, making him fall. Cade leaped on him, ready to shut him up with his fist. The gun pressing against the back of his head stopped him. He stood and backed away.

Frank rose and brushed off his clothes. "A sudden decision like that can be your last, Ramsey."

"Hold it right there."

Sheriff Morgan Thomas stood poised with his own weapon pointed at the two men with the pistols, his clothes wet from helping with the fire. "Drop the guns, boys." The men didn't move. "Do it, or you'll be seeing the doctor tonight. Or the undertaker. My aim's not that good anymore."

The pistols thumped on the ground.

"Very good. Now back away." The men moved to the edge of the crowd. The sheriff holstered his gun, picked up the two on the ground, and rammed them into his belt. "Now, Mr. Easton. You want to tell me what you think you're doing?"

Frank crossed his arms. "Your job, I believe." He motioned toward Cade. "I caught the culprit for you."

The sheriff's gaze swung to him. "Cade?"

Cade snorted. "You know I didn't do it, Morgan. I wouldn't, no matter what."

Frank stepped between them. "Now, Sheriff, you can't let your friendship stop you from doing your job."

Morgan's eyes narrowed. "Don't tell me how to do my job, Easton."

"Then arrest him, and we won't have a problem."

"Show me your proof and I'll do just that."

"Morgan!" Cade said.

The sheriff held up his finger but didn't take his eyes off Frank. "You got the proof, Easton?"

"Well, I...we argued."

"You argued?" Morgan tucked his thumbs in his holster. "About what?"

Frank motioned toward the burned lumber. "Cade saw that I was building my livery across from his and got mad."

"He got mad."

"Yes."

Morgan planted his fists on his hips. "I'm mad right now, Mr. Easton. Does that mean I could have done it too?" Frank remained silent. "Is that all you have?"

Frank opened his mouth and then clamped it shut.

Morgan gave a nod. "That's what I thought."

Frank held up one hand. "Wait. I thought I could smell that greasy substance used for wagon wheels. That's probably what he used to start the fire."

Morgan shook his head. "And he's the only one around who would have that on hand? Try again, Mr. Easton. Admit it, you don't have any evidence."

"But you still have to—"

"Cade?" The sheriff elbowed Frank out of the way. "Would you come with me please?"

Cade held out both hands. "Morgan—"

"Just come with me."

Morgan headed toward his office, and Cade followed. Frank started trailing them.

"You're not invited, Mr. Easton," Morgan said.

"Sheriff—"

Morgan spun on his heels. "Look, Frank, your presence isn't needed. And quite honestly, not wanted."

Cade almost laughed at the shock on Frank's face.

"All right, Sheriff. But if you don't arrest Cade, then you sure better arrest that black man he has working for him. One of the two did this."

Morgan stood with his fists clenched. "Are you through?"

"Yes."

Morgan nodded and then continued on toward his office. Cade took long strides to catch up. He entered the sheriff's office when Morgan held the door for him.

"Morgan—"

"Have a seat."

Cade sighed and did as told. Morgan turned the flame higher in the lantern before he set on the desk the two pistols he'd taken off the men, then flopped onto his chair and rubbed his eyes.

"You need to hire some help, Morgan."

"Yeah. Trust me, I'll be sending out notices in the morning." He leaned his arms on the desk and sat staring at Cade, almost as if he were waiting for something. "What happened, Cade? You stand too close to the wrong side of a horse?"

Cade tried to smile but it wouldn't come. "No, I didn't. And I didn't start the fire either."

"I know that."

"Then what am I doing here?"

Morgan flipped his hat onto the desk and ran his fingers through his hair. "I thought it would be the quickest way to calm that mess out there. Plus I really do need to ask you some questions." He raised his hand when Cade opened his mouth. "I believe you, Cade, but I still have to ask where you were tonight. And I need to know your side of that argument with Frank. That way I'll have answers if anyone asks."

Cade sighed. "All right. After arguing with Frank about his choice of locations for his livery, I went home and had an argument with my father."

Morgan gave a slight shake of his head. "Oh, Cade."

"I know. But this time, Mother heard us and gave us both a lecture. I doubt either of us will do that again."

"Well, good for her. I always said she was a smart woman. At least you have solid witnesses. All right, now I want to know more about this thing with Frank."

"There's not much more to tell. Like I said, I didn't like his choice of places to build. Then I told him I thought the only reason he was doing anything in this town was to put money in his own pockets."

Morgan's brows rose again. "What'd he say to that?"

"He told me that I'd be rid of him if I talked Grace into leaving with him."

"What?"

"I know. There's no way I'd put Grace in his hands. I don't trust him, Morgan."

Morgan nodded. "There's something about him that seems off. Can't put my finger on it."

"This next bit of news might help. He attacked Grace today."

Morgan all but came out of his chair. "What?"

Cade held up both hands. "She's all right. Apparently, Belle showed up and whacked him on the head with her basket."

Morgan grimaced. "That's not good. Frank could cause her a great deal of trouble for that."

"I know. That's part of the reason I wanted to tell you about it. Belle's afraid he'll get revenge."

"Maybe not. I doubt he wants to deal with the ridicule he'll get if the men find out a black woman bested him. Either way, I'll check on things. What about Grace? She want to press charges?"

Cade shook his head. "I wish, but I doubt it. I think she'd just like him to go away."

"I can understand that. My work load seems to have tripled since he showed up." He shoved his chair back. "All right, Cade. I'm sure things have calmed out there by now. Go on home. I'll talk to Frank so he won't cause you any more trouble. But I'll have to call on Joseph. Frank will insist since I'm letting you go." He put his hand on Cade's back when he stood. "No, I don't think Joseph did it either. But I still have to talk to him."

"I'll go with you."

"Now, Cade—"

"It's just for Joseph's sake, Morgan. I don't want him to get concerned or anything when he sees you."

Morgan hesitated. "All right, let's go. But don't look so happy or I might change my mind."

Cade opened the door and stepped out, only to slam into Dexter Kemp. He helped keep the man from falling before letting him go.

"Dex, what are you doing out so late? Your wife all right?" Cade knew Dexter's wife would soon deliver their firstborn. By the look on the man's face, he could be the one having the baby.

"I've been robbed!"

❋ TWENTY-THREE ❋

C ade grabbed Dexter's arm again. "You hurt?"

"Did you see who did it?" Morgan's question rolled right over the top of Cade's.

Poor Dexter's face glowed a ghostly white in the light of Morgan's lantern. His Adam's apple bobbed a couple times before he shook his head.

"Nope. I got there afterward. I noticed the side door was open as I ran past to see about the fire."

Frank, who had been leaning against a pole not far from the sheriff's door, turned toward the crowd still standing near the pile of burned lumber. "This man said he's been robbed."

Cade's hands curled into fists as Frank strolled closer while the rest of the throng surged their way, torches in hand. He hadn't thought of Frank as a stupid man until now. But then, the lout thrived on attention, and this was just another way to gain more.

Frank stood in front of Dexter, all but elbowing Morgan out of the way. "Was it your home that was robbed?"

"No, my shop."

"What kind of shop is it?"

"Leather goods." Dexter finally turned and faced Morgan. "Sheriff, they took five pairs of boots, some holsters, and my two best saddles. Those saddles were ordered and mostly paid for. I can't afford a loss like that."

"Five pairs," Cade said. "Same number of men we suspect is in the group that damaged the buildings."

Morgan nodded. "I caught that too."

"Wait, wait." Frank gave a sarcastic laugh and waved his hands. "You're trying to make everyone believe this is the same bunch that's been terrorizing this town?" He stepped between Morgan and Dexter. "Look, Mr.... ?"

"Kemp. Dexter Kemp."

"Mr. Kemp, did they take your money too?"

"No, sir."

"That's what I thought. It was probably some kids or local thugs hoping you'd do just what you're doing...blame the crooks."

Dexter frowned and shook his head. "They didn't get my money because ever since the land office was robbed, I haven't left my money at the shop."

"Wise move, Dex," Cade said. "Morgan, I'm guessing they used the fire as a distraction for the theft. It's what they've been doing from the beginning."

"Who's 'they,' Cade?" Frank wore a smug grin. "You trying to take the suspicion off yourself again?"

"How about we check Dexter's shop for anything the thieves might have left behind?" Cade said.

Morgan thought a moment, then nodded. "Looks to be a busy night."

They headed down the boardwalk with Frank and his mob close behind. Morgan followed Dexter and Cade into the leather goods store and managed to shut the door in Frank's face, leaving him peering through the window. His look of astonishment transformed to fury.

More than an hour later, Cade forced one foot in front of the other as he headed home. All their investigating brought a mixture of good and bad news. They found nothing at Dexter's shop. By lamplight, searching for any signs left behind was like trying to pull a splinter from a finger with one's eyes closed. Several footprints could be seen, but it was impossible to prove who they might belong to or when they were left.

Deciding to wait until morning to look any further, Morgan led the way to Joseph's house, thankful the crowd had lost interest and gone about their business. After questioning Joseph, relief rushed through Cade when they discovered Joseph and Belle spent the evening with Matt and Rebecca Cromwell. Morgan didn't want to disturb the Cromwells so late at night and decided to verify the alibi after a good night's rest.

Cade could have just finished wrestling a bull by the horns—and lost—he was so tired. Each step grew heavier than the last. In mere minutes he'd be climbing the stairs to his bed...if he made it that far.

"Well, if it isn't the stable boy."

Frank's voice froze Cade's leaden feet. In the dim lamplight, only Frank's outline could be seen. Cade moved across the narrow street to face his irritant.

"What are you doing here, Frank? Come to accuse me of something else I didn't do?"

"I just came to see if you'd given anymore thought to our earlier conversation."

Cade tilted his head. "Which part? The one where you're going back to Pueblo or the part where you're moving your new livery to the other side of town?"

"I never figured you for one who'd play dumb, Ramsey. Or maybe you're not playing." Frank leaned forward, his beady eyes gleaming in the flickering light. "All I want is Grace. Let me have her and all your troubles will be over."

"She's not mine to give. But even if she were, I'd do whatever it took to keep you from getting your grubby hands on her. She deserves better."

"Like you?" Frank snorted. "Look, Ramsey, I intend to have her as my wife, and I'll do whatever is necessary to make that happen."

Frank's two henchmen stepped from the shadows, both carrying rifles. They cocked their weapons.

"It'll take more than that to scare me off, Frank. Don't think the sheriff won't look you up first if something happens to me. You've already stirred that nest. I doubt it'll be your last mistake." He turned on his heel and headed toward home. "Go ahead and shoot me in the back. I'd like to see you explain that to Morgan."

Frank's curses followed Cade across the street. "This isn't the end of it, Ramsey. You haven't heard the last from me yet."

Cade entered the house, closed the door with a soft click, and leaned against it for support. With everything in him, he'd fight to keep Grace from falling into that evil man's hands...or die trying.

Grace threw the last of her belongings into her bag, snapped it closed, and dragged it from the bed. It was time to move on. Not for her sake this time but for Cade's. Her mind was made up the moment Bobbie told her about the fire and confrontation between Frank and Cade the night before. None of it would have happened if it weren't for her. Friends were paying the price for her presence. That problem could be easily fixed.

Grace placed the note she'd written earlier on the table for Bobbie to find and paused long enough for one last look around. She pushed back the regret threatening to make her change her mind and headed out the door.

The barn never seemed so far away. She prayed Tim Martell would be inside or at least nearby. He'd be the easiest one of the wranglers to convince not to say anything to Jace and Bobbie before she had a chance to leave. She didn't need any argument. They didn't understand who they were dealing with. Frank could be mean, and when he really wanted something, he wouldn't give up, no matter who it might hurt. She was living proof.

The cavernous barn seemed to swallow her the moment she stepped inside. The thought of hiding out in the huge building trickled through her mind until she remembered the creepy things that crawled around in the dark. Suppressing a shudder, she moved to the back where the horses were stabled.

Grace peeked around the corner and breathed a sigh of relief. Tim stood outside one of the stalls scooping some nasty-looking refuse into a small cart. This time she couldn't stop her body from quaking. Step by careful step, she made her way toward Tim. He looked up moments before she reached him. Sweat ran down the sides of his face and dripped from his chin.

Tim lifted his hat long enough to run his sleeve across his forehead. "Grace? What brings you all the way out here?" His gaze dropped to the bag in her hands before returning his focus to her eyes. "Going somewhere?"

"Actually, yes. And I hoped you'd be the one to take me there."

His eyes narrowed. "And where would that be?"

"Town." The answer sounded more like a question. Time to be more assertive. "I'd like to leave now, if I can." Still too weak. "Would you take me?"

Tim stared for several moments. Grace silently begged him not to turn her down.

"All right. Just let me hitch the buggy and tell Jace I'll be away for a bit."

"No!" At Tim's raised brows, Grace took a deep breath to calm herself. "Jace and Bobbie don't know I'm leaving, and I'd like to keep it that way for now. I don't need any questions or arguments, Tim. I just need to leave."

Tim took the few steps between them and peered down into her eyes. "You don't need to run, Grace. You have plenty of friends here who would help you. I'm one of them."

"If you're truly a friend, then do as I ask. Please. Just take me to town so I can be on my way."

He examined her face, his own showing his uncertainty, and then he nodded. "All right. Give me a few minutes to get the buggy hitched."

Good to his word, Tim had them on their way off the ranch a short time later. They hadn't been on the road long before he turned to her. She cut him off with a raised hand.

"No questions. And I'd appreciate it if you don't say anything to Jace and Bobbie. I left a note on the kitchen table. Please let that be the way they learn of my departure."

She could see Tim's struggle to hold his questions. He finally clamped his mouth shut and leaned back in the seat.

He flicked the reins. "I'm assuming you want to be dropped at the depot to catch the next stage out?"

"That's right."

He peered at her from the corners of his eyes. "And if one isn't leaving today?"

"Let's just pray there is."

Not another word was spoken the remainder of their trip. Tim never even said anything as he helped her from the buggy and followed her to the depot window. He stood silently by as she bought her ticket for the next stage out, which didn't leave for over an hour.

Grace asked the station master to watch her bag, and then turned to Tim. "Could I bother you one more time?"

The slightest smile pulled at the corners of his mouth. "You're no bother. What can I do for you?"

"Give me a ride to Joseph and Belle's house on your way back to the ranch? I'll say my good-byes, then return to catch the stage."

He bumped his hat back on his head. "You sure I can't—"

"No, you can't. I'm determined to leave."

He gave a slight shake of his head. "So I see."

He helped her back into the buggy and left her at the Klines' front door with nothing more than a tip of his hat and a warning to be careful. She didn't spend much time pondering the terse good-bye, but turned to greet Belle when she heard her name called.

"I didn't expect you today, Grace. Why you in town?" Belle led her into the house and motioned her to sit at the table while she went for the coffeepot and two cups.

Grace waited until Belle sat before answering. "I came to say good-bye."

Belle leaned back, her frown reaching all the way to the crease in her forehead. "What you mean 'good-bye'? Where you going and when you be back?"

For the first time since her decision, Grace's throat tightened. "I'm not coming back."

"What? It's that mean man Frank, ain't it? He's making you run again."

Grace tried to smile. "Did you hear about the fire last night?" Belle nodded. "Well, trust me when I say it's Frank's way of making me change my mind about becoming his wife."

Belle tilted her head. "I don't understand."

"If he can't get through to me by charming or threatening me, he'll use my friends against me. Whatever it takes, he'll do."

Belle shook her head. "But folks here loves you. Sure thing they'd help you with that Frank."

"That's what you don't understand." She reached for Belle's hand. "Frank won't stop until he gets what he wants, even if it means tormenting people until they break. I plan to leave before it gets any worse. Cade has become Frank's target. He doesn't deserve what will happen to him if I stay." She squeezed Belle's hand and stood. "I'd better go. I don't want to miss the last stage out of town."

Belle rose and pulled her into a long, hard hug. "You be careful, Miss Grace," she whispered into her ear before holding her at arm's length. "And you stay in touch. I wants to know where you is so I can let you know when it's safe to come back." She rubbed her belly. "And when my youngun arrives." She shook her head when Grace tried to argue. "Not another word. You hear? Just do as I say."

"All right. I will."

With tears building during one more hug, Grace was in a rush to leave before she broke down and sobbed. She tore herself from Belle's arms, hurried to open the door, and plowed right into Cade's broad chest.

TWENTY-FOUR

Grace gasped from the shock of the collision as well as the surprise of seeing Cade. He grabbed her arms to keep her from falling. She pulled away in alarm as she met his eyes. How did he know?

Movement in the yard caught her attention. She shifted just enough to see past Cade. Tim stood next to the buggy while holding the reins of another horse. She narrowed her eyes at him.

He looked down and toed the ground with the tip of his boot before meeting her gaze again. "I only said I wouldn't tell Jace and Bobbie. You never said a word about not telling Cade."

Tim climbed onto the saddle of the horse and galloped off toward the ranch, leaving the horse and buggy behind. Grace turned her accusing eyes to Cade, whose stern eyes stared back. The battle of wills continued with neither giving any indication of giving in. Belle finally stepped up to them.

"Why don't you all use the kitchen to work this out? I'm sure something out here is demanding my attention for a spell." She stepped off the porch, then turned back with a wide smile. "It shore is good to see you, Cade."

Grace scowled at her until she disappeared around the corner. She'd deal with Belle later.

Cade motioned her inside, but Grace shook her head.

"I don't want to miss the stagecoach."

"Then you'd best scoot inside because I have no intention of letting you leave until we talk."

Grace resisted the urge to stomp her foot and moved to the table, helplessness plaguing her every step. Men got their way only because of their strength. She refused to believe they'd outsmarted her. The only flaw in her plan was being too trusting.

Cade pulled a chair out for her. "Might as well have a seat."

"I don't intend to stay long."

He eyed her for a moment and then shrugged. "Suit yourself." He moved to another chair between her and the door before taking a seat.

She fumed. Did he really think she'd try to escape? All right, so the thought had skittered through her mind before reason returned. But did he have to be so obvious about the fact that he'd read her mind?

She plopped onto the chair. "Say what you came for so I can get going."

He crossed his arms and stared her down. "Why are you running again, Grace? You should know by now it won't solve a thing."

She met his eyes, and the warmth she found there stirred her to the core and made her want to give in.

Avoid his eyes. Don't look at them again.

She dropped her gaze to his lips. That was no better. They looked soft yet strong at the same time. She wondered how they would feel…

Stop it, Grace! Look away, for pity's sake!

She focused on the table and busily arranged her handbag on her lap, giving her time to pull herself together. "Actually…" She cleared her throat. "I think it will solve everything."

"No, it won't. Frank will only follow you again and transfer the trouble to yet another town and the people living there."

The truth pulled her gaze back to his for a brief moment before she again looked away. "So you admit I'm the reason there's trouble here."

"That's not what I said." He leaned forward. "Look at me, Grace." He waited. "Please."

She couldn't resist. He sounded so sweet. His face showed his concern. She took a deep breath and strengthened her resolve.

"I have to go."

She tried to stand, but he stopped her with a hand on her arm. "Why?"

"It's what's best for everyone."

"I don't believe that." He squeezed her arm. "I want you to stay."

Why, exactly? For what reason? To what end? She wanted to ask, but those words wouldn't come. "I can't."

His hand slid to hers and caressed the back with his thumb. "You can. Grace, you're surrounded by friends here. We can help you fight this man. You go someplace else where no one knows you or cares for you and you'll be on your own. With no one to help you, Frank has a better chance of winning."

Cade cared? Isn't that what he just said? Or was she reading too much into his words? "But look what he's doing to…this town." She'd almost said *to you*. "He'll stop if I'm not here."

"If you stay, we can fight him together."

She liked the sound of that. She peered into his eyes. "How?"

"Our sheriff already distrusts him. Between him, me, Jace, and Bobbie, we can come up with a way to make him leave." He paused. "No, I don't know how just yet, but trust me, we'll win." He squeezed her hand. "Please stay. I'll do everything I can to protect you."

He wrapped her hand in both of his. They were big hands. Strong hands. Capable hands.

"I want you to stay, Grace."

She stared at him a moment longer, and then sighed. "All right."

The grin stretching across his face sent a thrill through her.

"Thank you. Now, let's head to the depot, retrieve your bag, and get you home."

Just like that. But at least Cade did consider this her home. That was enough…for now.

Cade couldn't take it any longer. He'd spent the morning trying to concentrate on his work only to repeat several tasks or force poor Joseph to clean up his messes. It was time to give up and put his mind to rest. In minutes he had his horse saddled and headed toward the Double K ranch.

Since he and Grace had talked at Joseph and Belle's house the day before, he couldn't get thoughts of her out of his mind. She'd taken root and refused to shake loose. Truth be told, he'd been in this condition since the day he'd found her hiding in the bed of his wagon. Since then, the roots had only grown deeper until they'd reached all the way to his…

Stop it, Cade. Get a hold of yourself.

He urged his horse on faster until they entered the ranch at a gallop. Not a single wrangler was in sight. Cade reined to a stop. The place looked abandoned. Jace had assured him someone would be around at all times to keep an eye on Grace. And Jace's house raising was only a week away with more work to be done on the flooring before then. The solitude of the ranch sent an alarm from Cade's scalp to his toes.

After one more glance around, Cade spurred his horse to the front of the old house. He jumped from the saddle to the porch, rapped on the door, and waited. He was about to break down the door when he heard a shriek. He grabbed his pistol from the holster and raced around the side of the house.

Almost to the back, a chicken fled past him clucking, wings fluttering, a trail of feathers strewn in its path. Cade charged around the corner just in time to see a large stick fly through the air and bounce off the ground before launching at his face. The sharp end struck him near his upper lip before he could bat it away.

Hand over his mouth, Cade looked up to find Grace, all red-faced, running toward him with another stick in her hand. Her steps slowed to a stop when she saw him. The stick dropped to the ground.

After another quick glance around, Cade shoved his pistol back into the holster. "Grace, what in tarnation are you doing?"

One hand went to her hip while the other pointed behind her. "Do you know what that rotten chicken did to my garden? Look at it. Just look at it, Cade. I'll be lucky if I can get even half a crop." She spun to look at the devastation again before turning back to him. "Stupid chicken. If I ever get my hands on that scrawny neck—"

"I doubt it'll stop running until it reaches the next territory. Jace and Bobbie better get used to eating only beef and pig. I doubt you'll ever be able to catch a chicken again." He motioned around with his free hand, the other still trying to ease the pain from his mouth. "Where is everyone? Did you run them off with a stick too?"

"Of course not. I just…" She frowned and headed his way. "What's wrong with your face?" She stopped in front of him. "Let me see."

He wasn't about to let her near him. "I'm all right."

"Sure you are. All men walk around with a hand on their face." She grasped his wrist. "Let me see."

He gave in and allowed her to take a look. He nearly smiled when she gasped.

"You're bleeding." She untied her apron and held it toward his mouth. He pulled away. "Now, Cade, you're gonna have to trust me for once."

He wanted to howl with laughter, especially since it was Grace who caused the damage in the first place. Like an obedient child, Cade leaned down a bit to let her tend to his wound. She dabbed at the cut with gentle pressure, biting her lower lip as she worked.

He stared at her eyes, watching as they examined his mouth,

making his gaze drop to examine hers. The delicate outline of her top lip left him wanting to trace it with his finger.

He realized she'd stopped her ministrations and now looked him in the eyes. Her breathing was as shallow as his. He studied her face until he could stand it no longer. With only a second's hesitation, Cade leaned to claim her lips with his own.

He pulled back and looked into her eyes. Her face remained tilted toward him and her lips were still parted. He cupped her cheeks in his palms and thought he'd never felt so weak. Her hands slid up his arms to his shoulders as he leaned in for yet another taste of heaven.

Ending the kiss with a huge sigh, he smiled, his face still very near hers. "You can nurse me back to health anytime you want."

Pink tinged her cheeks as she returned his smile. "Spend much time near me and you may get your wish." She bent and picked up the stick. "I did that to your lip, didn't I?" When he nodded, she lifted her arm to show her muscle. "Guess I'm stronger than I thought."

He squeezed her bicep and grimaced. "Who knew trying to kill chickens could add so much strength. Remind me never to make you mad."

"Don't sprout any feathers and you'll be fine."

He'd never be fine again. Her flirty look made him want to kiss her all over again.

"There you are." Bobbie's gaze moved between Cade and Grace. She halted her steps. "Am I interrupting something?"

"No," Cade and Grace said together, sounding much too loud.

"Of course not." Grace brushed back some strands of hair that had escaped from her bun. "I was just..." she wrapped her apron back around her waist, "chasing chickens."

"And caught Cade?" Bobbie laughed and moved closer. She took another longer look at Cade. "What happened to your face?"

Cade reached up to cover his mouth as he cast a glance at Grace, only to let his hand fall back to his side.

"Oh, no. You got in Grace's line of fire again?" Another laugh. "I thought you'd learned by now."

Grace stepped in front of Bobbie, hands on her hips. "Now, hold on—"

"Relax, Grace. We all know Cade's accident prone."

Cade started to protest, but at Bobbie's wink, he grinned instead. "Where was everyone? Jace told me he'd be around the place getting ready for the house raising."

"We sent a couple men to Pueblo for more lumber. We knew we'd need it sooner or later. The rest of us were scattered around trying to get far enough in our work so we could spend a few extra days on the building project." She led the way to the front of the house and stopped next to Cade's horse. "Which is why I came searching for Grace. I've been talking to Beans about the meal when everyone gets here. He said he'd take care of cooking the beef and beans."

"Great." Grace ran a tentative hand along the neck of Cade's horse. "So what does that leave me to do?"

"Not much, really. Most of the ladies in town will bring desserts and other side dishes."

Cade flipped the stirrup over the saddle to check the cinches. "At least you didn't have your heart set on chicken. You may never get to eat that ag—"

Grace tossed the stirrup back at him, then aimed one of her mean faces his way.

Bobbie's mouth twitched as she eyed the two of them. "That's all right. At least for now. Beans said he'd think about adding a pig to the spit if I talk nice to him."

"Well that's easy enough." Cade untied the rein from the hitching post. "Just do what you did to get him to raise that calf last year."

"What did you do?" Grace said.

When Bobbie ignored the question, Grace turned to him. "What'd she do, Cade?"

"I have no idea. She wouldn't tell anyone, and Beans refused to say. Only smiled a bit when asked."

Grace turned back to Bobbie. "Come on, Bobbie. You have to tell me."

"Oh, no. At least not in front of Cade. I may need to use that technique again, and I don't want him spilling it to Jace."

Cade climbed onto his saddle. "What if I promised not to tell him?"

"I wouldn't believe you," Bobbie said.

"Wise woman." He tipped the brim of his hat. "Ladies." He looked Grace directly in the eyes. "It was a pleasure."

Without a glance back, Cade headed his horse toward town. Pleasure was an understatement. He couldn't remember enjoying anything so much as kissing Grace. But what was he thinking? He shook his head. That was just it. He wasn't thinking.

Cade smiled at the memory of Grace's sweet lips. Maybe he should stop thinking more often. His whistle tortured the poor horse's ears all the way back to town.

TWENTY-FIVE

People wandered like excited ants all over the ranch. The scene reminded Grace of the day she'd arrived in town after several of the buildings had been damaged by explosives. Except instead of the low-spirited gloom of that day, this time, everyone showed up with a party atmosphere. Women mingled with the men while children chased each other around the yard, some climbing on the stacks of lumber.

Grace scanned the grounds once again hoping to see Cade, but he had yet to show. She hadn't seen him since they'd kissed. All four of her fingers against her lips, she recalled the feel of his that day. She hoped he didn't regret it.

As she went about her duties overseeing the food as it arrived, she continued to glance at the bridge leading from the road to the ranch. Much as she didn't want to admit it, she couldn't wait to see Cade. Just getting to see him again would be more of a feast for her eyes than all the food on the tables would be for her stomach.

"Why you keep staring at the road like that?"

At Belle's whispered question, Grace turned with a smile and gave her friend a hug. "I was looking for you."

Belle waved her finger under Grace's nose. "Don't you be telling no fibs like that. I knows better." She squinted at Grace. "I ain't never seen your eyes sparkle quite like they do now."

Grace grabbed Belle's arm and led her away from the ladies. "Keep your voice down or you'll make me the center of everyone's rumor mill."

"Well, you gonna tell me what made your eyes all cheery or you gonna make me guess? Cuz I can think of only one thing that would make you look so pleased with yourself. I bet it was that—"

"Hush, Belle. I don't need everyone hearing your thoughts about my face."

Belle examined Grace's eyes, her own growing wide. "Mercy sakes. He done kissed you, didn't he?"

Grace glanced around, then led Belle even further from the crowd before turning to face her. "Would you please keep your voice down?"

"He did, didn't he? Well, good for him. He shore took his sweet time."

"Belle!" Though Grace wanted her to stop talking, she couldn't keep her own grin from appearing.

"Morning, ladies."

Grace gasped and turned.

Cade tipped his hat, then moved a couple steps closer and leaned toward them. "If I didn't know any better, I'd think you two were telling secrets. You gonna let me in on it?"

"Good to see you, Mr. Cade," Belle said. "Enjoy your day." And then she left them alone.

Grace wanted to grab her arm and pull her back, but she stood frozen and couldn't think of a thing to say, so she looked everywhere but at Cade.

"My lip is almost completely healed now, Grace, so it's all right to look at me."

His husky voice stopped her heart. She peered up into his eyes. Her knees weakened at what she saw. If there weren't so many people around, she'd be the one to initiate a kiss this time.

"It's good to see you, Cade."

He opened his mouth, but Jace's shrill whistle kept him from speaking.

Jace waved one arm over his head to get everyone's attention. "If ya'll are through wasting time, I think we should get started."

A cheer went up as all the men followed him to the work site. Cade glanced their way, then leaned toward her ear. "Hold that thought. Maybe we can sneak some time together later."

He tugged at a wisp of her stray hair before heading off to work. As he walked away, a part of her left with him, and she knew she'd never feel complete again until they were together.

"Well, wasn't that just cozy and heartwarming."

Frank's breath seared the same ear Cade had whispered into. She shifted away. He moved with her and grasped her elbow. "Don't get your hopes up too high, Grace. The only man you'll ever be with is me."

He kissed her cheek and walked away. She grabbed the edge of her apron and scrubbed the spot raw, but the damage was done. Frank made certain the women saw the kiss. Worse, so had Cade. His frown before turning his back and her humiliation burned worse than any fire she'd been near.

Belle rushed to her side. "That man gonna go too far one day." She hooked her arm through Grace's and led her toward the food. "I done fixed my basket so's I can whop him good again if need be."

The memory lightened Grace's mood. She'd worry about explaining to Cade what happened when there weren't so many people watching and listening.

Cade slammed the nail head even with the board in three strikes. He had never put up a wall so fast. All he had to do was picture Frank's face on the nail.

Who'd that man think he was? And why didn't Grace slap him when he kissed her?

The next nail went in so hard, the hammer left a deep dent in the wood. Once he'd finished his part of the wall, he took a step back and wiped his brow with his sleeve. He glanced around the yard and spotted Grace standing at the tables laughing with several ladies from church. The kiss didn't seem to bother her as much as it did him.

He moved inside the house to work on another wall. He lifted a board from the stack of lumber and held it against the beams. A minute later, he reached for another board.

Jace grabbed the other end and helped move it into place. "You trying to put up this wall or knock it down?" They exchanged a look before Jace grinned. "Fast is good. I'd like this house finished sooner than later."

He clapped Cade on the back and moved off to help one of the younger men. Cade stared for a moment, and then shook his head. He'd been acting like a fool and falling into the same trap of letting a woman weaken his defenses. He should have learned the first time around.

"Watch out!"

Cade glanced up in time to see a board about to hit him. A quick turn to the side and it landed inches from his right foot. He looked up again to see who'd been so reckless. Frank peered down and gave a slight shrug.

"Sorry. It slipped."

The reason for Frank's presence became clear. Cade didn't relax the next couple hours until Jace whistled everyone to a stop to enjoy a hot meal and cold water. After washing up and loading a plate with meat and bread, Cade sat as far from Frank as he could. Joseph plopped next to him, his plate heaped higher than Cade's.

"Bet you wishin' you back at the livery. Leastways you won't get a board dropped on your head by nobody."

"You saw that, huh?"

Mouth full, Joseph nodded and then swallowed. "Nobody working near him now. Cain't trust him."

With a snort, Cade shook his head. "They don't need to worry about him. Frank has only one target here." He peered at the menace who had eyes only for Grace. "Make that two."

He caught sight of Jace and Bobbie at the end of the tables waiting their turn for a plate. She held up her thumb, and Jace gave it a quick kiss, making Cade smile. A good many men had sore thumbs too. Jace's hand dropped to her stomach and he leaned close to whisper in her ear. She smiled and placed her hand over his. Cade's heart filled with joy for his friends. When would they make the announcement?

Some of the ladies rounded the tables with refills of water and platters of food. Grace carried a pitcher. Cade grabbed his glass, prepared to drain it so she'd come his way, but Frank emptied his glass first and waved her over.

After a slight hesitation, Grace headed toward Frank and stopped a full arm's length away. He held out his glass, but as she poured, he drew it closer until Grace had to take a step toward him to keep from spilling. In the blink of an eye, Frank had his arm around Grace's waist and pulled her against him.

Cade leaped to his feet ready to send Frank back to Pueblo with one punch, but Joseph grabbed his arm and tried to yank him down.

Grace dumped the pitcher of water over Frank's head. The crowd howled with laughter. Cade expected Frank's temper to show, but after looking around, Frank joined in their amusement. He stood, his arm still holding Grace, and planted a kiss on her cheek. She swung the pitcher at Frank's head, but he easily batted it away.

Frank tossed his head back with another laugh before letting her go. "I guess she doesn't like me to display my love publicly."

Grace scowled at Frank then stomped away. Cade moved to go after her, but Joseph again grabbed his arm.

"Best let this calm some. Things is stirred up enough without you adding more of a boil." Joseph nodded at Belle, and she scurried to follow Grace.

Much as Cade wanted to be the one to console Grace, he'd look for a chance to check on her later. Until then, he'd do his best to make sure Frank didn't go anywhere near her again.

Half an hour later, the sound of pounding hammers again filled the air. At some point, Grace had reappeared, smile back in place. With tables cleared of food, the women now took turns bringing fresh water to the men while others relaxed or entertained the children. Cade paused to take in the peaceful scene, yet in his mind and heart raged a battle. Had Grace been completely up front about her relationship with Frank or was there something yet to be learned? The kisses and familiarity left many doubts.

Hours later, the sun deep in the western sky, Cade glanced around him at the progress of Jace and Bobbie's house. They'd be pleased, not only with how many men showed to help but at how much had been accomplished. At this rate, they'd be moved in long before the first snowfall.

Joseph motioned for his help to lift one of the last inner walls in place on the second floor. They walked their hands up the boards, moving forward as they pushed the wall up against the braces. Two other men stood ready to start pounding in the nails.

"Whoa. Help!"

Cade craned his neck at the shout. Frank stood on the rafters above him, one arm flailing as he tried to keep his balance. Seconds later, both Frank and the roof beam he'd been trying to hold tumbled down.

Cade let go of his end of the wall and attempted to break Frank's fall. He took the full brunt of Frank's weight, and they both were slammed to the floor. The beam smashed onto Cade's shoulder and caught Frank right below his neck.

In moments, men were lifting the beam from them and crowding around to help. Frank moaned nonstop. "Don't touch me. It hurts."

Cade pushed to his knees and rubbed his shoulder. He'd feel that hit for days. No doubt Frank would feel his much longer, but as far as Cade could tell, he was fine—though by the show he was putting on for everyone, he was only moments from death.

Women raced up the newly built steps to see if they could help while some men lifted Frank onto a pallet to carry him down to a wagon waiting to take him to the doctor. Grace pushed through the group and looked to be holding her breath until she saw him. Her shoulders sagged and she attempted a smile.

"Grace." Frank reached out one arm toward her. "Help me, Grace."

The men lifted him from the floor and headed toward the stairs. Frank continued to call out for her. She looked from Frank to Cade, then back again.

"You're all I have, Grace."

As Frank passed her, he grasped her hand. With one last glance at Cade, Grace trailed alongside Frank, her hand still in his.

And for the second time in his life, Cade watched the woman he cared about walk away with another man.

❋ TWENTY-SIX ❋

Grace sat at the table tracing the wood grain with her finger. If she got any sleep tonight, it would be because of God's mercy only. The look on Cade's face as she left with Frank haunted every thought, every breath. She'd lost him and now there was no need to stay. And this time, he wouldn't try to stop her from leaving.

Bobbie entered the kitchen and stopped. "I thought you'd be asleep by now." She moved to the cupboard and removed a glass. "What's wrong?" After pouring some water, she sat at the table with Grace.

"How's your thumb?"

Bobbie smiled and took a drink. "Don't want to talk about it, huh?" She ran her finger around the lip of the glass. "I guess you wish Frank wouldn't have shown up."

Grace looked her in the eyes but didn't say a word. Talking wouldn't solve a thing.

"Jace and I considered running him off, but decided extreme dislike wasn't a good enough reason for asking him to leave. I'm sorry, Grace."

"It's not your fault. I blame Frank." She slumped in her chair and dropped her hands in her lap. "He came with a goal, maybe two, and managed to accomplish one of them."

"Which was…?"

After a deep breath, she rested her elbows on the table top, using its strength to hold her up. "To drive a wedge between Cade and me and maybe get rid of Cade in the process."

"And you think he succeeded?"

Grace closed her eyes and saw Cade's expression again. "Without a doubt."

Bobbie grasped Grace's arm until she looked up. "Then go talk to Cade. You'll see him in church in the morning. Talk to him after the service."

"And if it doesn't help?"

"You won't know until you try. And besides, it sure couldn't hurt." Bobbie rose and gave her a hug. "Get some sleep, Grace. Tomorrow might be the biggest day of your life."

Grace woke the next morning surprised to feel rested. She took extra care getting ready for the morning service, not that looking her best would help any but it might give her a bit more courage. Finally inside the church, she glanced around for Cade, but he hadn't arrived yet. She dropped on the pew next to Bobbie and received a pat on her leg.

"He'll show. He rarely misses church."

Bobbie's assurance ran through her mind over and over throughout the service. The pastor's words hummed in her ears as the minutes ticked by, but still there was no sign of Cade. With the final amen, Grace turned a full circle in search of Cade. Disappointment raked her heart, and regret bruised it further.

"Don't give up, Grace." Bobbie gave her a quick hug. "I'm sure there's a good reason he couldn't be here. Stay in town until you get a chance to talk to him. I'll make sure you have a way home afterward."

Grace's lips trembled as she tried to smile. "Thank you, Bobbie."

Belle appeared and looped her arm through Grace's. "Have dinner with us. I made way too much for us to eat."

"Speak for yourself." Joseph nudged his wife. "But I'll share anyway." He held out both elbows for Belle and Grace. "I can smell it from here. Let's go."

Grace nodded to Bobbie and followed her friends to their home, barely able to join in their banter. When there was a moment of silence, she forced out the question uppermost on her mind.

"Joseph, do you know why Cade didn't make it to church this morning?"

"I shore don't, Miss Grace. I figgered someone showed up needing help. And you know Mr. Cade. His big heart won't let him say no."

She nodded. Cade did have a big heart. But was it big enough to forgive?

They spent the afternoon chatting. The turmoil stirring Grace's mind didn't allow for much rest. Joseph must have noticed. He finally slapped his thighs and stood.

"Think I'll go check the livery." He leaned and kissed Belle's cheek. "Be back soon."

Grace closed her eyes and set her rocker moving with her toes. With any luck, she might fall asleep and get a break from her turbulent thoughts.

"Where's your faith?"

Grace stopped rocking as her mind went back to the past. "It disappeared years ago."

"Why?"

She shrugged. "I had no reason to hang on to it."

"But why?"

Grace sighed at Belle's persistence. "What has God done to make me believe He cares? Look at what happened over the years. Look at what's happening now."

Belle gave her a tender smile. "You can't blame God for man's decisions. He lets us choose for ourselves." She paused. "You'd rather trust man than God?"

"Man didn't choose to make my mother sick. God did that." Grace eyed Belle's odd expression. "What?"

"Sounds like you finally forgave your mama but shifted your anger to God."

She thought about that for a moment. Mama couldn't help being sick, but God was supposed to be loving and all-powerful. He could keep bad things from happening, and didn't. "God has proven Himself untrustworthy. Why shouldn't I be angry?"

"Why you think God owes you anything? All we deserve is death, sinners that we are. But God loves us too much for that, and He proved it with the sacrifice of His Son." Belle shook her head. "I don't know how anyone gets through tough times without God. Much better to go through them with Him by our side. If you gonna blame God for the bad things, you best praise Him for the good too."

Grace leaned her head back and again closed her eyes. Tears loomed.

Forgive me, Lord.

She rose and crossed to Belle. "Thank you for holding me accountable. A true friend tells the truth, and you didn't hold back."

Belle accepted her hug. "I only reminded you of what you already knows." She motioned to the rocker. "Now get you some rest. I knows I need some."

Grace wanted to ask if she was so much of a chore that she wore the poor woman out, but refrained. A renewed energy ran through her. A much stronger sense of hope.

"I can't rest, Belle. I need to talk to Cade."

"Now?" Belle peeked out the window. "It's getting too close to dark. You should wait for Joseph."

Grace smiled and hugged Belle one more time. "It's not that close to dark, and I want to catch Cade today. Having to wait until tomorrow will keep me from sleeping tonight."

"But it's not safe."

"You worry too much. I'll be fine."

"Grace—"

"I'll be fine. I'll stop by Cade's house first. And if I have to go to the livery and still don't find him, I'll go back to the house and wait. I promise."

Before Belle could argue or stop her, she raced out the door. With long, fast strides, she closed the distance between Belle's house and the Ramseys'. When no one answered her knock, she nearly ran to the livery.

The big front doors were closed, but the smaller door appeared partly open. She gave it a push and it swung wide. She stepped inside. The mixed scent of smoke and manure made her wrinkle her nose. The shadowy interior sent a shiver down her back, but determination moved her forward.

"Cade?" No answer. "You in here, Cade?"

A glow at the back of the livery pulled her further inside. The horses shuffled and snorted in their stalls. A blast of smoke made her cough and set her eyes to watering. She continued to the back, stopping only when she saw flames dancing around the base of what looked like a furnace. The fire spread fast, gorging itself on the mounds of straw strewn on the floor. In seconds, the flames shot toward the walls.

The horses began kicking their stalls and the sounds coming from them sounded more like children screaming than whinnying. Grace spun and ran to the door.

"Help! Someone help me!" She coughed. "Help! There's a fire."

She glanced both directions and didn't see anyone. Heart pounding, she unlatched the big doors and shoved until one side opened. Then she ran back inside to the stall closest to the fire and opened the door. She stood back praying each horse would find its way safely outside.

With a quick glance behind her, she saw the flames racing up the walls. She moved to the second stall and repeated the action.

Wide-eyed, this horse nearly ran her over before turning and darting toward the big doors.

Three more to go.

Grace worked as fast as she could and managed to get two more released before the smoke blinded her. She coughed until she gagged. Her lungs burned. She tried to take a breath, but inhaled only more smoke, making her choke again.

Grace refused to let any horses die. She dropped to her knees, hoping to find some air, then forced herself to stand. She ran her hands along the stall walls and managed to find and lift the latch to the last pen. As the horse raced past, a shadow loomed and something hard smacked against her head.

She went down, and her world went dark.

❖ TWENTY-SEVEN ❖

The sight of smoke against the evening sky had Cade's head swimming and his ears pounding as he raced down the street. His livery sat below the plume. He'd been gone only about 20 minutes. Everything was fine when he'd sent Joseph home. He knew without a doubt he'd banked the fire in the furnace. What had happened since then?

As he reached the livery, a horse ran out through the large doors. He took a step back. How did the animal get loose? Cade shoved the doors further open. Smoke billowed from within, making his eyes burn and fill with tears.

Except for the snapping and crackling of the fire, the silence from inside was ominous. Why weren't the horses shrieking? Did they all somehow escape like the first one?

He made his way to the back by running his hand along the stall fronts. Why were all the stall doors hanging open?

His toe caught something large, and he put out his hands to break his fall. Then he turned to see what had tripped him. The feel of cloth and soft flesh sent chills over his skin. He scooped the body up in his arms, and the skirts from a dress tangled in his hands. What was a woman doing here? He headed toward the door, coughing over and over as he shuffled his feet to keep from tripping again.

He finally reached fresh air. He tried to yell for help, but his throat burned from inhaling too much smoke. He knelt and blinked several times to see who lay in his arms. With a vigorous rub, his vision cleared.

Grace?

Blood oozed down her temple and cheek and some ran into her hair.

Men ran toward him from every direction. Cade looked at each face praying one belonged to the doctor. He tried to clear his clogged throat, but it had tightened even further at the thought that Grace had been hurt in his livery. He finally recognized Pete, who knelt next to him.

"Get Doc." He coughed several times. "I need Doc."

Pete patted him on the shoulder and stood. "I'll get him."

As Pete ran for help, several men scooped water from the trough in front of the livery, forming a bucket brigade in what appeared a feeble attempt to get the fire out. Flames shot from the back and left side. With all the wood and straw acting as fuel, Cade knew he'd have to say good-bye to his livery.

He peered into Grace's face, then pulled the kerchief from his pocket to stem the flow of blood from her temple. Her head lolled against his bicep and made her look helpless and fragile. What was she doing in there? How long had she been there? Did she see what happened? Worse yet, was she somehow involved?

His mind refused to accept his last thought. His stare moved to her throat as he sought a pulse in the dimming light.

Please, God. Help her.

And then he saw it. The steady throb on the side of her neck. Relief made him sag. With one finger, he gently pushed strands of hair from her face.

"Cade!" The doctor rushed toward him, bag in hand. He dropped to one knee and scanned Grace's face, pushing aside her hair for a better look. "I can't do this here. Bring her to my office so I can examine her properly."

Pete stuck an arm under Cade's to help him to his feet. With long, ground-eating strides, Cade headed down the street. The doctor barely made it to the door ahead of him. Cade laid her on the first bed he came to, taking great care with her head. He'd never seen her so still. Despite the large swelling above her temple and the blood that still oozed, her face looked so peaceful.

Cade was about to sit on the side of the bed when Doc elbowed him aside. "Excuse me, Cade. I need some room to work." Doc leaned over Grace and started his examination, but stopped and turned. "You need to leave, Cade. Go help put out the fire or something. You can check on her later."

"Doc?"

"Near as I can see, she should be fine. I'll know more once I get a chance to look her over."

Cade nodded, took one last glance at Grace's face, and headed out the door. Pete stood on the boardwalk and ran with him to the livery.

"Any idea how it started, Cade?"

"No." But that would be one of the first answers he sought.

The fire still glowed a dull orange against the night sky, though not as bright as he would have figured. Probably because there wasn't much of the livery left to burn. That thought made him want to stop, not ready to see a heap of ashes, but he pushed on.

Cade hesitated for only a moment at the sight of his livery. Half the men in town had turned out to help, and somehow they had managed to douse a good deal of the fire, giving him a glimmer of hope. He ran to lend a hand and get a better look at the damage.

Word spread that the water troughs in front of the livery were empty. They'd have to rely solely on the well out back. That would slow their fight, but no one seemed ready to surrender.

Cade ran to the well to give a break to the poor man who'd been cranking out buckets of water. He spun the lever to allow the large wooden bucket to drop. He heard the splash and started turning the handle as fast as he could. Time disappeared as he repeated the process too many times to count. He didn't stop until the next man in line didn't take the full bucket. Cade shoved the bucket against the man's chest.

"It's out," the man said. "I don't think we need any more water."

Cade shifted so he could see if any of the livery still stood. In the lamplight, he saw the outline of the building. To his amazement, only part of the back and side of the livery had burned. The front had been spared. Even so, he doubted he had the money to rebuild. But with all the men clapping him on the back with congratulations, their cheers invaded his gloom and brought a smile.

He grabbed the handle of a lantern on the ground near him and wandered inside to look around. He stopped at the forge just as Jace ran through the front doors.

"I got here as fast as I could." Jace glanced around before meeting Cade's gaze. "There's a lot left. That's good news."

Cade could manage only a half smile. "Yeah. That's good."

Pete and Sheriff Morgan Thomas joined them with more lanterns and held them high. Pete turned a full circle with his. "Still too dark to see much. Can't really tell how it started."

Cade moved toward the front. One stall to his right had burned. The doors to all the others stood open. That still struck him as odd. Had Grace turned all the horses loose?

A large beam lay charred and smoking on the ground. He pointed to it. "That must have been what raised the lump on Grace's temple."

Jace moved to his side. "Bobbie's with her now. How about we call it a night and go check on Grace? We'll come back in the morning when we can see better and try to figure out what happened."

Cade stood looking around several seconds. Nothing more could be accomplished here until daylight. With a nod, he followed Jace and Pete to the doctor's office wondering if Grace was as damaged as his livery.

TWENTY-EIGHT

Pain throbbed. Someone touched her. Grace winced. She attempted to move her hand to push them away, but the weight of her limbs made the action impossible. She moved her lips to tell them to stop hurting her head. Her tongue stuck to the roof of her mouth. Her throat burned.

Burned. Mind spinning, she tried to open her eyes. Why wouldn't they open? She needed help.

Fire!

The word wouldn't come. She moaned and turned her head. The move only brought torture. A fog wrapped her mind.

"Grace."

No.

"Look at me, Grace." Cool fingers touched her cheek. "Open your eyes, Grace."

This time, her effort was met with success. Light filtered through her lashes. A shadowy figure leaned toward her. Grace blinked trying to clear her vision.

"There you are." Bobbie's voice sounded soft, relieved. "Welcome back. You scared us."

Nothingness pulled at Grace again, where there was no pain. Her heart must have moved to her head. Her temples throbbed with each beat. And why was it so hard to breathe?

"Hey," Bobbie called as if from a distance and grasped her hand, "don't leave us just yet. Come on, Grace. Let me see those eyes again."

With great effort, her eyes fluttered open. Then she forced her lips apart. Now if she could just get her tongue loose.

"Would you like a bit of water?"

She nodded and instantly regretted the action. Someone lifted her head a couple inches from the pillow. Cool water dribbled down her chin as more made its way into her mouth. When it hit her throat, she started coughing. Lightning flashed behind her eyes. A cool cloth dabbed her face.

"Ready to try again?"

"No." Did that croak come from her?

"Do you have any pain, Grace?" That was the doctor's voice.

"My head."

"Anywhere else? Arms or chest?"

"No. My head." What was wrong with her, and why did it feel as though a herd of horses had trampled her skull?

Horses!

She forced her eyes open again. "Horses." The word scraped her throat. She thought she tasted blood. "The fire. Bobbie, there's a fire."

Bobbie grasped her hand. "It's out, Grace. The fire's been put out."

Grace closed her eyes and ran those words through her mind over and over until they made sense. Somehow, they'd found the fire...and her. Did she get all the horses out?

"The horses?"

Another gentle squeeze of her hand. "They're all safe. They've all been rounded up and put in the corral."

She blinked, then kept her eyes open so she could see Bobbie's face for the next question. "The livery?"

Bobbie glanced away, but only for a moment. "It's damaged, but at least half of it's still standing."

Not the news she'd hoped to hear. Fading fast, Grace fought off the fog. "Cade?"

Bobbie turned to look over her shoulder. "He's fine."

Cade was here? Grace tried to see and moaned at the needles piercing her eyes and brain. Tears formed.

Footfalls came closer. A warm hand touched her arm. "I'm right here, Grace."

Cade's tender voice brought more tears. She fought to maintain control so his face wouldn't be a blur. With another flurry of blinks, her view of Cade cleared. His hair stuck up in several places and soot blotched his face, yet he'd never looked better.

"You're a mess."

Cade grinned. "Why, thank you. Would you like a mirror?"

She smiled through her tears. "No."

He leaned closer. "Doc says you're gonna be fine."

"Really? Then maybe he'd like to change places." She licked her lips, but her dry tongue couldn't moisten a thing. "Could we try the water again?"

As Cade and the doctor held her head and shoulders, Bobbie tipped the glass to her lips. Water never tasted so good.

After laying her head back down, Cade again moved into her line of vision. "Do I have you to thank for saving my horses?"

"All but one. Do I have you to thank for saving my life?"

Rather than the expected grin, Cade frowned. "But all the horses were released."

Grace closed her eyes trying to remember everything. The action brought relief and she didn't want to open them again. Maybe they could finish all the questions later.

"Grace?"

The voice wasn't familiar. She pried her eyes open and found the sheriff standing beside Cade.

"Do you feel up to answering a few more questions?"

No. She sighed. "Sure."

"Did you see anyone in the livery?"

"No."

"Why were you in the livery?"

Grace glanced at Bobbie, who nodded. "I...wanted to talk to Cade." She turned to see his brows rise. Thankfully he didn't ask why. She wasn't ready for that conversation any longer.

"Was the fire already going when you entered the building?" the sheriff said.

Grace closed her eyes again. Sleep called to her and she ached to answer the call. Weights kept her lids closed. The fog rolled toward her.

"Miss Bradford?"

No one called her by that name. The thought forced her lids open.

"What?"

"I said, was the fire already burning when you arrived at the livery?"

She looked at Cade. He seemed as intent on her answer as the sheriff.

"Yes, it was. I smelled the smoke as soon as I opened the door. I saw the flames after I walked inside."

Cade squatted next to the bed. "Where were the flames? Where did it look like the fire started?"

"At that big brick thing near the back of the livery."

"The furnace?"

"All the straw around it was burning. It spread pretty fast toward the wall and that first stall."

Cade frowned. "Straw?" He glanced up at the sheriff before returning to her. "I don't keep straw around the back of the livery. There wasn't any straw anywhere near the furnace."

Sleep begged for Grace to join it. She wanted nothing more. The desire to help Cade made her hold it at bay. "There was straw, Cade. Mounds of it. And it burned fast. I called for help, then started turning loose the horses. I had trouble with the last one."

Cade put his hand on her arm. "I'm sorry the beam fell on you."

Is that why her head hurt so? She didn't remember a beam. What was the last thing she remembered? She recalled each horse, one running into her. The last one? That's right. She did manage to open the door.

Her eyes popped open. "It wasn't a beam that hit me."

Cade's brows furrowed. "Then what did?"

Her mouth dried even more. "A man."

Cade's hand gripped her arm tighter. "Who, Grace? Who hit you?"

"I don't know. All I saw was an outline of a man in a hat. In the shadows."

"What color?"

She wanted to cry. Someone tried to kill her. "I don't know. It was too dark. The smoke was thick. All I saw was a man in a hat, and I only saw that because of the flames."

"Tell me what happened. Can you do that?"

"I think so. I got to the last stall and opened the door. As the horse came toward me, I saw the shadowy figure in a hat and then felt pain. The next thing I know, I'm here."

Her heavy lids dropped closed again. She struggled to stay awake long enough to mull over the details and blocked out the murmurs around her.

The livery was already on fire when she arrived, so they weren't after her. She must have walked in on them, making them hide. That meant they were trying to hurt Cade, and there was only one person in town who wanted Cade out of the way. Oh, no. What had she done? She hoped Cade would forgive her.

Tears burned her eyes, and she reached for Cade's hand, but he'd stood to talk to the sheriff. Jace and Pete were there too.

Bobbie, still sitting on the side of the bed, reached out and touched her face. "Grace? Are you all right?"

Cade turned at the question and again crouched next to her.

"Grace?" He ran a knuckle along the corner of her eye and caught a falling tear. "Are you in pain?"

If he only knew. Her heart threatened to shatter into pieces. Her lips trembled, but she had to say it. "I'm sorry, Cade."

"Sorry? About what?"

"I—I should have left town."

He stared for several long seconds, then his eyes hardened. "You think Frank did this, don't you?"

She hesitated before nodding.

Cade's nostrils flared. He stood. "I knew it." Without another word, he turned and strode from the room.

Grace looked from Bobbie to the sheriff and back again. "You've got to stop him." Her head threatened to explode. "Sheriff, you've got to stop him before someone gets hurt."

Sheriff Thomas, Jace, and Pete hurried out of the room.

Grace closed her eyes. *Lord, please protect Cade.*

"I should have left."

Bobbie squeezed her hand. "Don't say that."

"I should never have let Cade talk me out of it." Tears burned their way down her temples. "This never would have happened if I'd left."

"You don't know that."

A cool hand touched her forehead. "How're you feeling, Grace?" The doctor's deep voice vibrated through her head.

"My head hurts. Is there some way to take away the pain?"

"Everything I have will make you sleep, and I need to be able to wake you up every hour."

She'd never been so exhausted, and the doctor planned to wake her every hour? Well, if he planned to annoy her, then she'd return the favor and ask about Cade each time.

Please God, keep Cade safe.

TWENTY-NINE

Cade headed straight for the hotel. It was the best place to start, but more than likely, the scoundrel could be found spreading his lies and nonsense to anyone willing to listen. This town needed to open their eyes and see the truth.

He heard Jace call his name, but he had no intention of letting his friend stop him. He shoved through the hotel doors. Frank Easton sat in the lobby with his hired guns, a cigar propped between his fingers. The smoke curled in lazy coils, much like Frank's grin.

"Well, well. We finally have a fourth for our poker game, boys." Frank motioned to a chair. "Have a seat, Cade. I'd love to separate you from the few coins in your pocket."

Cade heard Jace, Pete, and the sheriff enter, but he ignored them. "So burning my livery wasn't separating enough of my money from me?"

Brows raised, Frank took a puff on his cigar. "I guess I don't know what you're talking about." He looked at his two men. "Do you?" Both shook their heads. "Well then, I guess you'd better explain. You say your livery burned?"

"You know full well it did, since you did it."

Frank snorted. "Since I was here all night, that's not possible."

He motioned to his men. "Isn't that right?" Again, the men nodded. Frank spread his hands. "See?"

"They'll agree to anything, including burning buildings, if you pay them enough."

"You need more proof?" Frank turned to the hotel's proprietor. "Mr. Mahoney, these men and I were here all evening, were we not?"

"Yes, sir."

Cade examined Silas Mahoney's face for the truth. The man showed no fear or deception. "So you found another accomplice. Did he report to you how he almost killed Grace?"

Frank didn't respond, but his expression spoke of his fury. Once he'd regained control, he stood, his approach casual.

"What happened?"

"You can ask your employee all about it."

Frank puffed on his cigar and blew the smoke at Cade's face. "I don't know what you're talking about. Will she be all right?"

"No thanks to you. Come on, you coward. I dare you to step outside."

Frank's hired guns pulled their pistols.

"All right, Cade, that's enough." The sheriff pushed between them, and Jace and Pete grabbed Cade's arms and led him from the hotel.

"Look, I understand how you feel," Jace said, "but if you keep this up, you'll end up dead. Let the sheriff handle it."

"What can he do? He's got no proof. At least not yet. Someone has to stop that criminal."

Sheriff Thomas strode through the door and stepped in front of Cade. "It better not be you. Everyone knows how you feel about Mr. Easton. If something happens to him, they'll demand I arrest you."

"You can't be serious."

"I'm just telling you what it looks like right now, Cade. Let me do the investigating. You stay out of it, for your own good."

"Stay out of it? How can I do that when Frank keeps putting me right back in?"

"This is your warning, Cade. Don't do anything that will put you behind bars." The sheriff headed down the boardwalk, then looked over his shoulder. "Go home, Cade."

Jace patted Cade's back. "I have to agree with him. If Frank gets hurt, all fingers will point to you. Best thing to do is let the sheriff handle this. You know he's on your side. He doesn't like Frank any more than you do. I'm going to go check on Grace and see if Bobbie is ready for a rest. Want to come along?"

"I'd better get home too," Pete said. "It'll be morning all too soon, and I'm sure Annie's waiting to hear some news."

"You two go ahead," Cade said. "I'm too restless to get any sleep. I think I'll just wait in the livery till morning. That way nothing more can happen to it, and once there's enough light, I can look around for any sign of who started the fire."

Both men promised to return at first light to help. Cade headed toward the livery, his steps heavy. Once inside, he lit a lantern and wandered around the remnants of his business. At least the part of the livery that would have cost the most to repair still stood. For that, he could be grateful.

He held the lantern high and checked the stability of the loft. Even though it held the most straw and hay, the loft looked solid, almost untouched.

Thank You, Lord.

Cade was about to climb the ladder when a rustle at the front door made him pull his pistol.

"Hold up, boss." Joseph stepped into view, his hands up. "They ain't no need to shoot. Not just yet anyway."

"Joseph?" Cade waved him in. "What're you doing up at this hour?"

"Belle." Joseph's teeth gleamed in the light of the lantern. "Least I'm gonna blame her when she complains 'bout how tired I am all day tomorrow. We done heard about the fire and what happened to Grace. Belle say she can't sleep anyhow, so she might as well sit with her friend." Joseph strolled around the livery, looking at the damage and running his hand along the stalls. "I left Belle at Doc's. Jace told me you was here, so I figured I'd come sit with you." Joseph turned and faced him. "And don't go telling me to go home. Look what happened the last time you said that."

Cade smiled. "Well, I don't aim to make the same mistake twice. Thanks for coming."

The two hunkered down into the straw piled in the loft. Cade doubted either would get any sleep, but he appreciated the silence Joseph offered. Maybe the quiet would allow Cade's mind to get a bit of rest.

"Come on now, Grace. You gots to show me them eyes."

Belle's voice, though soft, demanded obedience. Grace wanted to refuse. She'd been awakened so many times, it would take days to feel rested. But from the past several hours with Bobbie, she knew she wouldn't be allowed to return to painless sleep until she'd opened her eyes and had a brief conversation. Belle's cool hand on her forehead forced her eyes open only to see Belle's dark ones mere inches away.

"You practicing your mothering skills on me, Belle?"

"Well, look at you. Gets a knock upside the head and she turns all sassy like. Keep up that sass an' you might find a lump on the other side. If I was a betting woman, I'd lay money your mama laid many a swat on your backside."

Grace would have laughed except for the memory of the pain that would bring. "Then you'd lose your money, because I was a good girl."

"Uh-huh, and that lop-eared goat, Jonah, has a genius brain in his hard head."

Her laugh refused to be smothered. "Oh, Belle. Don't make me laugh."

"Mm-hmm. Whom the Lord loveth…"

Grace managed a grin. "Then you'd better get ready for a good spanking of your own, because He sure dotes on you."

Belle's cackle echoed in the room as she moved to the window and slid the curtains open. "Peers to me the doc has nothing to worry about no more. You as feisty as ever."

Grace stared at the light coming through the window. "What time is it?"

"Almost seven." Belle returned to sit on the side of the bed. "How you feeling, Grace?"

"Better." But not by much. Though it no longer felt like her heart throbbed inside her head, the pain still remained.

"Then why you squinting? The light hurt your eyes? You want me to close them shades again?"

"No. I like seeing the sunrise."

Belle rearranged the pillow and bedding. "Anything I can get you? Some water maybe?"

"That would be good." A few swallows later, and Grace's throat felt much better. "Have you seen Cade? Is he all right?"

Though Jace had told her at some point during the night that Cade was fine, she needed to hear it again, this time from a woman.

"I ain't seen him, but I knows my Joseph is with him, so he must be fine."

Only seeing him for herself would set her mind at ease. She heard someone enter the room and soon the doctor came into view. At least someone looked well-rested.

"Watch her, Doc," Belle said. "She's a bit sassy this morning."

"Really? That's good news. Tells me she's feeling better."

"Or maybe it should tell you I'm sleep-deprived, what with all the wake-ups during the night."

"Mm-hmm. Like I said…sassy."

The doctor only grinned as he peered into each of Grace's eyes before removing the bandage from her forehead. His probing fingers made her wince.

"Do they teach you in those fancy schools how to inflict pain at the same time they teach you to heal, Doctor?"

"Nope. That's just a side benefit we gain from grouchy patients."

Belle cackled. "Looks like the good doctor doesn't need my help with you after all," she said. "I think I'll go home and get some rest so I can come back and pester you some more."

Grace wrinkled her nose at her friend. "Get some for me too."

When they were alone, the doctor turned serious. "How does your head feel? Still throbbing or has that calmed some?"

"It's not as bad."

"Good." He added ointment to her wound, then covered it again. "I guess I can let you sleep longer now. Anything I can do for you?"

"Can I get off my back? It's getting sore."

"Not a problem."

He helped her roll to her side, then pulled one side of the curtains closed, darkening the room a bit. Though she wanted to stay awake for a while, her eyes drifted closed.

She woke to singing. It didn't sound like Bobbie or Belle. Who was in her room? She forced her eyes open and saw only a chair and a wall. Then she remembered rolling to her side. She cleared her throat, and a face appeared before her.

"Mrs. Ramsey?"

"At least your memory is intact. I wondered since it had been so long since you'd been by to see me." The following wink let Grace know the woman was teasing, at least a little.

"I'm sorry. But are you supposed to be out of bed?"

Ella Ramsey made a tsk sound. "See, if you'd come by sooner, you'd know I've been out of bed for a few weeks." She sat on the chair. "I'll stop teasing. Is there anything I can get for you?"

"Just some company."

Ella sat back and made herself comfortable. "That much I can do." After eyeing Grace a moment, she leaned forward just a little. "Are you sure you're feeling all right? You're so pale."

"Unlike you. You look great."

Ella's tinkling laugh made Grace realize how much she missed visits with this dear woman. No wonder she and Grace's mother had been good friends. It didn't take much to make either of them happy.

"You've not gotten any better at changing the subject, dear." She shook her finger at her. "But I'll let you get away with it again…this time."

"Thank you." It was easy to see where Cade received his charm. He had a good teacher. "I heard you singing."

"Oh, I'm sorry if it woke you. Sometimes I can't seem to help it."

Grace held out her hand and Ella took it. "I didn't mind. I liked it. Reminded me of when my mother sang while she worked in the house. Always so happy. Like you." She examined Ella's face, tracing the smile lines around her eyes and mouth. "Even in the bad times."

Ella only nodded. But the nod didn't tell Grace how they could be happy no matter their circumstances. She figured the credit would be given to God, but that still didn't explain the how.

"Do you still have pain in your hip?"

"Sometimes, but it's bearable. Why?"

"Are you sure you should be here?"

"Are you trying to get rid of me?"

Grace smiled. "No. Never."

Ella gave her a penetrating look. "Ask your question, dear."

Yep, just like Mama. "How do you keep your joy through all the tough times? I know you're going to say it's because of God, but that doesn't tell me how."

Mrs. Ramsey didn't answer right away. By the distant look in her eyes, Grace suspected she had taken a moment to pray. Then Ella enveloped Grace's hand in both of hers.

"I have joy, Grace, because of all God's given me. I wake up every morning and remind myself that no matter what happens through the day, no matter how many mistakes I make or how many times

I disappoint Him, He'll still love me. He proved that when He sacrificed His only Son for me. How can I not feel joy?"

That sounded too easy. "You can tell me that after what happened, breaking your hip and being laid up for so long, you never got angry with God?"

Ella smiled. "I won't tell you that I didn't question God's reason for the accident or fear what might be the result of it, but I never stopped loving Him." She scooted forward in the chair, her eyes intent. "God never promised life would be easy, Grace, but He did promise to be with us through everything. All we have to do is look to Him and accept His help. God doesn't pick and choose when He'll be with us and love us. He never leaves us and He loves at all times. We can't just praise Him when things are going good, Grace. We need to praise Him at all times, through the good and the bad."

"So it's a matter of heart and mind," Grace said.

"Exactly." Ella squeezed her hand. "Rather than get angry and bitter over being laid up, I used that time to realize that the possible reason I was flat in bed was that I needed to work on my relationship with the Lord. In my pride, I started relying on myself, giving myself the credit for how well things were going. And since I wouldn't listen to God's gentle urging to change my ways, He used a different method to get my attention. And it worked. I don't think I've ever been as close to my Lord as I am now."

"And you never worried about your future, whether or not you'd ever walk again?"

Mrs. Ramsey patted the back of her hand. "I don't know how many times God tells us in His Word not to fear, but it's often, which means He wants us to take that to heart." She reached to caress Grace's cheek. "Trust Him in all things and at all times, Grace, because nothing is impossible with God. Use His strength, and you can do and get through anything."

And that was her problem. She had quit trusting anyone but

herself, and even that was a risk on any given day. She smiled at Ella. "Thank you."

"You're welcome. Get some rest, Grace."

She closed her eyes, but sleep eluded her as her mind replayed Ella's words. God didn't owe her a thing. Her Lord had already paid in full with His life. But she owed God everything. Somewhere along the last several years, she'd forgotten that fact while feeling sorry for herself.

Forgive me, Lord.

As peace filled her, sleep came for a visit.

❖ THIRTY ❖

Weary in body and spirit, Cade pushed through the door to the doctor's office. He spotted his mother in the chair staring at Grace. Before he could say a word, she waved away his question.

"I'm fine. I wanted to be here. Your father will be here soon to take me home."

He leaned down to kiss her cheek. "Any pain?"

"Not much at all."

Which meant she was hurting, but it wouldn't do him a bit of good to scold her or try to take her home right now. She was strong-willed and this visit seemed to mean a lot to her. He understood. Grace had that effect on people.

He squatted next to the bed to get a closer look at Grace. Her face flinched from time to time. "How is she?"

"Better, I think. We had a nice chat. You just missed it."

He caressed her cheek with the backs of his fingers and swept aside a few strands of hair from her face, wishing he could as easily brush aside her pain, or take it for her. As much as he fought his feelings for her, she managed to counter and best each of his battles with a smile, bat of her lashes, or even one of her silly mishaps that caused him some pain of his own. With a sigh, he sat on the floor next to his mother and leaned against the wall. She laid her hand on his shoulder.

"You're in love with her."

"No, I just…" He realized last night as he thought about Grace that he started falling in love with her on the trip from Pueblo. He took a deep breath. "You're right, I am. After Kim, I never wanted to love again. It hurt too much. But Grace is impossible to resist."

He rubbed his finger over the spot where she'd cut his lip with the stick. "I don't know if Mrs. Bradley knew what she was doing when she named her daughter, but Grace is anything but graceful. She's blackened my eye, got me stepped on by a horse, made me tangle with a goat, busted my lip, and gave me too many heart attacks to count. As much as I wanted to run in fear from her, I sought every chance I could to spend time with her." He shook his head. "My feelings for Grace are much deeper than anything I ever felt for Kim. I know they are because when I'm away from her, a part of me is missing."

"Sounds like love to me," Ella said. "So, what do you plan to do about it?"

Cade rested his head against the arm of her chair, and his eyes drifted shut as he pondered her question.

The clomping of boots brought Cade to his feet. His father entered the room, and Cade glanced down at his mother and wondered how long he'd been asleep. His father's gaze swept over him before looking at his wife.

"You ready to go?" Victor said.

"I can't leave Grace alone."

"She won't be. Doc's in his office."

"Oh. All right." Ella propped her hands on the arms of the chair, but before she could stand, Cade hooked his arm under hers to assist. She kept hold of his hand. "Are you coming home with us?"

"Not yet. I still have a few things to check on." He wouldn't get any help from the sheriff for a while. He was too busy trying to find out who killed a stranger just outside of town.

"Did you find any evidence of who started the fire?"

Cade took a deep breath. "No, not a thing. But I'm not giving up yet." He dipped his head and kissed his mother's cheek. "I'll be home tonight."

He took one last look at Grace. In the next few days, they needed to talk. Until then, he'd keep praying for God to give him the right words.

Grace sat on a rocker on Bobbie's porch, her legs draped with a blanket at Bobbie's insistence even though the day was plenty warm. She didn't think she'd ever been so coddled and wondered if Bobbie was afraid of losing her. The thought made her smile. It felt good to be wanted.

That led to thoughts of whether or not Cade wanted her. She hadn't seen Cade since he ran out of the doctor's office in search of Frank. Many had told her of his visits, but he always came when she was sleeping. She craved time with him.

The thought of Frank made her stomach churn. The man was a beast, though he could be quite charming when it suited his purposes. His alter-ego was what scared her most.

"You feeling all right?"

Grace looked up at Bobbie. "Yes. Why?"

"You had such a sour look on your face. I wasn't sure if you were in pain or if my cooking wasn't sitting well."

Grace had to laugh. "Your cooking isn't as bad as you think."

Brows high, Bobbie wrinkled her nose. "I'll let you try to convince Jace of that." She sat in the rocker next to Grace. "So, what did put such an odd expression on your face?"

"Frank. I just don't understand why the people in town can't see him for who he really is."

"He never lets them see his other side."

"Yeah, I've come to that same conclusion."

As if thoughts of the man conjured him up, Frank rode across the bridge and up to the house with his horse and buggy. Grace exchanged a look with Bobbie, who had her hand on her pistol.

Frank tipped the edge of his hat. "Afternoon, ladies."

He got out of the buggy and approached the porch, stopping short of the steps. His eyes went to Bobbie's pistol for a moment before looking at Grace.

"Grace, I really need to speak with you. It's about your father. Do you feel up to a brief chat?"

"Is something wrong? Is he sick or hurt?"

Frank glanced at Bobbie. "I'd prefer we speak in private, if you don't mind."

"It's up to you," Bobbie said, "but if you want to talk, I won't be far. All you have to do is grunt, and I'll be back with gun in hand." She spoke the last loud enough for Frank to hear.

"All right, Frank. I'll talk to you." Grace gave Bobbie a look she hoped would let her know not to wander far.

"I'll be right around the corner."

"Thank you, Mrs. Kinkaid." Frank climbed the steps of the porch, then sat in the rocker Bobbie had vacated. "And thank *you* for agreeing to talk to me. It's very important."

"So you said. Tell me about my father."

Frank leaned over the arm of the rocker, his face more intense than she had seen in a long time.

"He's in a lot of trouble, Grace."

"What do you mean?"

Frank ran his finger across his mustache, and right away, she was on the alert. This had something to do with money. "Your father is about to lose everything…and possibly end up in jail."

"I don't understand."

"I didn't think you would. This will take some time to explain, so please bear with me." He eyed her bandage. "Are you feeling well enough for this?"

"Just get on with it, Frank. I'll let you know when I've had enough."

"Yes, of course." He cleared his throat and turned the rocker in order to face her better. "Awhile back, your father came to me with the dream of owning a mine. I believe you knew about that."

"Yes."

"Well, between the two of us, we came up with a way to make his dream come true. He put up his gunsmith business as collateral for a mine he'd checked into and thought would have the best chance for a big payoff. In order to have enough money, he also had to put the mine up as an additional guarantee."

She didn't know much about banking, but she was certain Frank made sure he'd come out of the deal with plenty of money to line his pockets. "And I guess you signed off on the loan."

"I did. It had every appearance of being a sound deal for the both of us."

"Uh-huh." She wouldn't trust Frank with her next breath. "So what went wrong to put my father in so much trouble that he may end up in jail?"

"The mine turned out to be worthless." He planted his elbows on his knees. "Listen, Grace. I've been more than fair with your father. I gave him time to come up with the money and even tried to figure every way he could come up with enough to pay off the loan and still have some kind of business. But there's just no way."

He pulled his hat from his head and turned it in his hands. If she didn't know him better, she'd think he was nervous. He cleared his throat again, the hat almost spinning in his fingers.

"Except one."

"What do you mean?"

Frank glanced around before looking her in the eyes. "You."

She stared. "Me? I don't understand."

"I came up with a plan and talked to your father. He said he'd agree to it if you did."

He wasn't making any sense, and her patience was wearing thin. "I still don't understand. What *plan*?"

"Marry me, and I'll drop the loan. Become my wife, and your father will own the gunsmith business free and clear."

Shock took hold, leaving her speechless. All she could manage was a tiny shake of her head. Marry Frank? Not a chance. Not ever.

He reached over and touched her knee. "Don't say no, Grace, or I'll be forced to call in the loan. And since your father can't pay, and the value of the shop and the mine can't cover the loan, your father will go to prison. Marry me and you'll save your father's life, because there's no way he'll survive even a year in prison."

Frank was more evil than she had ever imagined. She shoved his hand from her knee. "You're despicable. How could you even come up with such a diabolical plan?"

"Because I want you for my wife." He dipped his head to see her face. "Don't say no, Grace, because I won't stop there." He sat back in the rocker, his expression looking more like the Frank she knew. "After I take your father's shop and gold mine and put him behind bars"—he pressed his hat back onto his head—"I'll go after Ramsey."

The last remark jerked her head up to examine his face. He meant every word. What he'd already done to Cade was just the beginning. He wouldn't stop until Cade was completely broken.

"Why?" The question came out in a whisper. "Why me?"

Frank stroked one side of his mustache, a slight smile on his face. "I've decided you're to be my wife, Grace, and I won't stop until you bear my name and my child."

The image he presented was revolting. She took several deep breaths to calm herself. *Please, God. You promised to be with me at all times. I need You now. Help me.*

"So, what's your answer, Grace?"

Tears welled, but she refused to give Frank the pleasure. "I don't see as I have much of a choice…which is just the way you wanted it, isn't it, Frank?"

"Is that a yes?"

She closed her eyes, hoping God would show her a way out. She saw none. The freedom she fought so hard to gain and keep dwindled to a vapor before it disappeared.

"Yes."

"Good." Frank rose and kissed the top of her head. "Wise decision. I'll get back with you about when we'll leave for Pueblo. I'll give you enough time to mend before you have to pack and say your good-byes. In the meantime, I'll be planning what I can of our wedding from here, starting with making sure the church is available. I'll want the whole town in attendance. My aunt can help with some of the other details." He squatted in front of her. "Don't look so sad, Grace. Not only have you made me the happiest man alive, you'll be closer to your father, who'll be more than pleased with our union."

He patted her hand and stood. "Get better soon, Grace. Get plenty of rest. We have a long trip ahead of us." After a quick kiss to the back of her hand, he placed it on her lap and descended the steps. "Have a good evening, Grace."

As he climbed into the buggy and turned the horse, she knew she'd never again enjoy a good evening. Frank had seen to that. But if it meant her father and Cade would enjoy evenings for the rest of their lives, that would be the one piece of joy she could hang onto in the midst of despair.

THIRTY-ONE

Cade farmed out his last few horses to men in town who had small stables, then he returned to the livery and wrapped the reins around one of the posts inside. Jace had promised to clear a small area on his ranch where Cade could work until he could re-build. He'd have to fix up some kind of makeshift forge, but at least he could take some of his tools out there to get started.

Cade took one last look around to make sure he hadn't forgotten anything. He hadn't seen Grace in four days, and he couldn't wait to have at least a short visit with her. Maybe he could wrangle a meal with the Kincaids. And then maybe he and Grace could finally have that talk he'd wanted. He took a deep breath and blew it out hard, hoping to calm his nerves. He tied the canvas bag filled with tools to his saddle and led the horse outside.

Frank stood propped against the hitching post out front, clouding an otherwise bright day.

"What do you want, Easton?"

"Oh, now don't be that way, Cade. Not when I've got good news to share."

"I don't care about your news." He flipped up the stirrup to check the cinch, then climbed onto the saddle. "Excuse me."

"Hold up." Frank grabbed the reins. "I just wanted to give you your own special invitation to the wedding, especially since you've been such a good friend. I figured it's the least I could do."

Cade yanked the reins to free his horse. "I don't care about you or any wedding you may want to invite me to." He heeled his horse to put distance between him and Frank.

"You wouldn't want to disappoint Grace, would you?" Frank called after him.

Cade stopped his horse and turned it back. "What did you say?"

Frank beamed. "Grace and me. We're getting married. She said yes two days ago." He crossed his arms. "Funny, I thought you'd have heard by now. She didn't tell you?"

Shock and anger raced through Cade. He turned his horse and trotted out of town. When he was certain Frank couldn't see him, he heeled his horse into a gallop, as if he could outrun the ache in his heart. This couldn't be happening again. Not again. Not with Grace.

Grace wandered through Bobbie's old house, dust cloth in hand, in a feeble attempt to stay busy. In two days, she'd be leaving for Pueblo with Frank. In ten days, she'd become Mrs. Frank Easton.

That thought didn't sicken her now as it had when Frank first forced her into agreeing to be his wife. After spending two full days in prayer, God had granted her peace, and she smiled as she remembered the answer she'd received. In all God's loving grace through the sacrifice of His Son, His loved ones received life. And through Grace's sacrifice of her freedom, Daddy and Cade would receive life as well. With that discovery came peace, and God's love would get her through the coming years as Frank's wife.

A knock at the door pulled Grace from her reflections. She opened the door only to have Belle rush past her, clucking her tongue with each step before she turned and planted her hands on her hips.

"You done gone and lost your mind, girl. That's the only explanation for you agreeing to marry that mean ol' Mr. Frank." Belle pointed her finger at Grace's head. "I don't know what he done, but I aim to undo it, and quick."

Grace closed the distance between them and put her arm around her dear friend to lead her into the kitchen. She'd miss Belle. Once there, Belle pulled away and faced her again.

"Spill it, girl. Tell me what happened to make you do such a crazy thing." She crossed her arms and tapped her toes. "You know you can't do this, Grace. That man gonna make you miserable, if not kill you outright."

Grace leaned against the doorframe and shrugged. "I saw no other way, Belle." She put up a hand when Belle's mouth opened. "Let me put that another way. Frank gave me no other choice."

"I don't understand. There's always more than one choice."

She motioned for Belle to have a seat at the table, then she moved to the stove to stir the stew she'd made earlier from the leftover roast.

"I used to think that too." She propped one hip against the counter in order to see both Belle and the pot. "I was wrong."

Belle peered hard at Grace. "Why aren't you upset? At the very least, you should be screaming and tearing out your hair or sobbing your eyes out."

"I almost got to that very state." She faced Belle and smiled. "But God saved me…again."

Belle rose from her chair and headed toward Grace, arms outstretched. The two hugged for several long moments, then Belle held her at arm's length and peered into her face.

"I see it now. That unspeakable peace. But still, how can you be so calm?"

Grace made a face. "I'm not all that calm. I haven't been able to eat since I said yes. And sleep is pretty hard to come by."

Belle patted her cheek. "Well, least you starting to seem more normal than I first thought."

"Normal flew out the window long ago for me, Belle."

"Still, I can't let you marry that beast of a man."

The side door rushed open and slammed against the wall, and both women jumped. Grace turned and caught the brunt of Cade's fierce glare. For the first time, her resolve weakened right along with her knees. She dropped onto the closest chair and propped herself against the table. For days she had longed to see Cade, and now that he was here, the sight of him pierced her heart.

"Is it true?" Cade's chest heaved. "Are you going to marry Easton?"

Mouth suddenly dry, Grace couldn't swallow. She managed a feeble nod.

His throat worked several times. "You had to let *him* tell me? Why didn't you come to me?" He shook his head and looked as if he was about to say more before he gave a helpless gesture with his hands, turned, and walked out.

Grace opened her mouth to call him back, but his name stuck in her throat. Though she'd hurt him now, in the long run, she'd made the right choice. She would have to keep telling herself that until Frank dragged her out of town.

She shared a look with Belle, who sat at the table next to her and grasped Grace's hand.

"You better do some explaining. That man," she whispered, pointing out the door, "loves you, and you just busted his heart like shattered glass."

And Grace's heart joined his all over the floor in pieces.

THIRTY-TWO

Tim Martell helped Grace onto the stage platform before return-ing to the wagon for her trunk. He placed it at her feet, then stood up to face her.

"You sure you want to do this, Grace?"

He'd tried to talk to her a few times on the ride into town, but she not only refused to talk about it, she couldn't. She'd get choked up every time she tried to speak. This time, she looked him in the eyes and nodded.

"Thank you, Tim. For everything." He was a good man.

He touched the rim of his hat with thumb and finger. "You take care of yourself, Grace." He squeezed her hand, then climbed onto the wagon seat and clucked at the horses. After one last look back, he headed toward the ranch.

Grace stood on the platform, unsure of what to do next. She con-sidered briefly having the station manager watch her trunk while she went in search of Frank, but decided against it. If he wanted her, he'd have to come for her. She moved to the bench and sat.

Oh Lord, make Frank change his mind...please.

But there he was—Frank and his two shadows striding down the boardwalk toward her. Sporting a wide smile, he approached her and clapped his hands, rubbing them together as though he'd just won a large pot playing poker.

"You ready?"

She motioned to the small trunk. "All my worldly possessions."

"I can fix that. I'll buy you all new dresses. Lots of them. I want my wife to be the best dressed woman in all Pueblo." He turned to his hired guns. "Men, get the horses. You can follow us. My future bride and I are riding in style in the stagecoach."

The men left, and Frank dropped on the bench next to her and leaned close. "One more week, my dear, and we'll be husband and wife. I know I've said that a lot, but I'm thrilled beyond words."

If only he were beyond using words. He hadn't stopped talking yet. A rumble from down the street made them both turn that direction. The stagecoach had arrived. Grace fought tears so Frank wouldn't see them.

Once the coach had come to a stop next to the platform, Frank jumped to his feet and held out his hand to her. She placed hers in his, and he led her to the coach. While they waited for a couple to disembark, Grace glanced up and down the street, getting one last look at the town she'd come to love.

The sight of Cade standing in front of the bank staring at her made her breath catch in her chest. She didn't know what she expected from him, but to have him turn and enter the bank without a nod or smile felt like a dagger to her heart. If only she could talk to him...

She stood frozen to the spot. No. Nothing she could say would take away his hurt or change the outcome.

"What's wrong, sweetheart?"

She shook her head, unwilling to let Frank know how much seeing Cade had affected her. He'd only gloat.

Frank led her forward and helped her inside, then instructed the driver to load her trunk and retrieve his from inside the station office before joining her on the seat. Much too soon, the driver climbed onto his seat and set the coach in motion. Grace's eyes involuntarily moved to the bank. Cade stood at the window watching them. The sight of him would no doubt be burned forever into her memory.

I love you, Cade, and I always will.

Cade swallowed around the lump in his throat. He had thought watching Kim ride out of his life was difficult, but this pain was much harder to take. Worst of all, he didn't understand. Grace told him, and it showed on her face and in her actions, that she had nothing but contempt for Frank. Yet she just rode past with that very man on the way to becoming his wife.

The last two days, he'd fought with himself too many times to count about whether to confront her, try to dissuade her from going through with the wedding. And too many times to count, he talked himself out of it. The memory of her face when he went to the ranch to see if Frank's news was true haunted his every thought. She never made a move toward him, no effort to help him understand. And the expression on her face let him know he'd be wasting his breath if he tried to stop her.

"You all right?" Pete's voice was low and concerned.

Cade turned and walked a few steps away from the window. "Yeah. Sure."

Pete eyed him for several moments. "You sure you want to talk about a loan right now? We can wait until tomorrow. Longer if you need some time."

Cade ran the offer through his mind a few times. If he were honest, he didn't want to talk about money right now. Maybe not for some time to come. All he wanted was to get away for a while. But running never solved anything. He remembered telling Grace that very thing months ago.

He shook his head. Grace had filled every part of his life. Not a day or a thought would go by when she wouldn't pop into his mind. But he'd have to learn how to deal with those moments. Besides, he wasn't ready to go home and face the multitude of questions his mother was sure to ask, or the condemnation and disappointment he'd see in his father's eyes.

"Let's talk about the loan." He clapped Pete on the back and headed toward his office.

Almost an hour later, Cade left the bank with several options Pete had given him to consider.

Still not ready to go home, he climbed onto his saddle and headed for the Double K ranch. Not only would it help pass the time, but he'd also burn off some unwanted energy, maybe even keep from thinking about Grace for a spell. Besides, he needed to finish setting up the area Jace had set aside for him and his black-smithing tools. Not exactly the ideal situation, but it would do until he decided for certain about his future.

THIRTY-THREE

Grace stood before a long mirror as some stranger measured her and held fabric after fabric against her body. How did Frank expect her to make any decisions about a wedding dress mere hours after they'd arrived in town? The way he was racing through plans and choices with such determination, she had to wonder if he was afraid she would back out of their agreement.

"That's the one." Ida Easton, Frank's aunt, sat in attendance like a regal queen. Her eyes went from Grace to the mirror and back before she stood to touch the fabric. "This is absolutely beautiful. Makes me wish I were getting married again." She hid her titter behind her gloved hand. "What do you think, my dear? Do you agree this is the perfect fabric for your wedding dress?"

Grace examined herself in the mirror, trying to picture what she'd look like wearing all white in three days. "It's lovely." And it was. If only…

"It's settled then." Mrs. Easton pulled some bills from her reticule and pressed them into the dressmaker's hand. "When will it be finished?"

Grace stepped from the platform and moved into the small curtained room to get dressed. She didn't want to hear any of the wedding plans sure to come up in the next few minutes. She hoped all that would be required of her from here on out would be to show up at the church on time.

As she slipped into her old dress, her mind wandered back to Rockdale and the Double K ranch. What was everyone doing right now? Better yet, what would she be doing if she were there?

Stop it!

Those thoughts were sheer torture, and she needed to quit thinking that way. Those days were gone. Time to focus on the future, no matter how bleak it might be.

"Are you ready, dear?" The curtain was flung back and Mrs. Easton's pinched face looked very much as though she'd been kept waiting for hours.

"Yes." Grace hurried with the last few buttons before scooping up her tattered satchel. "Are we finished?"

"Not by a long shot, dear." Frank's aunt scurried toward the door with tiny steps, her wide hips pitching from side to side with such force, Grace was sure if a child walked by, it would be knocked to the ground. "We still have several errands to run. This wedding won't plan itself, you know."

Grace took several long strides to catch up. "Will I have time to see my father?" Frank hadn't given her even a moment to stop in and say hello.

"I'm not making any promises, dear. My nephew has us on a very tight schedule. I've been running myself silly since we received his wire with the news of his impending wedding." She paused long enough to hook her arm through Grace's, probably more to make sure she kept up or didn't run off than to show affection.

As the woman prattled on, Grace's mind wandered, though she managed to give an occasional nod and murmur when needed. She thought she might actually come to like her future aunt. Though she could be annoying at times and could talk the legs off a team of oxen, she seemed to have a tender heart, and that might make the rest bearable.

Grace hoped to make a quick stop at her father's gun shop at the end of the street. She looked that direction and spotted her father and Frank talking a few buildings down and across the street.

Before she could tell Mrs. Easton, the woman yanked Grace the opposite direction. "Before I forget, we need to stop in at the bakery and place an order for the reception."

Grace took one last glance behind and caught her father looking at her. But then Frank put his arm around her father's shoulders and led him away. With her own arm firmly held and being pulled by Mrs. Easton, she had no chance to get away.

Not hearing a word of the woman's blather, Grace let herself be dragged along as she tried to come up with a way to escape in order to talk to her father face-to-face. She had the feeling something very strange was going on.

Cade shut the side door as quietly as he could. So far, he'd managed to avoid an inquisition by coming home late or showing up when others were visiting. Cowardly as it was, talking about Grace was the last thing he wanted. He pushed through the kitchen door and headed for the stairs.

"Cade?"

The breath he'd been holding left him in a gust at his mother's voice. He turned toward the office and found her standing inside, next to his father. No more putting off the inevitable. He crossed the foyer, entered the office, and kissed his mother on the cheek.

She grasped his arms in her hands, held him at arm's length, and examined his face. "How are you? Besides being worn out from avoiding me."

He managed a weak smile. "I've been better." She'd see through anything less than the truth. "How about you? Still having pain?"

"I'm fine. It's you I'm worried about." She motioned to a chair. "Why don't you sit and talk awhile?"

He shook his head. "It won't do any good. It'll just take some time to heal, like the last time."

"But this isn't like the last time, Cade. You said so yourself."

He glanced at his father. He'd never be able to speak from his heart with his father listening. He took a breath. "I think I'll just go to bed. Sleep seems to help the most." That wasn't exactly true since sleep eluded him better than he avoided his mother. But he was through talking. He headed for the door.

"Cade?"

His father's voice stopped him. He turned, looked his father in the eyes, and waited.

"I owe you an apology. Several, actually."

Cade was about to wave away the apology, but the still, small voice in his heart told him to remain quiet and impassive.

Victor's chest rose and fell with every breath, as though summoning the words from a deep place inside. "I've been praying that God would let me see you through the eyes of others."

"And what have you seen?"

Victor's expression softened. "A man full of kindness and generosity, son. Ready to offer help even at the most inconvenient of times. Honest, good, and decent. The kind of man a father can be proud of. You're the man I wish I had been over the years, and I can't stand seeing you suffer like this."

His father stared at the floor, shoulders slumped, looking like a broken man. Cade's mouth worked but no words came.

"I'm sorry, son. I apologize for not being the father you wanted… deserved. For not being here for you when you needed me most." His voice broke. Tears formed in his eyes and overflowed.

Cade went to him and put a hand on his shoulder.

"For berating and belittling you when you needed support and encouragement. I began hating myself for the man I became, and I think I took out all my self-loathing on you." He gave a helpless gesture with his hands, and then looked Cade in the eyes. "I've earned your hate, but I hope that someday you can find it in your heart to forgive me."

His throat tight and burning, Cade stared at his father for several long moments, then pulled him into his arms. Another pair of arms came around them. Cade looked down to find his mother in tears. He stepped out of the way and stayed quiet while his parents held each other.

She finally pulled back. "You don't know how long I've prayed for this day. That you and Cade would work things out and show the love I knew you had for each other."

Victor took her hands in his. "I need to apologize to you too."

"No."

"Yes." He caressed the backs of her hands with his thumbs. "I allowed jealousy and resentment to put a wedge between Cade and me, and I allowed greed to keep me away from you."

He turned back to Cade. "I'm afraid I have another confession to make." He took a deep breath and let it out slowly. "I believe Grace being here, her running from her father and Frank, is a direct result of something I did."

"Something you did? What could you have possibly done…"

His mother looked from Cade to her husband. "Victor?"

His father released his mother's hands and sank onto the chair next to him. "Frank paid me to do a survey on Simon Bradley's claim. I didn't know who he was at the time. It was just another job." He shook his head. "It was the richest claim I've ever seen. When I told Frank, he paid me a great deal of money to lie about it." He propped his elbows on the desk and dropped his head into his hands. "I filled out the forms that said the claim was worthless. Right after that, I learned that Frank started pushing for a marriage between him and Mr. Bradley's daughter." He looked up at Cade and blew out a long breath. "I think he plans to kill Simon Bradley after the wedding to get his hands on that claim."

"Oh, Victor." Ella put her hands on his shoulders but looked up at Cade. "We've got to do something."

Anger, pity, and forgiveness fought for dominance in Cade's heart and mind. He wanted to slam his fist into his father's face and hug him at the same time. His father had changed for the better, but his old self put the woman Cade loved in danger. He had to save her, and prayed he wouldn't be too late.

He headed for the door. "I'm going to Pueblo."

"Cade, wait."

He swung around. "Don't, Dad." He held up his hand and then dropped it to his side. "Don't tell me to wait. I already lost Grace once. Maybe forever. I can't wait any longer."

"Cade, here…" His father opened the bottom desk drawer, pulled out a cloth bag, and tossed it to him. "Take this with you."

He opened the sack and peered inside. Money. Thousands of dollars. He looked back at his father for an explanation.

"It's everything Frank paid me to keep quiet. Use it to pay Mr. Bradley's debt. Then Frank won't have any hold on them, and Grace can be free."

"Thank you."

"Don't thank me. It's the least I could do. If it weren't for me, none of this would have happened. Now go! Before it's too late!"

Cade saddled two horses so when one grew tired, he could switch to the other. Hopeful for the first time in days, he prayed nonstop that he would arrive in time.

THIRTY-FOUR

Grace stood at the back of the church waiting for the music to start. Her heart trembled as much as her knees. She hoped they held her up as she walked down the aisle. Frank wouldn't appreciate being embarrassed on his wedding day.

During the last few days, she'd gotten to know Frank's aunt and uncle better. They were decent people—more thoughtful than Frank anyway. But Stuart Easton was as business-minded as Frank. He spent more time talking about making money than anything else.

Last night was the only chance she'd had to be with her father since she'd returned to Pueblo, and that time had been shared with the Eastons. If she didn't know any better, she'd think they were going out of their way to keep her and her father apart.

She glanced across the foyer at him. Even now, they were kept apart until the music started. Then they were to meet in the doorway for him to walk her down the aisle. He looked so sad, broken, and defeated. If only they could be alone for a few minutes. Maybe she could make him feel better.

The first notes rang from the piano, and her father turned to look at her then headed her way. He took her hands in his and pulled her toward him, then placed a kiss on her cheek.

"You look beautiful. Just like your mother."

Tears in her eyes, she gave him a trembling smile. "Thank you." She touched his cheek. "I love you, Daddy."

His eyes welled. "Listen, Grace. I need to—"

"Time to walk, Bradley." Frank's men urged them forward. "Don't keep everyone waiting."

They turned, Grace's hand on her father's elbow, and took the first steps into the church. The attendees rose, most of them smiling, all of them staring, some whispering to the person next to them. How many had showed up purely out of curiosity?

Unable to avoid it any longer, Grace looked to the front of the church. Frank stood waiting, his hands crossed in front, a wide smile on his face. He rocked up on his toes and bounced. As she drew closer, he wiped his mustache, first one side then the other, then licked his lips. She couldn't stop the shudder that raced through her. In a matter of minutes, she'd be bound to him and have to look at his face every day for the rest of her life. Her father patted her hand.

They came to a stop at the front of the church. Daddy kissed her cheek one more time before handing her over to Frank and moving to the front row. Once the piano stopped playing, the silence that followed screamed to be filled. The pastor stepped forward and offered a short prayer.

"Please be seated." When the rustling quieted, the pastor turned his attention to the bride and groom. "Frank and Grace, you both have professed to be children of God."

Grace glanced at Frank. When had they made that profession? She'd never seen this minister before today.

The pastor cleared his throat. "Ladies and gentlemen, we are here as witnesses to the union of Frank Easton and Grace Bradley. The vows they are about to take are legal and binding"

The words made her weak in the knees. Frank tucked his arm further under hers and leaned down. "This won't take long. Take some breaths to get you through. You'll be fine." He looked at the minister and made the motion to speed things along.

The pastor nodded and glanced over his notes. "Grace Bradley, do you take Frank to be your husband, to have and to hold from this day forward, for better or for worse, for richer, for poorer, in sickness and in health, to love and cherish, until death do you part?"

Grace swallowed hard. Did these vows count if she didn't love Frank? And would she ever be able to cherish him? She took a deep breath.

Frank squeezed her arm. "Answer him."

She licked her lips and opened her mouth, but nothing came out. Frank bumped her with his elbow. She dipped her head and swallowed one more time before looking up at the pastor. As she was about to say yes, a crash sounded at the back of the church.

Frank turned to see what caused the noise. Grace glanced up at him before looking back. Before she could see anything, Frank jerked her back toward the front.

"Keep going, Pastor." He leaned down to Grace's ear. "Hurry up and say yes."

More noises echoed from the back along with the crash of breaking glass. What sounded like fists smashing into faces came next, followed by cursing. Grace tried to look back again. Frank held her tight against him.

"Answer the pastor."

"Grace!"

She knew that voice. One she thought she'd never hear again.

"Grace, don't say a word. Don't marry Frank."

She yanked away from Frank and turned to the back. Cade threw one last punch to get rid of the man keeping him from her. Then he bent, picked up a bag, and stumbled to the front, wiping blood from his nose and mouth.

He stopped several feet from them. "Don't marry this man, Grace. He's a liar and a cheat. He deserves to be behind bars."

Stuart Easton stood and pointed his bony finger at Cade. "Now listen here, young man…"

Frank held up his hand toward his uncle. "I'll take care of this."
He looked at Cade and crossed his arms. "You'd better have a good
reason for busting into this private ceremony and making those accusations."

Cade tossed the bag at Frank's feet. "There's your reason."

Grace stared at the bag, then peered back at Cade for an explanation. He motioned to her father.

"You need to hear this, Mr. Bradley. This concerns you too."
Grace's father came to stand next to him. Cade gestured to the bag.
"There's thousands of dollars inside that bag, Mr. Bradley." Cade's
voice rose so everyone could hear. "That's what Frank Easton paid
my father to lie about the value of your claim. According to my father, that mine is worth more money than you can count."

Murmurs raced through the church.

Cade put his hand on Simon Bradley's shoulder and pointed at
the bag. "My father is giving you that money to pay off your debt to
Frank Easton. It should more than cover the loan." He looked into
Grace's eyes. "And you don't have to marry him."

Frank pulled Grace against him as he grabbed a gun from his
pocket and pointed it at Cade, who'd reached for his sidearm. "Don't
move."

"Or what?" Cade motioned to everyone in the church. "You plan
to shoot someone in front of all these witnesses? You'll hang before the
week is out." He put his hand on his pistol. "You may hang anyway.
How many of these people have you cheated besides Mr. Bradley?"

The murmurs rose once more.

Frank's hand moved to Grace's throat. "I may be in trouble,
Ramsey, but I can make sure you never get what you really came for."
He waved his gun at Cade. "Get your hand away from your pistol."

Stuart stepped into the aisle. "What have you done, Frank? If
you've done something to jeopardize my bank, I'll shoot you myself."

Frank's attention shifted to his uncle, and a gunshot went off, followed closely by a second.

THIRTY-FIVE

Women screamed, and most everyone ran for the back door.
Cade dashed up the steps and grabbed Grace in his arms,
holding her tight against him and putting himself between her and
Frank.

Frank's gun fell to the floor with a thud. Cade glanced behind
and found Frank clasping his hand over his shoulder. Frank stared
at Simon Bradley, his mouth dropped open, and then he collapsed.

Grace pushed away from Cade's chest far enough so she could
see. They both saw Grace's father holding a small gun in his hand
still pointed at Frank.

Cade held Grace at arm's length and looked her over. "Are you
hurt? Were you shot?"

Grace peered into his eyes and shook her head. "I'm fine." She
turned. "Daddy?"

Together, they walked to Simon. The poor man's hands were
shaking. His eyes never left Frank.

Cade reached out and grasped the gun. "Let me have it, Mr.
Bradley."

He released it with no hesitation. Cade thought he looked like
he'd aged ten years in the last few minutes. He placed Grace's hand
into her father's. "Take care of her for a while." Cade dipped his head

to look into the man's eyes. "Watch Grace for me." When Simon finally nodded, Cade touched Grace's cheek. "I'll be right back."

He strode toward Frank. His uncle crouched over him. Cade grabbed Frank's gun and the bag of money before checking on him. Frank lay writhing and moaning, but he was very much alive. The sheriff ran up to them and knelt.

"What happened?"

Now that the sheriff was here, most of the people who'd fled were filing back inside and angling themselves for a good look. Only one person was moving against the flow. The man looked familiar. Cade squinted then dropped the guns and bag next to the Bradleys and took off at a run. He swung around the crowd, grabbed Tim Martel by the shirtfront, and shoved him against the wall.

"What are you doing here, Martel?"

Tim strained to get free. Cade gripped the shirt tighter.

"Start talking."

Tim held his hands out. "All right." He looked around. "But can we get out of this crowd first?"

Cade glanced around, then motioned toward the front of the church. He stopped Tim before they got too close to Grace and pointed to a pew. Cade waited for Tim to sit, then propped on the pew in front of him, blocking any attempt to escape.

"Now, let's hear it."

Tim squirmed and rubbed his palms together. "I'm…I was…" He glanced at Frank, then back at Cade. "I work for Frank."

"What?"

Tim leaned back and held out a hand. "I had to. He threatened to take my land and throw me in prison. When I tried to back out of his plan, he threatened to hurt my family."

Cade relaxed. Tim was but another of Frank's victims. Maybe. "Explain."

Tim slumped in the pew. "I moved my family here and signed a loan with Frank for a nice piece of land north of here. The next thing

I know, Frank came out to my place and said he was calling in the loan, that if I couldn't pay, he'd take my land and have me tossed in prison for years." He lifted his hands in a helpless gesture before letting them drop to his lap. "He offered a way out by telling me that if I did a job for him, he'd give me more time to pay off the loan." He peered up at Cade. "I felt I had no choice."

His story sounded all too familiar. Frank was evil. "What was Frank's plan?"

Tim took a deep breath. "I was to find Grace and bring her back."

The day Cade found Grace in the back of his wagon ran through his mind. "You the one who shot at us?"

Tim nervously rubbed his palms on his pants. He finally nodded. "Yes. But I wasn't trying to hit you."

"You came mighty close for trying to miss."

"Yeah. Sorry about that."

Cade glared at Tim until he looked away.

"Then what?"

"I went back to Frank and told him Grace was with someone and that I was done. I wouldn't hurt someone for him." He gazed at Frank and shook his head. "That's when he told me he'd hurt my family if I didn't finish the job." Tim blew out a breath. "He ordered me to follow the two of you and let him know where you ended up, that I was to stay in touch by wiring him with any news about Grace." He shrugged. "The best way to keep an eye on Grace was to work for the same people."

"Why you? Why not have his two hired guns do the job?"

"I used to be a gunfighter. How he learned that, I don't know, but he said I was perfect for the job. Plus, he didn't need to pay me to do his dirty work."

"A gunfighter, huh. Why not just shoot Frank?"

"Because that wouldn't have solved the loan problem. I didn't know if his uncle was in on it."

The last several months raced through Cade's mind. He landed on one thought. "You the one who burned my livery and hurt Grace?"

"No, sir." He held up one hand. "I give you my word. I'd never do anything like that."

"Do you know who did?"

Tim looked away. "I don't know for sure."

"Tell me who you think it was."

Tim hesitated for several moments. He finally looked Cade in the eyes. "That man found dead outside of Rockdale. Frank was furious when he found out the man he'd hired from the gang had hurt Grace and could have easily been killed."

"The gang?"

Tim nodded. "Reed Murphy's gang."

Cade stared at Tim. Reed used to be a schoolboy friend. Cade couldn't believe Reed had changed so much as to hurt people. "Why do you think it was Reed?"

"Because he works for Frank too."

"But he hasn't even been around town."

"Yes, he has. He just stayed out of sight, him and his gang. In fact, if you were to talk to his folks and they told the truth, they'd admit Reed and his men have been around. Not all the time. Just whenever Frank wanted them to cause trouble." He rubbed his thumb and fingers together. "Frank paid them well."

Reed's gang burned my business. He dropped onto the pew next to Tim and shook his head. "Unbelievable."

"I'm sorry, Cade. I wish I'd done more, but fear for my family…" Tim gave another helpless shrug.

Cade's anger grew. No doubt, Reed and his men were involved in every fire, explosion, and theft in town. "Where can I find Reed? Do you know?"

"I have a fair idea. He's been bragging about stealing from miners and prospectors whenever Frank didn't need him."

"He told me he had a claim that paid well."

Once Tim gave him the directions to find Reed, Cade stood and held out his hand. "Go see your family. I have a feeling Frank's uncle will work out some arrangement about your loan just to stay out of trouble."

Tim stood and shook Cade's hand. "You're not going to tell the sheriff?"

"About what? As far as I'm concerned, you're just another of Frank's victims. I'll explain everything to Grace and the Kincaids."

Tim strode out of the church without looking back. Cade would have loved to see his reunion with the family, but he had more work to do.

Grace stood, a frown on her face. Cade joined her and her father. She pointed toward the door. "Was that Tim?"

"It was. I'll tell you about it later."

Loud moaning drew their attention to Frank. The sheriff had his arm under Frank's back and was lifting him from the floor. Once he had Frank on his feet, the sheriff led him toward Grace and Simon. He jerked Frank to a stop in front of them.

"I understand you might have some grievances against Mr. Easton, here?" At their nod, the sheriff motioned toward the door. "If you'll follow me, I'll get it all written down once I have him behind bars."

"Sheriff, once you're through with Frank here, you may want to wire Sheriff Morgan Thomas in Rockdale," Cade said. "He'll have another list of charges to add."

The sheriff gave a nod. "I'll do just that. Thank you, son."

Simon held out his hand to Grace and prepared to follow the lawman.

"Sir." Cade reached for Grace's arm. "If you have no objection, I'd like to speak with your daughter for a moment. I'll see she gets to the sheriff's office safely."

Simon looked at Grace for an answer. At her nod, he reached to shake Cade's hand. "Thank you for everything, young man. I owe you and your father my life."

"No, sir. We owe you an apology."

With a wave of his hand, Simon patted Grace's cheek before trailing the sheriff outside. Most of the gawkers followed.

Cade peered down into Grace's eyes, and all thought and words disappeared. Now that she was safe, he was at a loss. How had life gotten so complicated? He had once been so sure of Grace and her feelings for him, but now his jumbled emotions left him confused. Seeing her in a wedding dress didn't help.

He motioned for her to have a seat and filled her in on why Tim was at the wedding. After answering all her questions, he finally had to say what kept distracting him throughout their conversation.

"You look beautiful." And she did, more so than ever before.

Her face pinked. "Thank you."

He stood and helped her to her feet, then strolled down the aisle. He'd keep his word and make sure she made it to the sheriff's office unhurt. What happened after that was up to her.

Outside the jailhouse, Cade was about to open the door, but Grace stopped him, her hand on his arm. He examined her face, waiting, hopeful of what she might say.

"I appreciate everything you did. I think Daddy was right. You saved his life."

He shook his head. "No, but I think I understand now that that was what you were trying to do. My father was pretty sure Frank intended to kill your dad once you two were married."

Grace's hand covered her mouth. "Frank assured me that if I married him, my father would be fine."

"I don't think Frank has any idea how to tell the truth."

Grace looked at him as if she expected something. "What's next?"

If only he knew. He wasn't about to offer his heart again. It already carried enough scars. "You're free now, Grace. Free to do what you want. I'm sure your father would love to have you back, as I'm sure the Kincaids would too. You became invaluable to them." *And to me.* "Everyone in town enjoyed your company."

She stood quiet, her eyes flashing as she looked into his. He silently begged her to say the words he'd longed to hear. He received nothing.

Finally, he leaned and opened the door.

"Stay safe, Grace."

And with a tip of his hat, he walked away.

THIRTY-SIX

What? *Stay safe?* That's all he had to say?

At first, Grace stood in stunned disbelief. But as Cade's long strides lengthened the distance between them, she moved on to heartbreak and then anger. How could he just walk away? What about the kisses? Did they mean nothing? Didn't *she* mean anything to him?

"Grace?" She turned at her father's call. "You coming in, dear?"

She took one last glance at Cade's retreating back, then entered the jail.

An hour later, she walked into the home she'd known for so many years. The very house where she'd nursed her mother until her death. The home she'd fled in search of freedom. Now, she'd found what she sought…and hadn't gained a thing. What she wanted most had ridden away.

Her father tossed the bag of money onto the table, pulled out a chair, and dropped onto it as if he had no more strength. The poor man had been through so much more than she had. Before she could go to him, someone knocked on the door. She crossed the room and turned the knob. Seeing Frank Easton's uncle Stuart standing there, she almost slammed the door in his face. After a moment's hesitation, she motioned him inside.

Stuart moved to the table. "I won't take much of your time," he said to Grace's father. "I've just been to the bank, where I pulled your loan from Frank's files." He dropped a pile of torn paper on the table. On top of that, he laid the title to the gunsmith shop and mine. "As far as I'm concerned, Simon, your loan is paid in full. I can only apologize for all that's happened to you." He turned to Grace. "And to you too, my dear." He shook his head and tears welled. "I had no idea my nephew could be so evil. And you're not the only ones he tried to manipulate and steal from." He lifted his hands and let them fall again. "I'm so sorry. I'll not fight any charges you may decide to file against my bank."

With that, he headed for the door. Simon grabbed the bag of money, stood, and rushed to his side. "There will be no charges, Stuart. I'll not make you pay for your nephew's crimes." He held out the moneybag. "That also means I pay my debts."

Stuart held his hands away from the bag as though it would bite him. "No, sir. I won't take it."

"At least let me pay the loan on my shop. I think that'd be fair to both of us."

Tears ran from Stuart's eyes. "I can't thank you enough for your generosity."

Simon dumped the money onto the table and counted out hundreds, then handed them to the broken man. "I trust you'll deal as fair with me when I bring in the gold I expect to find in my mine?"

Stuart's mouth dropped open.

"I'll take that as a yes." Simon walked him outside and they said their good-byes.

When he reentered, he looked much happier. He returned to the chair he'd vacated and patted the seat next to him. Grace moved to his side and wrapped her arms around his neck. She'd never been more proud of her father. She planted a kiss on his cheek and sat next to him.

"I love you, Daddy."

He smiled. "I love you too, dear. Now, tell me about Mr. Cade Ramsey."

Her heart crashed at her feet. "What about him?"

"Oh, dear. It's worse than I imagined."

She stared at her father. "What do you mean?"

He tilted his head. "I may be old, Grace, but I'm not blind. I saw the way you looked at him. The way your eyes sought him out. It was very much the way he looked at you." He bumped her with his shoulder. "You love him, yes?"

There was no denying it. Grace blinked back the tears. "Yes," she whispered.

"And is he coming for you later?"

She tried to smile. It wouldn't form. "No. He said his good-bye at the sheriff's office."

"I don't understand. The way he looked at you—"

"Was as a friend. That's all." If Cade had any feelings for her at all, she had killed them when she left with Frank.

"I think you're wrong, Grace."

For the next several minutes, Grace explained to him what had happened since she'd left home. She owed him that much. From hiding out in Cade's wagon all the way to when they'd kissed, Grace didn't leave out a detail or feeling. When she finished, her father took her hands in his and smiled.

"You must go to him, little one. As much as I'd love to have you with me for years to come, I can't come between you and your love."

"I can't, Daddy. Cade doesn't want me. If he did, he wouldn't have walked away."

Daddy turned to face her fully. "You're talking about a man who raced almost a hundred miles to keep you from marrying the wrong man. If that's not love, Grace, then I've been a foolish and stupid man since I met your mother."

"But you adored Mama."

"Exactly, my dear. Which is why you should believe me when I say young Cade loves you. He just may not know it yet."

"Even if that's true, Daddy, I killed that love when I left him to marry Frank. The look on his face as we rode away broke my heart."

"Then you need to go back and mend what's been broken." He tapped his finger on the end of her nose. "Remember, I've seen what a good nurse you are. You kept your mama going for years." He turned and scooped the remainder of the money back inside the canvas bag. "I want you to take this with you and give it back to Cade. Tell him I want him to use it to rebuild his business."

"He won't take it."

"Then you must find a way to convince him." He set the bag on Grace's lap, then cupped her cheek in his palm. "I believe in you, Grace. Now believe in yourself." He stood. "I'm going in for a rest. This has been a harrowing day." He took a few steps and stopped. "Go buy a ticket for tomorrow. Then come home and get some sleep. I have a feeling you might need it."

"Thank you, Daddy."

As he disappeared into his bedroom, hope sprang to life in Grace's heart.

After wiring a brief message to Sheriff Morgan Thomas about the news he'd learned from Tim Martell, Cade headed west into the mountains with the intent of bringing Reed Murphy in to get what he deserved. He tried to keep his mind focused on what was ahead so he wouldn't dwell on Grace. Most times, his plan failed.

Part of him thought he should have laid everything out for her, told her of his feelings, and let her do with them what she felt was right. But each time that thought popped up, he struck it down just as fast.

Though he understood her desire to do what she could to protect her father, he still couldn't comprehend how she could marry a man like Frank without even trying to talk to him first. To let him find out about their marriage from Frank was...well, almost unforgivable. He thought they had a better relationship than that.

He snorted. Of course he'd forgive Grace. He already had. Though her decision had hurt him more than he could describe, she was an honorable woman, and he loved her with a deep and unshakable love.

Cade rode far into the night before stopping. He and his horses needed a rest. His thoughts needed a rest, but they never seemed to tire. He allowed himself to doze only for a short time, then he was back on the saddle again before dawn.

As he rode higher into the mountains, Cade could feel the air changing, now much drier and thinner. In spite of the turmoil of the last few days, he could still appreciate the beauty of God's creation.

That beauty was shattered by gunfire. Cade heeled his horse into a gallop and headed toward the sound. He slowed after a bit to check if he could hear anything more. Voices echoed through the trees. Cade recognized one. Reed.

He dismounted and tied his horses at a distance. He pulled his rifle from its sheath and slipped through the trees as quickly and quietly as he could. He slowed to a crawl as the voices became louder.

"Just hand over the gold you found, and we'll leave you in peace."

Reed. His voice sounded calm and soothing, but Cade knew he couldn't be trusted.

"We don't have any gold."

"You're a liar! All the prospectors up here have gold."

Cade moved to where he could better see how many men he'd have to face. Reed and his three friends, all with guns, stood around a young family. Cade moved some grass and recognized the family as the young man and woman who had traveled with him and Grace. What was their name? Woods. That was it. Layton and Katie Woods. They were supposed to be long gone, traveling west with the wagon train. And they had a baby. Where—?

Just then, the baby began to cry.

"Shut that thing up." One of Reed's friends took a step closer and nudged Katie with his gun barrel. "You hear me?"

Reed waved the man back. "Leave her alone, Deuce."

"I hate that noise." Deuce bumped the woman again. "Do something!"

Katie dug around in a basket until she found what she sought and stuck it in the baby's mouth. The child went silent.

"That's better. Now, tell us where you've hid the gold."

Layton held out his hands. "I already told you, we don't have any."

Deuce placed his gun barrel against Layton's head. "I won't ask again."

Cade knew if he didn't act soon, Layton Woods would have a hole in his head. He glanced around for the best angle and decided he'd have to make do right where he sat.

As quietly as he could, Cade pulled the hammer back. But the click was still too loud. Reed and all his men crouched as they turned their guns toward him. One fired wildly. The rest waited, peering intently into the woods. Cade waited for the next move. It came when Deuce swung his gun toward the baby.

Cade fired. Deuce went down. The rest of the men shot toward him. Cade rolled behind a tree. When the shooting slowed, he took careful aim and squeezed the trigger. Reed's gun fell, and he howled as he grabbed his arm.

His face in a grimace, Reed motioned with his good arm. "There's only one shooter. Go get him."

The last two men fired toward Cade as they moved forward. With the tree as protection, Cade remained where he was and kept firing. Another man yelped and grabbed his thigh. Only one left. Cade aimed again.

Click.

Cade threw the rifle aside and reached for his pistol. The last man was almost on him. A bullet whizzed past his ear. A torrent of gunfire came from his left. The man glanced that direction, then ran the other way. Cade stayed put, not sure who was firing.

"You can come out now, Mr. Cade."

Joseph?

Cade rose to his feet and stepped into the clearing. Joseph and Morgan grinned at him.

Joseph raced after the one trying to escape. The sheriff headed toward Reed, cuffs in hand. "Thought you might be able to use some help."

"You thought right. Glad you showed." Cade covered the short distance to the Woods family. "You three all right?"

"Sure are, thanks to you…again." Layton held out a trembling hand. "Ramsey, wasn't it?"

"Yeah, Cade Ramsey."

He dropped to one knee to see the boy, who chewed on a piece of dried beef as though it were the best thing since peppermint sticks. Drool dripped from his chin as he gave Cade a toothless grin.

Cade ruffled the boy's hair. "He looks fine."

He stood and stared at Reed, trying to find the words he'd planned to say when they met up. In the end, he turned and walked away as Reed flung all kinds of venom at him. Cade let it roll off. Instead, a smile formed. As far as he was concerned, one long chapter of his life had just ended. Time to see what the next one brought.

THIRTY-SEVEN

Grace accepted Joseph's help getting into the buggy he had waiting. She took her time arranging her skirts and making sure she hadn't dropped her bag in the transition.

"Oh, quit wasting time, Grace, and go get your man." Belle stepped into the buggy to give her one last hug. "I'll be praying the whole time."

Grace held her tight, hoping to gain some of Belle's courage. Belle patted her back and pulled away. "It gonna be fine. You'll see."

Grace took up the reins and gave them a flick. Or maybe her trembling shook them. Either way, the horse had her moving to what she hoped was her final destination. She took a deep breath. She'd never been more nervous than she was this moment.

As she'd wired Belle with her plans and then packed for this trip, she'd been filled with nervous energy. But until now, she hadn't felt sick to her stomach. She prayed again for the Lord to give her courage and the words she needed to win Cade's heart. Because right now, she still had no idea what she would say.

She reined the horse to a stop at the top of the creek bank before crossing the bridge to the Double K ranch. She needed a moment and took several deep breaths as she scanned the ranch hoping to catch sight of Cade. Then she checked her bonnet and skirt before flicking the reins and heading toward…what? That question would be answered soon enough.

She crossed the bridge and rode up the other side as she'd done so many times over the last several months. Yet this time was so much different. Especially from the first time she'd crossed it. Cade had been at her side and then left her there. Would today end the same way with Cade leaving her standing there…alone?

She chased the thought from her mind and stopped the horse at the barn. Cade was nowhere to be seen. She wrapped the reins around the hook, then climbed from the buggy and retrieved the bag.

As she turned to enter the barn, she ran smack into someone's chest. She looked up into Cade's face and lost her breath. The bag dropped from her fingers.

They both bent to recover the bag and bumped heads. Grace couldn't believe she'd hurt this poor and wonderful man again. She reached toward him to rub the spot she'd hit. Instead, she poked him in the eye. He pulled away, covering his eye with his hand. She reached out to comfort him and apologize. What she heard made her stop.

He's laughing?

She scowled, her hands planted on her hips. "Are you laughing at me?"

He took a breath and swiped his sleeve across his eyes. "That I am."

She tried to stay mad but couldn't. Only moments ago, she'd recalled how similar her arrival here had been. A giggle escaped. She held out her hand. He stepped back. They both smiled.

Cade shoved his hands into his pockets. "It's good to see you, Grace."

His deep voice touched her soul. "You too."

He glanced toward the house. "You here for a visit?"

By the grace of God, she was here for so much more. "In a way." Time to jump in and pray she floated. "I came to see you."

"Is that right?"

He wasn't going to make this easy. She deserved worse. "Yes. And for the very reason I went looking for you at your livery that day… a lifetime ago."

He nodded. "Feels like years." The knot in his throat bobbed.

"I'm sorry." She cleared her throat and started again. "I had something I wanted to tell you that day. Something I need to say today."

She looked into his eyes and saw the rims had turned red and it wasn't from poking him. "I know I have no right, Cade, and that I've hurt you deeply." She twisted her hands together. "But I have to tell you that I…that I love you."

He didn't move. Not even a smile. All the hope she'd held in her heart drained into a heap at her feet. Her father was wrong. Not all hurts could be nursed back to health.

Grace licked her lips, her mind scrambling for a way to save the relationship. She dropped her hands to her sides and shrugged. "I just thought you should know." She turned to leave, but then faced him again. "Do you love me, Cade…even a little?"

He took the two steps separating them and pulled her into his arms. He rested his chin on top of her head.

"I love you more than a little, Grace. You own my heart. I don't think it's belonged to me since you nearly got us killed by that pack of wolves." He held her away and peered into her eyes. "But I can't marry you. Not now, anyway." He gave her another hug. "But you have no idea what it did to my heart just now to hear you say you love me."

She pushed back until she could see his face. "You love me?"

"With everything in me."

"But you won't marry me?"

"I will, but not until I can provide for you."

Her heart swelled until she thought it would burst. She turned to retrieve the bag and gasped. Jonah stood over it, chewing on the strings that held it closed.

"You rotten goat! Get away from there!" She took a couple of steps toward him, waving her arms at the beast, but stopped when he shook his horns at her. "Cade, do something. That dumb goat is eating all your money."

Cade moved to her side. "All my money? What money?"

She pointed as though he should already know. "That right there. It's from Daddy. He wanted you to have it to rebuild your livery. Now, get it away from that goat!"

A slight smirk on his face, Cade crossed his arms and nodded toward the goat. "And what happens if I get hurt?"

She caught the look in his eyes and raised her brows. "You've never complained about my nursing in the past."

"But that was when you were the one who did the hurting."

She smiled at him. "What if I promise to kiss you to make it all better?"

Cade grinned. "Well, if the past is any indication of our future, you'll be doing lots of kissing to nurse my wounds."

Her mouth dropped open. He put his fingers under her chin and pushed it closed.

"But I'm looking forward to every painful moment." He planted a kiss on her lips before going to tackle Jonah.

Grace touched her fingers to her lips and smiled. Daddy was right after all.

Jonah moved closer, and she backed away from the tussle between Cade and the beast.

"Where do you think you're going now, Runaway Grace?" Laughing, Cade wrested the bag from Jonah, then gave her chase.

She ran, but he caught up quickly, pulled her into a tight embrace, and claimed her lips again, and forever.

1. Grace ran from her troubles rather than stay and face them. Was running right or wrong? Why or why not?

2. Grace had trouble dealing with her mother's sickness and death, and she felt disappointment with her father because he insisted on an arranged marriage. Cade was upset with Reed and several of the town's residents because of their dislike of Joseph. He also grew angry with Frank's actions toward him and Grace. Why do trials often reveal weaknesses in ourselves we didn't know we possessed?

3. Though Cade tried to make everyone believe he'd gotten over his role in his mother's accident, he still carried a great deal of guilt. Why is it so difficult to forgive ourselves even when we've been forgiven by God and others?

4. Grace's father wanted her to marry a man she didn't love. Have you ever been forced into a situation you were opposed to? How did you respond? Would you do things differently now if you had the chance?

5. Examine the relationship between Grace and Belle. How did

this friendship help or hinder the two of them? Look at your closest friends. Are they a help or a hindrance to your faith? How can having godly friends make you a stronger Christian?

6. The relationship between Cade and his father was strained at best because Cade felt unloved and betrayed. Can you recall a time when a loved one let you down? How did you handle it? Has the relationship been resolved?

7. Greed played the largest part in Frank's actions. What were some of the subtle effects of his greed? Under what conditions might you be tempted to allow greed to take root in your own life?

8. Grace felt like an outsider because her mother was too sick to teach her feminine ways. Have you ever felt like an outsider? If so, how did you handle or get over those feelings?

9. Grace thought God didn't hear her prayers. Have you ever felt this way? What are some ways you've dealt with those feelings of unanswered prayers?

10. The struggles Grace faced with her parents sent her running and she landed in Cade's arms. Can you look back at your life and see how God brought good from a difficult situation?

=== **About the Author** ===

Janelle Mowery is the author of several novels, including *When All My Dreams Come True,* Book 1 in the Colorado Runaway series. When not writing, reading, and researching, she is active in her church. Born and raised in Minnesota, Janelle now resides in Texas with her husband and two sons, where she and her family raise orphaned raccoons, look at beautiful deer, and make friends with curious armadillos.

Visit her website at www.janellemowery.com

Enjoy this excerpt from *When Two Hearts Meet*
Book Three in Janelle Mowery's Colorado Runaway series
Available now at a bookstore near you

March 1874 Colorado Territory

Rachel Garrett stuck her head out the stagecoach window and received a face-full of dust. She ducked back inside and laughed as she coughed and sputtered. *Well, that's one way to be greeted into my new home.*

The incident didn't quash her excitement. Nothing could, although she had to push away the memory of her mother's tears as she said good-bye to her parents. Rachel clung to the knowledge that her arrival marked the beginning of her new lifework, the fulfillment of a dream, and the end of the trouble that had haunted her the last four months.

Her heart pounded as she took in the sights. She'd never been farther west than her home in Missouri, and everything she saw held her spellbound, from the plains of Kansas to her first glimpse of the glorious Rocky Mountains.

The town looked bigger than she expected. While many of the buildings they passed gleamed with new lumber, some structures looked rough, as though left over from the earlier years and kept patched together. The bleak sight caused her to wonder about the proprietors. Another bout of apprehension struck, but she tamped it down. Her teacher and mentor, Doctor Freeman, assured her he was sending her to the best town and doctor in the West.

They left a small church behind. Rachel's gaze remained fixed on the whitewashed spire long after the rest of the building faded from view. Once she left the doctor's office, she would go back and meet the pastor. Maybe he could use someone to help out around the place when she wasn't working. The surroundings lacked flowers and shrubs, minor touches that would make it welcoming to strangers like her.

The sound of clanging brought her attention back to the scene in front of her. They passed by a livery and a general store, as well as a hotel and eatery. Several women bustled down the boardwalk, and men lingered outside the feed and hardware shop. Rachel held fast to her seat, wishing the coachman would slow down so she could take in more of the scenery.

As though the driver read her thoughts, the stagecoach slowed and then stopped in front of the depot. Within seconds, he opened the door and held out a dirty, calloused hand to help her onto the platform. She smiled and thanked the man, then looked down the street to see what she'd missed.

Music from a couple saloons drifted toward her. Though they tended to keep people in her profession busy, she didn't like that they appeared in every settlement. She was thankful the sheriff's office stood nearby to help keep most of the ruckus to a minimum.

Rachel scanned the street looking for her new place of employment. Doctor Barnes wrote that his main office stood next to the barbershop. She looked the direction they'd come, but didn't recall seeing a barbershop. She took a couple steps before her travel bag rushed past her head and hit the ground in front of her feet. She drew a deep breath and looked up.

"Sorry, ma'am." The driver didn't look a bit sorry as he shrugged. "Watch the head and feet, little lady. Your trunk's coming next."

Rachel backed up to wait for her trunk to descend in the same manner as her bag.

"Hold up, Frank."

A young man appeared from the shipping office next door and hurried across the boardwalk toward them. He climbed on the back rail of the coach and helped the driver ease the heavy chest onto the platform. When he straightened, he tipped his hat and smiled as if helping damsels in distress were an everyday occurrence.

The young man wiped his palm on his trousers before offering his hand. "Afternoon, miss. I'm Chad Baxter."

Rachel examined Mr. Baxter's face as she shook his hand. Merriment danced in his brown eyes as well as a hint of interest. No doubt most women enjoyed his attentions.

"Thank you, Mr. Baxter."

"Oh, come now." He placed his other hand over hers, and she gave a gentle tug to pull her hand free. He tucked his fingers into his pockets and leaned toward her.

"Mr. Baxter is my father's name. Call me Chad, Miss—" Chad raised his eyebrows.

Rachel studied him a little longer. He seemed harmless enough, like a young pup eager for attention. "Rachel Garrett."

He grinned and rocked back on his heels. "Ah, Miss Garrett. I hope you'll call me Chad. I wouldn't want things too formal between us."

Her mother had been right. People were more forward in the West. Funny. Their bold ways didn't startle her as much as she expected it should. In fact, with his boyish approach, she fought the laughter that bubbled inside her at Chad's attempt at charm.

Chad tapped the trunk with the toe of his boot. "Do I dare assume this means you'll be staying in town awhile?"

Rachel opened her mouth, thinking Mr. Baxter needed to mind his business, when she noticed a man standing in the entrance of the shipping office watching them.

"Chad?" The older gentleman stepped out of the office and walked toward them. She could see where the young man received his good looks.

"Is my son being a pest, miss?"

Rachel smiled. "Not at all. I think he was welcoming me to town in his own unique way."

The man's brows rose. "Unique, huh? Well, knowing Chad, that's a mighty diplomatic way to put it." He held out his hand. "Richard Baxter. Welcome to Rockdale." His handshake was brief but courteous as he looked her in the eye. "Can my son and I help you with this trunk?"

Rachel glanced down the street. "I'm supposed to be staying in a small house near Doctor Barnes's home."

"Oh, so you're the new nurse we've heard so much about. I expected someone much—" Chad stumbled over his words as he shuffled from one foot to the other.

"Older?" Rachel finished for him with a grin.

"I can see I have more training to do." Richard laughed as his arm went around his son's shoulders. "And that you're more than capable of keeping him in his place." He motioned toward the trunk. "If you can wait, I'll have Chad deliver this for you after work. Doc's house is two streets over on the left. It's the big white one with black shutters. You can't miss it. His office," Mr. Baxter gestured the opposite direction with his thumb, "is halfway down and across the street."

"You're very kind, Mr. Baxter. Thank you."

"Not a problem." Richard squeezed his son's shoulder. "Chad, those crates aren't moving themselves." He turned back to her. "Nice meeting you, ah—"

"Rachel," Chad supplied, his gaze never leaving her face. "Rachel Garrett."

Richard grinned, winked at her, and bowed slightly at the waist. "Miss Garrett." He turned and entered his office. Chad gave her a sheepish grin, stooped to pick up her trunk, and followed his father.

Rachel grabbed her carpetbag and headed down the boardwalk. She already felt at home. Maybe their manners were less polished compared to those of her friends back home, but such friendliness was endearing. She passed the hardware store and met the stares of the men sitting on the benches as she offered a greeting. She nodded and smiled to the women who gazed at her through the dress shop window next door.

She hurried past the swinging doors of the saloon, her gaze locked on the white sign boasting Doctor Barnes's name. She wasn't supposed to start work for three more days, but hunger to see the office and love for her work carried her feet across the dirt street and up the steps.

Screams assaulted her ears before she reached the doctor's door. She hesitated, grabbed the knob, and held tight as the shouts from inside the office intensified. The nameplate nailed to the door read *Jim Barnes, M.D.* Dr. Freeman claimed Dr. Barnes was one of the best. She prayed he was right.

Another shriek from inside made her cringe. She took a deep breath, turned the knob, and entered. The man standing closest to her yelled that his wife was about to have a baby and the doctor needed to come to his house right away. Next to the man, a woman held a young boy with blood streaming from his nose. His tears made clean tracks down his grimy face. Another man pounded on a doorframe, begging for the doctor's help, though he didn't look hurt. Others with no visible signs of ill-health occupied the few chairs lining a wall.

Rachel peered through the doorway across the room that led into the examining area. Before moving that direction, she instructed the young mother to tip her son's head back and handed her a small white towel off a nearby washstand.

"Just use the cloth to gently pinch his nostrils closed."

She edged toward the examining room and around the man beating on the frame. A man bent over a padded examining table. A woman stood next to him. Rachel's heart skipped a beat. *Did the doctor find a replacement nurse before I could get here?* A scruffy-looking man stood at the end of the table wringing an already mangled hat. The patient on the table bellowed and tried to sit up.

The doctor, his sleeves rolled up, stood over him and pushed him back down. "Lay still, Walt. You're only making it worse."

"But Doc—"

The doctor beckoned toward the man with the hat. "Hold him down, Patch. I gotta put him under so I can fix this leg."

Patch clamped his hat on his head and leaned down to press on the patient's shoulders. The injured man fought against him. Rachel glanced at his leg, bent at an awkward angle below the knee.

She dropped her travel bag in a corner and approached the doctor. "Dr. Barnes?"

"Yes?"

The patient hollered and almost rolled off the table. Rachel moved to his head and grabbed the mask and ether from the small stand next to the table, placed the mask over the patient's face, and administered the ether. In moments, the man fell unconscious. The doctor looked up. Rachel couldn't tell if the expression on his face was shock or anger.

She pointed toward the patient's leg. "I suggest you get started. He won't stay unconscious long."

The doctor scrambled to do as she suggested. "Who are you and what do you think you're doing?"

"I believe I'm your new nurse, Rachel Garrett. I'm just putting into practice some of what Dr. Freeman taught me."

Dr. Barnes glanced at her as a slow grin spread across his face. "How is that old pain maker?"

"As ornery as ever. He sends his regards." She eyed the other woman who had tears running down her cheeks. *Must be the patient's wife.* Rachel motioned toward the waiting room. "Would you like me to help you here or get to work out there?"

The doctor gave her a look of relief. "Do you know how to deliver a baby?"

Rachel nodded.

He jerked his thumb over his shoulder. "Go with Henry there."

Rachel glanced at the man who looked ready to pass out.

"His wife is having a baby and needs help. Give Mrs. Cagle the ether. She can take over that job. My medical bag is behind my desk in the next room. It should have everything you'll need. When you're finished there, come on back."

"Yes, Doctor."

When All My Dreams Come True
Book 1

Bobbie McIntyre dreams of running a ranch of her own. Raised without a mother and having spent most of her time around men, she knows more about wrangling than acting like a lady. The friendship of her new employer awakens a desire to learn more about presenting her feminine side, but ranch life keeps getting in the way.

Ranch owner Jace Kincaid figures the Lord is testing his faith when a female wrangler shows up looking for work. Bobbie has an uncanny way of getting under his skin, though, and he's surprised when she finds a home next to his heart. But when his cattle begin to go missing and his wranglers are in danger from some low-down cattle thief, can Jace trust God, even if it may mean giving up on his dreams?